Mingling with the scents of gasoline and cutting fluid was something putrid.

An odor reminiscent of opening the family's summer cottage—the stench of a rodent tempted by D-Con that crawled behind the stove to die. Breathing through her mouth, she headed to the far corner where the odor was strongest.

She'd been fifteen when Uncle Walt bought the Empire glass beader. The day after Thanksgiving he'd dragged her along to a local factory where they were produced. It takes a two-handed tug to latch the beader's door shut to create vacuum. There's no way for an animal to climb up and into the machine. Still . . .

Rebecca wiped at the machine's tempered glass window with the sleeve of her shirt. She leaned closer, trying to peer through the haze of a hundred scratches. There was the engine block from a 20/25 and something . . . pale. Rebecca swiped at the window again and stared.

A naked, dead man stared back.

Rebecca had found the source of the stench.

It was indeed coming from a dead rat—the human kind.

JUDITH SKILLINGS

DEAD END

AVON BOOKS

An Imprint of HarperCollinsPublishers

This is a work of fiction. Names, characters, places, and incidents are products of the author's imagination or are used fictitiously and are not to be construed as real. Any resemblance to actual events, locales, organizations, or persons, living or dead, is entirely coincidental.

AVON BOOKS
An Imprint of HarperCollins*Publishers*
10 East 53rd Street
New York, New York 10022-5299

Copyright © 2004 by Judith Skillings
ISBN: 0-06-058298-7
www.avonmystery.com

First Avon Books paperback printing: April 2004

Avon Trademark Reg. U.S. Pat. Off. and in Other Countries, Marca Registrada, Hecho en U.S.A.
HarperCollins® is a registered trademark of HarperCollins Publishers Inc.

Printed in the U.S.A.

10 9 8 7 6 5 4 3 2 1

This book is dedicated to

Margaret Perkins Skillings
and to the memory of Neal T. Skillings

for their lifetime of love and support

Acknowledgments

While all the characters in this book are fictitious, the cars aren't. My sincerest thanks to Lynne and Whit Ball for allowing 946 to be the 3-Litre Bentley featured in this book—I promise to clean off the blood. Many thanks also to those who contributed inspiration and support: Bob and Bridgit Nurock, Stu and Noreen Spector, DiAnn Vick, Susan Giddings, Barney, and especially the guys at The Frawley Company.

I am indebted to my agent, Dominick Abel, and my editor, Sarah Durand. Without their guidance and support I'd still be writing for my own enjoyment. Of course, without the cooperation of my husband, I'd still be doing valve timings and not writing at all.

Author's Notes

The original Peking-to-Paris automobile endurance rally took place in 1907, sponsored by the French newspaper, *Le Matin*. In an attempt to prove that cars were reliable, five of them "raced" from present day Beijing to Paris. It took sixty days. The winner received a bottle of champagne. Since then, the rally has been re-enacted a handful of times in both directions, most recently in 1997. Seven years earlier it was called the "London to Peking" and crossed the continent heading east. A friend, Tom Troxell, made the trek in a Model T Ford. His stories of the trip will never fade.

A word in the spirit of accuracy: the terms Rolls-Royce and Bentley are adjectives. The cars should always be referred to as "Rolls-Royce motorcars" or "Bentley motorcars." They are not "Rollers," "Royces," or even Rolls-Royces. Or Bents. Regrettably, some of my characters don't know any better.

DEAD
END

Rebecca let the screen door slam.

She crossed the porch, strode down the wooden steps, headed toward the grove of black walnut trees with their leaves not fully unfurled. Maurice padded along behind. Rebecca had carried the cat home for company during the weekend. She made him walk back for the exercise. At the edge of the bridle path, she slowed to fish keys out of her jeans pocket—keys to the automotive restoration shop she'd been masochistic enough to accept as inheritance.

Monday. Memorial Day. Six days to go.

Rebecca pushed open the front door with her hip, letting Moe slip into the office. She tossed the keys on the desk, followed the cat's erect tail and swaying belly to the lunchroom. She had the coffeepot in her hand before the smell registered.

Mingling with the scents of gasoline and cutting fluid was something putrid. An odor reminiscent of opening the family's summer cottage—the stench of a mouse, tempted by D-Con, that crawled behind the stove to die.

Rebecca set down the carafe. Ignoring Moe as he bumped her leg, she reached into the circuit breaker panel, flipped on the overhead lights for the back room. The cold tubes flickered, then hummed in protest. She opened the door and en-

tered the silent machine shop, pinched her nostrils to keep
from gagging.

Moe watched from the doorway, his tail swishing the
floor.

"One quick sweep, then I'll feed you." Rebecca snatched
a broom. Breathing through her mouth, she headed to the far
corner where the odor was strongest.

She'd been fifteen when Uncle Walt had bought the Empire glass beader. The day after Thanksgiving he'd dragged
her along to a local factory where they were produced. Un-
adorned metal boxes, beaders use minute particles of glass
oxide impact beads and around eighty pounds of air pressure
to blast rust and peeling paint off car parts. Or from ten-
speed bicycle fenders—that was how Walt had trained her to
use a beader. The blasting area is five feet square. The sepa-
rate dust collector stands seven feet tall. Both rest on skinny
metal legs.

Rebecca swept. She retrieved a pile of bead silt, two split
washers and five hex-head screws.

No decaying rodent.

It takes a two-handed tug to latch the beader's door shut to
create vacuum. There's no way for an animal to climb up
and into the machine. Still . . .

She flipped the on switch. The motor whirred to life. Interior bulbs glowed with the harshness of an all-night diner.
Then one sputtered and went out. Hissing pressure sucked
the long rubber gloves into the beading area and suspended
them stiffly in dusty air.

Rebecca wiped at the machine's tempered glass window
with the sleeve of her shirt. She leaned closer, trying to peer
through the haze of a hundred scratches. There was the engine block from a 20/25 and something . . . pale. Rebecca
swiped at the window again. She thrust both arms shoulder-
deep into the black gauntlets. She spread the gloves apart
and stared.

A naked, dead man stared back.

The bloated corpse embraced the block from behind.

Knees hugged the metal, modestly obscuring his genitals. One foot pressed against the sealed door like a sprinter poised for the start of a race he'd never run. His wrists were lashed together. His left eye was shut. The right one glazed. Even in death his stingy mouth twisted into a leer.

Rebecca had found the source of the stench.

It was indeed coming from a dead rat—the human kind.

She shut her eyes, blotting out the gray-whiteness of death. Her head sagged against the cool front of the beader. The pulse of the machine merged with the throbbing tightness in her chest. Perspiration trickled down her temple into the corner of her mouth. *Not again.*

Her breath erupted as a gasp, forcing her to suck in the overripe odor of decaying flesh. She coughed and turned her back on the lifeless form in the humming machine.

Rebecca slid to the concrete floor and hugged her knees.

Dear God, not again.

Monday

Dead Blow

One

_____

"We having an open house? Or is he selling tickets to the policemen's ball?"

Rebecca forced herself to look up. Frank Lewes's rangy body blocked the sun, his face a dark void of shadow. She'd heard his Corolla drive in, the wrenching squawk of the driver's-side door, the rhythmic shuffle of his boots on the tarmac as he approached. She'd imagined his eyes flitting from the sheriff's patrol car to the open front door to his boss huddled on the cement stoop, belatedly guarding the shop. As ineffectual as the thrasher rustling in the dead leaves beneath the azalea.

She squinted at him. "We already gave."

"Uh-huh. That's what I thought." Frank peered over her head into the foyer. "You gonna tell me what's going on?"

"Frank—"

"Or make me guess? Val?"

"No, Frank. It's—"

"Paulie?"

"It's none of us. But it's bad."

"No shit." Frank glared.

Rebecca held out her hand. Her chief mechanic pulled her to standing with as little effort as if she were still a spoiled kid hanging around the shop for the summer. Frank had run the shop for her uncle and now did for her. On the step, she was level with him. Close enough to smell Head & Shoulders shampoo tinged with a dose of fear—Frank's Pavlovian response to the police.

He gripped her hand as if he could squeeze the news out of her. She didn't flinch. His intimidation was pure bluff. Always had been, like his silences. Frank claimed to have lost the knack of small talk in the state pen. Maybe. Or maybe he preferred to listen. Soak up people's chatter like a sponge attacking spilled milk. Wring it out late at night when he had time to consider more than just the words.

Rebecca's words were strained but unambiguous.

"Graham Stuck was murdered. Then stuffed into our glass beader."

Frank whistled. He dropped her hand, wiped his on the leg of his coveralls as he stepped back, leaving her in charge. "Mighty inconsiderate. Hope he didn't gum up the machine."

Rebecca and Frank watched in silence as Harry Tolland wheeled the remains of Graham Stuck through the doorway of Vintage & Classics into the blinding sunshine. Past retirement, Harry should have put away his surgical tools. He'd given up private practice, stepped down to assistant medical examiner for the county, but he couldn't open his fist and let go of the string. Which was okay with most everyone. With Harry, you knew which way the wind was blowing. He was an archetypal grandfather, if your grandfather brandished a scalpel—as sensitive to the anguish of the living as he was invasive to the secrets of the dead.

Harry maneuvered the stretcher outside. The gurney bounced off the doorframe. No one much cared, since the corpse wasn't complaining. Harry frowned, mumbled to the body. "Muddier than tobacco fields soaked by spring rains." The front wheels bumped down off the step. Frank caught the back end and eased it onto the tarmac. Harry nodded his thanks. "Too damn muddy by half."

Rebecca tore a ragged thumbnail off with her teeth. If that

was the aging coroner's assessment of Stuck's unnatural death, she was inclined to agree. Who kills a classic car mechanic—even a mediocre one who overcharged his customers? Why was Stuck in her shop instead of his own? Why put his body in the glass beader? Where were his clothes? Nothing made sense.

Sheriff Bradley Zimmer wasn't troubled by such philosophical questions. The town's second-term sheriff was still trying to adjust the uniform over his middle-aged spread. He corralled everyone in the lunchroom. Like most areas of the shop, the lunchroom was clean and functional. Vanilla walls, beige Armstrong tile floor, window set high in the front wall. Access to both the office and the machine shop. Butcher-block counter ran along a side wall holding a counter refrigerator, sink, microwave and Paulie's contribution: two-burner Bunn coffeemaker. The six-foot-long cafeteria table was white—not the most practical color for a shop—but Uncle Walt had figured that way you could see when it needed to be cleaned. In the corner, a water cooler belched as an air bubble erupted.

Rebecca crossed her right leg over the left, tucked her ankle behind to keep it from swinging. She clutched a mug of Paulie's coffee *du jour* with both hands. Mondays it was equal parts French Nut and Zanzibar Roast. The sheriff hadn't touched his, which upset Paulie, who hovered offering refills. Frank sat at the far end imitating a sphinx, avoiding eye contact. Maurice sprawled on the table, playing centerpiece. Presumably, Juanita was at Flo's Café waiting tables. Val was more than three hours late. The missing teen had been there eighteen months and was still on probation from a burglary conviction. Being late was not a good move.

Zimmer lurched over the table in Rebecca's direction. "You have no idea what Stuck was doing in your shop?"

"No, Sheriff. I didn't know twenty minutes ago and I still don't." Rebecca sighed. Moe stretched his legs, shoving Zimmer's notepad onto the floor. "He shouldn't have been in the shop, alive or dead."

"You didn't get along?"

"Why would we?"

"You were enemies?"

"We were business competitors. Maybe the shops were close, geographically, but we weren't. Why would we want him hanging around?" Rebecca shook her head, ducked beneath the table to retrieve the notepad. It was too odd thinking of herself as a business rival of a vintage car mechanic, even after six months running the place. Odd to think of herself at all in her present guise. At thirty-seven, she was no longer a reporter. No longer enmeshed in the drama of the DC scene. No grab-and-gab lunches at High Noon, swapping leads with Hayes. No evenings fishing the olives from designer martinis with those politically connected, trying to absorb more leads than you gave away. No trips out of town on the expense account. No need for a laptop, tape recorder, briefcase.

"You smash his brains in, strip him naked because he's hanging around? Was he harassing you, Moore?"

Rebecca slid the spiral-bound pad toward Zimmer. "I didn't kill him, Sheriff. No one here did. So unless you plan to arrest us, we're going to work." She pushed away from the table.

"Now, just you wait a—"

Rebecca didn't hear how long she was supposed to wait.

She clapped a hand to her mouth and bolted for the bathroom. Door closed, she dropped to her knees, gripped the rim of the white toilet and vomited the remains of raisin bran and too much coffee. It could have been worse. She wasn't that keen on cereal anyway. She felt blindly for the handle and flushed. Watching the water swirl away, she heaved again. She lowered her head to the rim and waited for the perspiration to subside.

All things considered, she was amazed she hadn't been sick sooner. Nothing like finding a putrefying body bright and early on a Monday morning. The second naked, dead male in less than a year. Head Tide, Maryland, was supposed to be her sanctuary, or her penance. So she'd rationalized it on the gray December day when she lugged cartons of books from the back of the rental van into her dead uncle's house. She didn't care which it was, as long it proved an escape from the ugly reality of an untimely death.

Now this.

Rebecca dragged herself upright. She rinsed her mouth under the faucet, splashed cold water on her face. Pale and drawn, clad in a denim shirt and faded jeans, she wasn't anyone's idea of a ritzy classic car shop owner. Five-six, one ten, she was slender like a long-legged foal. She had her father's high cheekbones, her uncle's broad shoulders, grandmother's wavy auburn hair, and moody gray-green eyes nobody claimed. Rebecca accepted that she looked like a suburban dance instructor. Or maybe the honey selling perfume in Saks. At the moment, either of those jobs had appeal. For a start, she wouldn't have to wear steel-toed boots. She dried her face with a paper towel and pitched it into the wastebasket.

"Gal, what do you think you're doing?"

Frank blocked her way as Rebecca exited the bathroom. The guys had moved from the lunchroom to the office. With the light from three windows, the office usually felt spacious despite its furnishings. A computer workstation sat in the corner, tall metal bookcases ran along the east wall and a scarred mahogany desk Walt had rescued from a defunct bookseller took center stage. At the moment, with Paulie and Frank waiting for her response, the room was claustrophobic—closing in, spinning, like those black and white scenes from Hitchcock's *Vertigo*.

Rebecca didn't have a good answer. What she thought she was doing was handling a crisis. Poorly, it would seem. She brushed past Frank to the desk and slumped in the swivel chair. Moe landed in front of her and offered himself as a pillow. "Where's the sheriff?"

Ignoring the question, Frank bent over the desk, nose to

nose with her. "Bad enough you make us come to work on a holiday. But that's cool. We understand—"

"So glad you do."

"What we don't understand is you making nice with the sheriff. Giving him the run of the place."

"Get real, Frank. Graham Stuck was lying dead out back."

"So? The man was nothing. You called us, we would've put him out with the trash. They empty tomorrow."

Rebecca peered up at Frank Lewes. She'd known him for almost twenty years and never realized he had a sense of humor. He was occasionally cheeky, but not comedic. At a guess, serving eleven years' hard time for homicide would stifle most men's humorous streaks. She sat back. Frank continued to stare. He wasn't joking. Inappropriate giggles threatened to surface like a diver's air bubbles. Why didn't she think of that? Just toss the cold, dead Graham into the dumpster like a spoiled leg of lamb and let the sanitation people deal with it. Voilà, no more problem. If she was going to make a go of it here she had to start thinking like a criminal. So pragmatic.

At least she hoped Frank was advocating efficiency. Not confessing what he would have done with the body if there had been time. She vaguely remembered Walt mentioning bad blood between Frank and Graham Stuck. A public argument last year that nearly escalated to blows over—over what? If she'd known she was going to be saddled with Vintage & Classics, she would have paid closer attention.

She shook her head. "Has the sheriff gone? Will someone tell me that?"

"Yup." The voice was Val's. Annoyance mixed with relief at seeing the teenager lounge against the doorframe. His tongue sucked at the gap in his front teeth. "Frank told the sheriff he might want to check the weapon for fingerprints. Eliminate us as suspects. That's what real cops do. Keep him from bothering us hardworking folks. He was way cool."

"The sheriff forgot the fingerprinting kit," Paulie said.

"That's great, guys. But Zimmer will return. Real soon

and real annoyed. So let's get to work." Rebecca gave Moe a pat and stood. "Because I have more surprises. While Harry was zipping up the corpse, Hal Lindeman phoned. He's staying in town and will be underfoot until the Hisso is finished. Plus, another car arrived Friday night after you left—a rush job." She held up a warning hand. "Don't give me any static. It's a Bentley 3-Litre to be rewired for the race. You'll recognize it. It's the car strung with bright yellow police tape, you know, part of the crime scene. The Bentley's owner is also in town."

She shooed them toward the back room. "That means, in addition to a smelly corpse and a narrow-minded sheriff, we have two unfinished cars, two anxious owners and six days until both cars ship for Paris. Any questions?"

Two

"Hey good-looking, what can Flo cook you?"

Mick Hagan lowered the plastic-covered menu. An over-permed, overdyed blonde waved a spatula at him and beamed her best. Her ample breasts oozed onto the gray Formica counter as she leaned forward to get a closer look.

"Special's grilled ham and cheese, french fries, pickle and the best joe in the county for three-fifty," she said. "Can't do better. How 'bout it?"

Mick dropped the menu and slid a toothpick from his mouth with the tip of his tongue. "Angel, how could I refuse an offer from the likes of you?" He tipped the chair away from the table to give her opportunity for viewing. The cook roared with delight. With a wink and a wave of the rag, she sent a tiny Hispanic girl over to his table with coffee, then waddled through the swinging doors to get grilling.

Mick sipped the steaming brew from a thick mug and tried to relax. Small towns gave him hives. Head Tide, Maryland, looked about as small as towns come and still rate a dot on the county tourist map. One wide main street, sidewalks, narrow storefronts with awnings—like small towns used to be before Wal-Mart reduced them to empty shells. Business ads on the place mat touted a newsstand, hardware store, hair salon, bakery, one lawyer, a Chinese restaurant, an insurance broker who worked out of his home and Flo's Café. The place was undoubtedly the town's social hub, spreading gossip faster than they dished out the club special on Thursdays.

The diner was half full. Most of the square red tables were shared by two women or long-married couples downing their meals without conversing. The up-at-dawn yokels had come and gone. Holiday shoppers hadn't tired enough for refueling. Picture windows were streaked where someone had cleaned them in a hurry. Screen door was hanging by one hinge. Typical small-town diner, Anywhere, USA.

When he'd walked in, heads had turned. Talking stopped. Mick didn't have to be wearing a sign saying "stranger." Regulars knew. They were equally sure he was in town to cause trouble. Not true. Mick was there to put trouble behind him. Or so he'd been convinced by the department's shrink.

The chattering had resumed fast and loud before Mick even took a seat near the counter. Most of it centered on a chubby kid in scrubs. He straddled a chair backward, straining it forward toward his audience.

"Dead as a possum on the center line. That's what Harry said. Stuffed into a beading machine over at Vintage & Classics. Been dead all weekend, most likely. Miss la-di-da Moore found him first thing. Couldn't have missed him. You should of smelled it. Swelled up like a sausage getting ready to burst." The teen chortled. He got up and shuffled to the counter, plopped down on a cracked vinyl stool opposite Flo. "Probably that runty kid Val did it."

In the kitchen, a plate shattered on the floor.

Mick gazed into his coffee like a fortune-teller looking for the future. He didn't know who had died. Didn't much care. Work provided him with a plethora of deaths: violent, ill-timed, senseless, occasionally accidental. What bothered him was the coincidence. He sided with Freud; or was it Jung? There are no coincidences. The sloppy teen had just tossed out one Mick couldn't ignore—a man had been found dead by Rebecca Moore.

That explained the cop cars parked in front of her shop.

Mick lifted his cup for a refill. The tiny waitress wasn't in the room. Flo came to his rescue, hip-checking her way between tables, plate in one hand, insulated carafe in the other. The smell of fried grease rose off the heavy china like steam on a winter morning.

"Don't let it put you off your feed, hon." Flo shook her chins, her earrings tinkling. "First genuine murder I can remember. This town's a peaceable place. I mean real peaceable."

Mick pried a wad of napkins from the dispenser and smiled up at Flo. "Then if a stranger checked into the local motel for a day or two, you figure he'd be safe?"

Flo giggled, dimples appeared. "Safe? Didn't take you for a door-locking man." She topped off his mug.

"What motel?" The teen hollered from across the room, trying to reclaim the spotlight. "Ain't none. Tell him, Flo."

"No motel?" Mick tore the corner off a triangle of toast.

"Nope. But you try the Great Wall Restaurant. Lu Chan's got a room over. Tell him I sent you. You'll be safe enough there."

"Unless you're charming, same as Graham Stuck." The suggestion came from a sour matron at a window table. "I thought he was real charming."

"Too charming by half," countered the man at the next table. "Ask any husband from here to Washington. You'll get an earful. That man would poke a hole in a woodpile."

Three

After a quick lunch which no one felt like eating, Frank
herded the mechanics into the machine shop. Paulie wanted
to cover the glass beader with a blanket like a shroud, maybe
get flowers to show respect. Val wanted to explain why he
was late back from the motorcycle races. No one listened.
As long as he was okay and in no more trouble than the rest
of them, they'd forget the infraction.

Rebecca remained in the front office. Dust danced in the
shafts of sun angling in through the front windows, spot-
lighting the bookshelves overflowing with abused car manu-
als. Thin, hard-covered owner's handbooks were wedged
between oversized shop volumes, victims to greasy fingerprints and torn pages. She should straighten them. Walk
across the room, fuss with them, arrange them alphabeti-
cally, or by model, by color. Do something to restore order.
Be productive, normal.

But she was afraid to move. Too easy to walk out the door
and never return. Take the cat. Let the shop and the cons
fend for themselves. Get out of town, away from what she
knew was coming.

She was too fidgety to sit still.

She paced into the bathroom, left the door open, the overhead off. In the half-light, the face in the mirror was a

stranger—the stranger she'd been ever since David's death had closed the coffin on her former life. How had the human resources director summarized it during the exit interview? "A good looker from a good family on the fast track in a demanding career. How the mighty have fallen." The biddy's smirk had been belittling, unprofessional. Rebecca had not responded. She'd pocketed the severance check and exited the *Post*'s headquarters through the main entrance. Eight months later her face still had little expression. Deeper frown lines, maybe, same mole on her left cheekbone, but not much life.

She wandered back to the desk, reached for the phone, then set it down. She had two choices. Call a lawyer for advice on keeping her staff out of jail. Or call her resident customers before they heard the gossip at Flo's. And say what? Even if she could track down Lindeman, or reach Shelley at the Sunset Marina between international calls, what would she say? She didn't have a clue as to who had murdered Graham Stuck or why. She couldn't reassure her customers that they wouldn't be in danger at the shop. Or promise that their cars would be finished on schedule—which was the only thing they cared about.

Legal advice would be easier to endure.

Rebecca flipped through the Rolodex. There were three law offices in Blue Marsh, the county seat, but Uncle Walt had stayed with Joachim Delacroix, Head Tide's only lawyer. He felt that Delacroix was sharp and honest. A nice surprise from a young man practicing law in a backwater town, where most locals shunned lawyers, instead settling disputes the old-fashioned way, with fists or a gun. Anyone with possessions worth squabbling over wrote his own will, or got his sixth-grader to do it on the computer at the public library. She hadn't talked with Delacroix since Walt's will had been probated.

The lawyer was not in his office. Rebecca asked Edna to have him call her as soon as he returned. Edna didn't ask what it was about. Undoubtedly she knew. In three hours a juicy story could circulate the entire town twice. With revisions.

Frank entered the office as Rebecca was leaving the message with Delacroix's secretary.

"You calling a lawyer?"

"We can use some legal advice. Don't you think?"

"No, I don't. Course I don't think we had anything to do with Mr. Stuck-up's death. Apparently you do. Which one of us you think did it? Me, because I strangled my wife thirty-two years ago? Paulie, because Stuck maybe spilled a drink on his Armani jacket? Or Val, 'cause . . . 'cause—shit, even if he was drugged up I can't think of a reason why Val'd hurt a snake, much less a person."

Rebecca raked her fingers through her hair. Did she think one of them had done it? No. Of course not.

Frank was overreacting. The guys would not have left the body to rot in the beading machine. As mechanics, they had too much respect for their equipment. As criminals, they would have deflected attention away from the shop, and themselves. Wouldn't they? Assuming they had sufficient time, and no wish to implicate her or each other. Assuming they were really as rehabilitated as her uncle believed.

Rebecca pushed away from the desk and rose. "Frank, there are other issues here." Like the desperate need to finish both cars on time. If they didn't, she wouldn't be paid. If she wasn't paid, the shop would deflate like a hot air balloon, putting the guys out of work.

"Sure there are, Reb." Frank stepped closer, slapped a bill for two cases of 20:50 weight oil on the desk. "Maybe you think we did it together? Offed a business rival just to make things easier for you? Is that it? First sign of trouble, you turn on us. Guess you ain't Walt's kin after all."

Rebecca jerked to standing. She wasn't turning on them. She was reverting to middle-class conditioning. In a crisis you call in professionals: doctor, lawyer, sheriff, plumber.

You pay their bills. They deal with the sewage. "Frank,
That's unfair."

"Yeah? So's life." He slammed the door behind him.

Well done, Rebecca. She started to follow Frank. The phone
rang.

"Vintage & Classics," she said, staring at the closed door.

"Rebecca Moore, how delightful that you called. What
small service may I offer?" Joachim Delacroix's voice
drifted through the receiver. There was a hint of the islands
in his speech, particularly when he was amused. "No, don't
tell me; let me guess. At Flo's they say that one of you has
flayed the competition in a torture machine reminiscent of
the Spanish Inquisition. Or is it 'filleted'?" He chortled.
"Thus, you need legal representation. Am I right?"

"Not guilty."

"It might interest you to know that our citizens are not
shedding tears over the freshly departed."

"After a weekend in the closed shop he was not fresh."
The rancid taste lingered at the back of her throat. Carrying
the handset, she wandered into the lunchroom for water.
"Who's the front-runner?"

"Opinions are divided, though Frank Lewes has the lead.
My favorite scenario is that Mr. Stuck broke into the shop,
hot for your seductive person. Frank defended your honor.
He was so irate at the man's audacity that he tried to remove
the offending, ah, shall I say 'tool' or 'equipment' in the
beading machine. Any truth to the rumor?"

Rebecca nearly choked. "Untrue. I haven't been accosted
since I moved here. I would remember."

"A civic oversight. I'll mention it to the city council." The
glee in Joachim's voice eased away some of her tension.

"You do and I'll be arrested for propositioning."

"In which case, I will defend you *gratis*."

"You may have to defend me *gratis* in this case. Assuming
we need a lawyer." She leaned against the counter. "Maybe
there's nothing a lawyer can do at this point."

"My dear, an attorney can always do something. At the very least, I can bill you for listening. Talk to me."

"As long as the meter's already running?" Joachim chuckled. Rebecca continued. "Okay. Our immediate problem is a 3-Litre Bentley. The sheriff has it cordoned off. There are specks on the door edge which could be blood, or ketchup, or raspberry jam. The car is a last-minute rush. We need access to it now."

Joachim sighed. "I've never seen a vintage Bentley up close. Will I lust after it?"

"Those with testosterone seem to."

"Then I must liberate it. I will speak to Judge Wagner without delay. Anything else?

"Zimmer thinks one of us is the murderer." Rebecca shuddered voicing the concern. She understood the sheriff's assumption. It was a natural place to start. If only he didn't stall there.

"Naturally, the path of least resistance. So, it cannot hurt to have a little free legal counseling. Oh, dear. I sound too charitable for a lawyer, don't I? So, perhaps not free. It will cost you at least two imported beers at Tony's. Shall we say six o'clock?"

Four

Rebecca returned to the office. She held on to the phone receiver while she ruffled the warm fur of the cat's belly with her face. "Do I call the widow, Moe? What should I say?"

For the second time in a year Rebecca envied Mrs. Bellotti, the immigrant who cleaned for her mother in Boston. On all topics relating to death, Mrs. Bellotti was the neighborhood rabbi. She gave advice on how much to spend for flowers; when to bring a casserole; which cards are in good taste. Each morning she opened the *Herald* to the obits, creasing the paper for a long read full of clucks and sighs. Mrs. B. lived for funerals, attending masses for people she barely knew. From the floral arrangements, she could tell the relationship to the deceased, and the degree of sincerity. Thanks to generations of Italian ancestors who transferred this insight to her via their genes, Mrs. B. was never at a loss for the right words of sympathy.

She alone would know what to say to the widow of a man whose naked body you found murdered in your building.

Rebecca dialed Vera Stuck's home number. After ten rings, the widow answered. She announced her name in a flat, soft voice.

Rebecca hung up.

Damn. What could she say over the phone? Through Walt,

she'd known Vera Stuck casually for years. Since Rebecca had taken over the business, they'd traveled in the same circles, to the same cities, the same events, knew the same people. If she was going to pay her respects, Rebecca would have to do it in person. She was sure Mrs. B. would agree.

Rebecca grabbed her car keys. She headed for the machine shop to tell Frank she was leaving and to make sure the guys were coping. And working.

They were. In silence.

No radio. No talking. Cleaning fluid gurgled, circulating through the Safety-Kleen tank. The wire wheel whirred as Val abraded the rust from bolts. Paulie stood back-to at a long bench, stripping the ends from black, cloth-covered wires. High overhead, the ceiling fans rotated without ticking, in unison for once. Not a hum from the thirty-foot-long double bank of fluorescent lights suspended above the workbenches.

No one turned to greet her.

To a visitor, they would look preoccupied with their tasks. Or in mourning for the dead man. To Rebecca, it was obvious that Frank had rallied the troops against their traitorous management. Punishment for permitting police interference or for calling a lawyer. At least she hoped that explained his churlishness. She slipped between the heavy fire doors into the car shop.

Frank was detailing the Hispano-Suiza H6. The overdrive had gone in without a hitch, which was a minor miracle. It would allow the car to purr at lower rpm while cruising at highway speed. Easier on the engine and less tiring for the driver. Frank had road-tested the car and was now touching up bolt heads with black lacquer to match the paint on the single overhead cam engine.

Rebecca watched him move the length of the engine. She clasped her hands behind her back as she had at thirteen, the summer Frank was cajoled into teaching her how an internal combustion engine worked. Then he had pointed out the components and their connections—crankshaft to camshaft, camshaft to tappets, tappets to push rods, push rods to rocker arms to valves. Today, he ignored her. The standoff continued until Rebecca tired of being snubbed.

"Frank—"

"Something wrong with what I'm doing?"

"It looks fine."

"Then what do you want?"

"To apologize for bringing in the Bentley without telling you." Frank grunted and returned to dabbing paint on linkage rods. "The owner phoned Friday, pleading with me to rewire the car. I couldn't turn him down."

"We can do it. None of us minds the hours."

"I mind taking in work on short notice. And I don't like pulling a car away from a competitor."

"Well, get used to it, boss. We gonna be seeing lots of his customers now." Frank slapped down the paintbrush. A glob of black splatted on the bench top.

Until that remark, the potential impact of Graham Stuck's death hadn't really penetrated. With Stuck out of the picture, the small group of vintage car restorers just got smaller. If no one from Vintage & Classics was convicted of murder, their slice of the pie should get bigger. That was good news. The bad news was it would smell like a juicy motive to the sheriff.

Five

Rebecca coasted to a stop in front of Stuck's house, pulled on the parking brake and shut down the car. Driving to Blue Marsh in the topless MGA had helped. The rushing air was cool, the sun warm on her face, adding needed color to her cheeks. A welcome break from arguing with Frank; an hour's escape from her customers. She reached for a hairbrush and worked the bristles through her shoulder-length waves. Dumping sunglasses on the passenger seat, she rummaged in her purse for a tape recorder or something to write on. Then remembered that this wasn't an assignment. It was a courtesy call. *Offer your condolences and get back to work.*

Other than the crunch of Rebecca's boots on the gravel drive, it was Sunday-morning quiet. No close neighbors. No kids playing or dogs barking. Vera's house stood on an acre of land, a solid, two-story structure from the early 1900s. It had narrow lemon siding, dark green shutters and a glassed-in porch along the back side. The grass smelled just-mowed, clipped like a military haircut. Symmetrical patches of dark earth displayed bearded iris, standing poker-straight.

Off to the right was a five-stall garage housing Graham's venture, Capitol Chassis. The business had been grandfathered into the residential neighborhood twenty years earlier, before the zoning committee got busy. The roll-up doors were shut. No sign of Billy Lee, Stuck's one full-time worker. Understandable if he didn't feel like tinkering with old cars with the boss lying in the morgue.

Rebecca rang the bell. A Rufous-sided towhee darted at fallen bird seed in the mulch of the flower bed. He'd had his fill and flitted away long before Vera Stuck opened the door.

Framed in shadow, the widow looked composed. In heels, she was the same height as Rebecca, with understated curves. Simply dressed in a deep chestnut skirt and matching cardigan, cream silk blouse. Her platinum hair was twisted and pinned up. Rebecca's jeans, blazer and wind-tangled locks couldn't begin to compete.

Vera raised an eyebrow, then shrugged. Clearly she wasn't expecting Rebecca. She said as much. With a slight hiccough she retreated to the dining room, leaving Rebecca to follow, or not. At the sideboard Vera raised a nearly empty decanter and splashed a dram of sherry into a stemmed glass. When she sat, she placed the drink on an end table beside a Waterford old-fashioned glass nestled in a crumpled handkerchief. Sunlight through the windows danced on the surface of the amber liquid and set the cut crystal sparkling, but it couldn't improve the gummy residue in the bottom of the second dirty glass. It was as out of place in Vera's immaculate sitting room as Rebecca.

She remained standing, hands in her jacket pockets. "Vera, I can't tell you how sorry I am."

Vera's mouth twitched, maybe a wince, or an attempt at a smile. "You have nothing to be sorry about, especially if you killed him. Did you? I'd like you a whole lot if you had." Vera punctuated the sentence with a dainty laugh and raised her glass in a toast. "Whoever killed him did me a favor." The next laughs were louder. And shrill.

The hair on the nape of Rebecca's neck tingled. She dropped down level with Vera, trying to recall basic first aid: symptoms and treatment for shock. She covered Vera's hand with hers. "Vera? Are you all right? Should I call someone?"

The widow's laughter devolved into a loud hiccough. She waved her free hand as if shooing a pesky fly. "Tell me why Graham was at your shop."

"Do you know, Vera?"

"At first I suspected he'd gone to meet you."

"Why?"

"The usual reason," Vera said.

"Business?"

"You mean car business?" Another shriek of delicate laughter. Vera patted Rebecca's hand and leaned back against the cushion. "Oh, no. My late husband hated working on cars. It's true. He adored the phony, monied people he met because of the cars. 'Lovely people to fuck.' That's a direct quote. And the chic places he got to travel. Loved the rich foods that bloated his belly. Wines he couldn't pronounce any more than he could afford. Adored all that. But he hated twisting wrenches. That's what he called it, twisting wrenches. Graham Stuck was a fraud." Vera hiccoughed again. "Fraud. But he never wasted time with an attractive woman on *business*."

Rebecca stood. "Believe me, Vera. There was nothing—"

"No. Nothing. I can't imagine you sleeping with Graham, or whatever, even if the sheriff can. You're too intelligent. He couldn't control intelligent women. Do you like to be controlled?" Her voice sank to a rasp. "I do, don't I? I must." Vera reached for the dirty glass and handkerchief. Turning it in her lap, she folded the linen over the lip and into the glass as if wrapping an awkwardly shaped gift.

Rebecca wasn't sure she should hear whatever Vera needed to unload. The widow was stressed and had been drinking, a lot. Whatever she said now she'd regret in the morning. Rebecca should leave.

But she couldn't repress her curiosity. Like the old percolator at the cottage, questions started to burp up slowly and demand attention. What kind of relationship had existed between Graham and Vera? Did she know where he'd been on Saturday before being killed in the shop? Did she suspect who had murdered him, and why? Could she supply a list of his enemies? Could she have killed him herself? Not that it was any of Rebecca's business.

Vera set down the padded glass, trading it for the stemmed one. She walked to the sideboard for the decanter, poured another splash. Smidgening her way through the bottle, the way Rebecca's mother smidgened her way through a caloric chocolate doughnut. Vera sipped, leaning against the Rococo sideboard.

"Bradley thinks Graham went to your shop to sabotage it. That nice black man must have caught him in the act and killed him."

"Why would Graham want to sabotage my shop?"

"You take business, money, away from him. He couldn't tolerate losing business—not to a woman."

"Vera—"

"But I think it was a lover. I'm certain he was having an out-of-town affair. Annapolis. Somewhere like that." She reclaimed her seat. And Rebecca's full attention.

"Annapolis? Why there?"

Vera flicked lint from her skirt. When she looked up, there was a faint blush on her cheeks. "I checked the mileage on the odometer whenever he went out of town. For a year it's been the same each trip: one hundred and two miles. Annapolis is the proper distance. It has everything Graham liked: good restaurants, expensive shops, boating. It's small enough to get around in on foot. Crowded enough on weekends to go unnoticed. It's where I would have chosen."

Vera pulled the cardigan close around her like a waif. The woman was hurting. It could be anguish over losing her husband. Or self-pity because of the way he died. To a private, well-bred woman, Graham's murder was excessively crude and much too public. Sort of like his life.

"Billy Lee said he left at three-thirty to visit a 'friend' for the weekend. I was playing tennis. I didn't expect him back until Monday. Today." Vera leaned forward, voice at a whisper. "The man could *not* juggle more than one at a time.

Sloppy with names. Couldn't keep his lies straight. A new one every few months, yes, but never more than one at a time." Vera blanched as another potential social gaffe occurred to her. "Do you think she'll show up at the funeral?"

Rebecca wondered how Mrs. Bellotti would have answered that.

Six

According to Flo, the sheriff's station was on 2nd Street in Blue Marsh, the next town over and the county seat. Didn't take long to get there. Follow Main Street away from town about two and a half miles. Slow down after the sign for Twin Pins Bowling Alley. Next left. Can't miss it.

Blue Marsh was a decent-sized small town. The center was marked by a grassy common with flowering trees, a kid's play area and a war memorial. Courthouse on one side, Baptist and Methodist churches opposite and a block of shops and eateries in between. Mick parked in a diagonal space across from the stores, next to a spot reserved for the sheriff. A tan Chevy Caprice filled the slot. The sheriff must be home.

Mick crossed the street. If he was deciphering the faded sign correctly, the brick sheriff's station had once housed Tulley's Hardware. Heavy door with ornate Victorian hinges said Tulley had done all right peddling nails and paint.

Inside, the place was too cozy, with mint-green walls and the smell of furniture wax. A female officer was on the phone. A young male leaned against the radiator reading a file. The scanner emitted regulation static, the volume turned low. No phones ringing or crazies screaming to see a lawyer, a congressman or the Lord God Almighty. Nobody in the holding cells.

The sandy-haired male closed the folder as Mick approached.

"Help you?" The question was polite, but edgy: one part arrogance, two parts inexperience. Rookies' attitude. Kids, desperate to become seasoned officers, having no clue as to the price they'd pay to get there. Mick pulled out his shield and flipped it open at eye level. The officer shifted his stance.

"You here about the murder?" He capitalized the *M*.

"Your boss in?"

"Yeah. What's the name?"

"Hagan. Michael Hagan. From DC." Mick didn't specify rank, department or district. He did unzip the L. L. Bean windbreaker he'd ordered for the trip. If the kid was curious, he could see that Mick wasn't packing. It was a gesture. Like a Roman shaking hands to show he didn't have a knife up the sleeve of his toga.

"Take a seat." The cop strolled to an office at the back.

Mick remained standing. He fished a cellophane-wrapped toothpick out of his hip pocket. The female officer, "S. Olson," hung up the phone next to her nameplate. She raised an eyebrow. Mick shook his head. No help needed; he was being served.

Sheriff Bradley N. Zimmer emerged from his office. He cracked his neck as he crossed the room. "Hagan?" Curt nod. "With the DC police, huh? Must see some excitement up there."

"Enough."

"Can't believe our little murder would bring you to a piss-ant town like this. How'd you hear about it? Can't have made the city papers. Something I should know about the vic?"

Hagan retrieved the toothpick. He assured the sheriff that he was in town on a personal matter. Though the murder was making the lunch rounds at the diner. Zimmer snorted and turned. He directed Mick to follow him into the office, shut the door and take a seat. The visitors' chair faced a pale wooden desk, the kind middle school teachers used in the fifties. It had seen a lot of idle doodling.

Zimmer cleared his throat. Nodded once to himself. "You homicide?"

"Was. On special assignment with the Feds the last eighteen months. Right now I'm on R&R."

Zimmer nodded again, sucked his lower lip. "Vacation, huh?" The sheriff pulled a stack of photos from the center drawer. He aligned the edges, slid them to the middle, like a deck of cards waiting to be cut. "Willing to take a look?"

The top black and white showed a middle-aged head with dark hair and a darker, splintered crater where the left side used to be. Mouth sagged open, his eyes frozen in a wide-eyed wink. Discoloration marks on the distended skin of the naked torso. Wrists lashed, hands pressed together as if in prayer.

Mick flipped through the rest of the stack. "Local hoodlum?"

"Businessman here in Blue Marsh. Found in a rival shop in Head Tide. Owner cut short the long weekend, discovered him this morning. Stuffed in a machine."

"That the machine?" Mick flipped out a photo showing a large metal box on legs with a two-by-three-foot window at eye level and two six-inch holes arms'-width apart beneath it.

Zimmer nodded. "Beading machine. Air gun inside for blasting off rust and such. That foot pedal on the floor makes it work."

"That didn't do the damage."

"Nope. Dead blow hammer. One of them polystyrene things." Zimmer stabbed at another photo with the eraser end of a pencil. "On the floor next to the workbench. Coroner says there's hair and bits of dried tissue on it."

Mick guessed Zimmer had done his homework at the Home Depot near the beltway. Post-It note on the photo spelled out the details. Mick knew the gist without reading. A dead blow hammer is designed to smack something immovable without the hammer rebounding. The head's filled with lead shot. The shot absorbs the energy. If you believe the spec sheets, it has three times the force of a standard hammer but requires no more effort to swing.

Zimmer tipped back in his chair. "A woman could kill with that thing."

Mick fanned the photos apart, selected a fuzzy one that showed the body inside the beader. "Couldn't have been hit inside the machine. You know where it happened?"

"We do. Harry spotted blood next to an old race car they got in the back room. Some on the floor and on the edge of the car. Not much, considering. Most of it pooled in the machine. Real mess. Best guess is Stuck was hit near the car, caught before hitting the floor, then carried—not dragged, no heel tracks—and dumped in the beader."

"Why not leave the body on the floor? Or take it away?"

The sheriff shrugged.

"You find the clothes?"

"Pushed down in the trash can out back. Weekend going-out-to-dinner clothes: Bill Blass jacket, shirt, trousers, loafers."

"Blood?"

"Yup. He was wearing them."

"Footprints?

"Too dry. Some tire tracks, but hell's bells, it's a car shop. You expect that. Vic drove a foreign station wagon, Subaru. No interest there. Usual glove box and under-the-seat junk."

Zimmer retrieved the photographs. He restacked them in numerical order. He took a deep breath and let it out slowly. "Your personal business—think it might leave you any free time over the next few days?"

"Could."

"Don't mind admitting I could use help, Hagan. Bad. I'm elected. Dale Hemphill, my number two, is the detective. Or was, until he forgot he was supposed to arrest drug dealers, not join them. Doing five to eight. Can't deputize you. No funds till state approves a replacement. But I'd be mighty obliged if you'd give this hick sheriff a pointer or two."

Mick leaned back from the desk. "Got any suspects?"

A slow grin spread over Zimmer's face. "Miss Moore and her gang of ex-cons."

"Rebecca Moore."

"Got to be involved. Homicide happened about midnight. They got security. One of them had to let Stuck in, else how'd he get there? Course they all swear they weren't near the place. Cons are always innocent. Right?"

"Prior offenders working at a fancy car shop?"

"Queer, ain't it? I'll get you their files. Frank Lewes strangled his wife. Val Kearney's a drugged-up thief. Paulson Antrim, well, he's a mite peculiar. Comes from a fine old family, which is probably what's kept his name out of the police blotter. And Moore—" The sheriff looked like he wanted to spit. "I don't know what Moore's story is, but I don't like the plot."

"You got a motive, Sheriff?"

"Not yet, but I will. Bet you me, Hagan, I feel like a fox waiting at the henhouse door. How about you join me for a chicken dinner?"

Seven

Rebecca downshifted and tucked the MG against the curb between a white panel truck and a dark SUV in need of a bath. Parking meters were bagged for the holiday.

Not yet five o'clock, but the take-out dinner crowd had descended on the Great Wall Chinese Restaurant. Those not attending a Memorial Day picnic or flipping burgers on the grill didn't feel like cooking. Rebecca pulled open the gloss red door to the odor of shrimp fried rice. With a nod at Lu Chan, she joined the line behind an electrical contractor and a mother of three under five.

Rebecca prayed Vera was right about an out-of-town lover. Preferably one with an out-of-control husband stupid enough to brag about putting a permanent end to his wife's affair. Or remorseful enough to confess to Stuck's murder and exonerate her workers. Someone Zimmer could lock up quickly without harassing her further. Barring that miracle, Rebecca hoped the lawyer would get the Bentley released so they could work on it. It would be worth a few beers at Tony's to accomplish that feat. But no amount of legal advice, free or not, was worth eating there.

The contractor left, large bag in each hand. Rebecca moved closer to the counter.

What was the bit with Vera and the dirty drink glass?

Maybe it had a crack and she was wrapping it before putting it in the trash? Considerate under the circumstances. Or was she preserving it? A souvenir of her late debauched husband. Why save a drink glass? Maybe she was just fidgeting.

One of the toddlers broke free from his mother's grip and headed for the front door just as it opened. The door swung so wide it nearly flattened the boy. It was pushed aside by a duffel bag, followed by a dark-haired stranger. He had long-lashed blue eyes and tense jaw muscles. Tight jeans over tighter muscles. He tossed Rebecca a nano-glance, then turned toward Lu Chan. With a flurry of nods and the wave of a chopping knife, Chan directed him up the stairs against the side wall. The man hesitated.

Toddler clinging to her thigh, the young mother stepped away from the counter to wait for her order.

Lu Chan called out. "Becca. You want soup." Rebecca swung toward Chan's voice and nodded. Peking hot and sour soup, same as always. She held up her hands four inches apart—small one. Chan smiled. "Same as always." He hollered the order to his daughter at the grill.

When Rebecca turned back, the man with the duffel bag had vanished.

The MG was running rough. Again. Rebecca blipped the gas pedal, let it idle in front of the shop. Could be old gas; she didn't drive it often enough. More likely it needed a tune-up. She couldn't remember the last time she'd tended to the car. It had been Walt's present for her seventeenth birthday. Since the previous owner had put a rod through the block housing, he got it cheap. He thought the '57 sports car was the perfect learning experience for his niece. Over the next four summers, Rebecca had restored the engine, rewired it in its original color scheme and had it reupholstered. She never got around to doing the paint or the chrome.

When she landed the job at the *Washington Post* and moved into a fringe neighborhood in DC, she'd left the MG behind. Walt had parked it in the corner of the barn, waiting for her return. Did he think she'd come back before he died, or know she wouldn't? Had he willed her the place to give her roots, or to protect his lifelong investment? Or maybe there simply wasn't anyone else to leave it to. She should be grateful, but Wolfe was right: You can't go home again. Nothing was the same here without Walt. Or anywhere else, since David. Another dead end.

Rebecca inhaled the aroma of pungent soup filling the car. Late-day shadows from the hundred-year-old maple cast dark streaks over Vintage & Classics, her legacy and albatross. The business was set well back from the street, made up of two buildings joined at right angles. One was a renovated tobacco barn in need of a refresher coat of carmine paint. The other was a low concrete building faced with tan stucco, wine-red doors that once matched the barn. The barn was longer, front and back. In the rear, where it extended beyond the machine shop, there was a door for taking out the trash. In the front, an aging wisteria clung to the building, pale gray branches bending outward toward the sun, laden with purple clusters.

The stucco portion housed the office, bathroom and lunchroom at the front. The machine shop ran along the back. Customers' cars were kept in the barn, which had two four-posted lifts and wide garage doors at both ends. The original sliding barn doors were at the back, a new rolling door with remote at the front. Access from the garage to the machine shop was via sliding fire doors spanning the eight-foot opening.

There was room for up to five cars with their doors shut. Right now the shop was overflowing if you counted the Bentley parked in the machine area. That should have been prosperous news. Plenty of work. *Ha.* Because of the deadline, only the cars entered in the Paris-to-Peking rally were being worked on, so there were only two potential sources of income. One was Lindeman's Hisso, and he wasn't paying yet—for which she should have her head examined. The other was the Shelley's Bentley on which they weren't allowed to work—thanks to its starring role in Graham Stuck's homicide. Cordoned off as part of the crime scene until Delacroix got it released.

She shut down the MG. It stuttered once, then died. As she entered the shop by the front door Val Kearney slipped out through the garage. He rolled the door closed behind him and bounced across the parking area. Short, with long blond hair and wide light eyes, he could be an elf in a Disney storybook. Next to Juanita, with her exotic coloring, they made a cute couple. Too cute. And too young. Having Juanita type and file three days a week was a great help. However, her proximity to Val was providing another managerial challenge to be addressed—someday. Predictably, Val ignored his Yamaha and headed down the street toward Flo's Café. Juanita's shift ended at six.

Rebecca set the Chinese soup on the desk and shrugged off her jacket. From across Main Street, a shaft of light bounced off the window, momentarily blinding her.

Paulie swept in to say goodnight. He handed her a stack of pink memo slips. Three were from the accountant, all with the same message: call ASAP. One each from Lindeman and Shelley. They were together "sightseeing."

"Mr. Shelley called first to make sure you *were* working on his Bentley. Mr. Lindeman called an hour later to make sure you *weren't*. I didn't tell them about the murder. I said to call back tomorrow—the shop was closed for the holiday."

Rebecca barely heard Paulie. Again, a momentary blot of brilliance shot through the window. She raised a hand to shield her eyes. Could be sunlight deflected by metal or reflecting off the glass of a lens. The storefronts across the road looked innocuous. No pedestrians in sight. A sedan pulled away from the curb. Only remaining vehicle was a dark blue Jeep idling in front of Henry's Newsstand.

"Need any supplies for tomorrow?" Paulie offered the same service every night. He drove in to work from the area of country estates, past the ubiquitous suburban mall with a store of every description. He loved to shop.

Rebecca smiled at him. It was hard not to. Decked out in a designer blazer and space-age metal glasses, Paulson Antrim III looked like a generous, rich kid slumming in a car shop. Which he was. She could still remember her uncle's call announcing the new employee and how glad she'd been that he wasn't a prior offender. Paulie played mother, made coffee and fretted. He wooed customers. Never forgot a single detail about their lives, their likes or dislikes. Everyone's instant best friend, though no one knew much about him. And possibly the loneliest person in Blue Marsh County.

"No thanks, Paulie. See you tomorrow."

"Ta." With a wave, he exited and closed the door softly behind him.

Rebecca edged away from the window. She watched as Paulie crossed the lot. Another flash made her blink. A second one followed quickly as Paulie pulled open the door to his baby-blue Cadillac.

She wasn't crazy: Someone had a lens trained on the shop. She was willing to bet the someone was sitting in the Jeep Cherokee with the driver's-side window eased down four inches. She didn't recognize the car. Couldn't see the license plate. Couldn't see through the tinted glass. It was dirty enough to be the one that had been parked in front of the Great Wall while she was getting soup. She recalled the dark-haired stranger—his quick glance at her and away.

Rebecca exited the building half an hour later accompanied by Frank. He was speaking to her, but just barely. The dusting of freckles across his cheekbones and liquid brown eyes didn't soften the lines around his mouth.

She assumed his mood was a reaction to Stuck's death and police interference. She knew Frank could be sullen from the dozen summers she'd spent in exile with Uncle Walt. The two men had worked side by side, as close as spouses: bickering yet loyal. The day Frank had nicknamed her Reb—short for rebel—Walt had explained how Frank had gone to prison for manslaughter. A crime of passion.

Walt warned her not to judge another person too harshly without knowing what he'd gone through. A conservative middle-class teenager, Rebecca nodded sagely, all the while thinking that murder was wrong no matter what. After years as an investigative reporter, she was willing to accept that there could be extenuating circumstances. As a boss, she prayed she wouldn't have to face that lesson again.

Frank locked the building behind them, folded himself into his faded Toyota and headed west to the farmhouse he rented on Hassan Field Road.

Rebecca crossed in front of the barn, then started up the footpath to her home next door. Once on the knoll, she glanced over her shoulder toward the far side of Main Street. The Jeep was still there, still idling. From her vantage, she could see the District license plate. Fishing a pen from her hip pocket, she wrote the number on the folded flap of the soup bag.

Eight

"Punctual, as well as pleasing to the eye."

Joachim Delacroix, Esquire, smoothed his tie as he rose. He stepped around the table to pull out the chair opposite for Rebecca. He was of mixed heritage with the kind of good looks that plateau at twenty and stay unchanged for life. Same for his manners. His mother raised him right. The old-fashioned courtesy was as out of place in Tony's as Delacroix's conservative suit. The combination gave Rebecca the fleeting illusion she was safe and protected. Like snuggling under a goose-down quilt on a snowy night in New England. The weather's still lousy, but you don't care as much. She was glad she had taken time to change.

"Thank you for agreeing to meet, Mr. Delacroix."

"How could I not? I couldn't let you go elsewhere for representation. I'm Jo. May I call you Rebecca?"

"Of course."

His eyes twinkled. "Besides, being seen with one of the principals in this year's most flagrant crime is good for my reputation."

"Being seen conferring with a lawyer is not good for mine. Unless you can exonerate us quickly."

Delacroix removed his eyeglasses, folded them into his

jacket pocket. "Which is why you're here. So, we get right down to business. Admirable. Please hand me five dollars."

Rebecca fished the money from her wallet. Joachim smoothed it on the sticky surface of the table.

"I'm officially on retainer. You're protected by client privilege. And the five dollars will take care of the first round of drinks. What may I get you?"

"Whatever you're having."

"Excellent. We'll not confuse the bartender."

In a seamless motion Delacroix stood, plucked the bill and turned toward the bar. Shoulders undulating with a big cat strut, he picked his way through forty-watt lighting and a wall of cigarette smoke. The room was dense with sweaty drinkers letting loose. Office help in short skirts and fuck-me pumps; sunburned yacht rats in jeans and Topsiders. Everyone looking for a few hours of drink-induced good times. They didn't mind contracting lung cancer or blasting out their eardrums in the process.

Given the noise level, confidential talk would be difficult. Pretending others weren't gawking would be impossible. Every stare and pointed finger brought back the goldfish-bowl existence she'd barely survived after David's death hit the papers. A reporter whose lover kills himself because of her investigation was fair game for the *Post* as well as its competitors. Since her newsroom had more personal dirt, and more recent photographs, they capitalized on the story of their star employee's downfall. She didn't blame them. Just herself.

Rebecca wished she'd asked to meet at the lawyer's office. Or not at all.

Delacroix returned with two frosted mugs. He drank deeply of the pale ale, leaned back and folded his hands low on his lap. "You may begin."

Rebecca shifted her chair to face the bar. Her eyes focused somewhere amid the high-priced brands. She described finding the body; recited the sheriff's questions; noted her employees' lack of alibis and her business interactions with the deceased. She touched on the shop's financial woes.

As she spoke, Delacroix gazed into his beer. When she finished, he drained it. "Very straightforward. Though, as with most engrossing tales, there are many layers. Those not revealed being the most intriguing."

"The only thing I'm not revealing is the extent of my panic." Rebecca played with the moisture on her beer mug as she scanned the throng of rowdy drinkers.

"Panic is most natural. You and your employees are being distracted at a time when work is critical. If you don't finish the cars for the race you will not be paid. Instead of good publicity, you'll be denigrated within the small community of exotic car aficionados. The shop—in which I think you take as much pride as your late uncle—is in financial distress and can't withstand a major blot on its reputation. Is that a fair summation?"

She nodded: fair and distressing.

Delacroix pushed aside his empty mug. "Then we'd best find the sheriff alternative suspects, hadn't we? And quickly. Another round?"

The question was rhetorical. Delacroix rose. Rebecca stopped him, clutched at his arm, digging her nails into his sleeve. "Jo, I left out my paranoid concern that perhaps Stuck wasn't the real target. One of us was. That some maniac is stalking mechanics, photographing us with a telephoto lens, following me around town—first to the Chinese restaurant, then here tonight—plotting his chance to kill again."

Delacroix bent protectively toward his client. "Rebecca, what are you babbling about?"

She scrounged in her purse for a scrap of torn brown paper smelling faintly of sesame oil. She pressed it into his hand and nodded toward a man lounging too casually against the bar. An urban cowboy leaning back on both elbows, scanning every face in the crowd.

"Him. Here's his license number. Check him out. Please."

Tuesday

→

Vintage Racers

Nine

Rebecca awoke with a start.

She listened, heart pounding, blood running cold.

The scream was not repeated. Of course not. The scream had been in the nightmare. Her scream. The scream she'd emitted upon finding David's lifeless body. The scream that woke her each night for weeks after it happened.

She flipped back the quilt she'd dragged out of the closet last night when she couldn't stop shaking and sleep wouldn't come. She refused to huddle in bed like a cornered mouse while the scenes from her old bedroom replayed like movie stills. Yellow light pooling on the waxed oak floor. Sheets twisted from lovemaking. David's limp legs falling off the edge of the mattress, bent like one of Dali's clocks. David's torso pinned to the headboard by the force of the blast. And don't forget the blood. Blood splattered everywhere: fanning the walls, dotting the ceiling, dripping down the black and white photographs framed above the bed—photographs of the Maine coast in fog, ponies wading near Assateague Island—photographs she later mangled, full of rage, because they had watched while David destroyed his life. And hers.

The nightmare had left her alone since she moved. It had stayed behind with her ex-job and former friends. In taking

over her uncle's shop she'd inherited enough worries to con-
sume her during the day. At night, she'd gone to bed too
tired to dream.

Now the nightmare had found her again. It was back, in
bloody Technicolor brought on by discovering another
naked, dead male.

At eight-thirty, the shop doorbell rang. Rebecca's hopes for
a productive morning faded. Shuffling through the invoices
layered on the desk, adding up the hours Lindeman owed
for, she thought about ignoring it. The bell sounded again,
long and impatient. She threw down her pencil and headed
for the door, mumbling a string of medieval tortures to be
used if there was a reporter at the door.

Nothing so benign. Sheriff Zimmer barged in, angrier
than a pit bull on a short chain.

"You have explaining to do, Moore. You lied to me."

He backed Rebecca against the desk. She slid sideways
and strolled to the kitchen. Moe jumped down to follow.

"Would you care for coffee?"

"Don't walk away, girl. You lied. You were here Saturday
night. In this building. At the time of the murder. I got a
witness."

Witness? Rebecca studied the sheriff as she reached for a
clean mug. Was he bluffing? Flo claimed he was too
unimaginative to bluff at poker. With both fists planted on
his hips, Zimmer filled the doorway. The immovable obsta-
cle waiting for an explanation, as incensed as if she were the
first suspect to ever withhold information.

Moe hopped onto the table and began licking a back leg.
When in doubt, cats wash. When in doubt, reporters—even
former ones—occasionally resort to the truth. "You may be
right, Sheriff. I did stop by the shop on Saturday evening.
For a minute or two. I'd forgotten."

"A minute, my ass. Twenty minutes, anyway. Guy who
delivers papers to Harry's ran out of gas. Saw your beat-up
sports car out front. Shop lights were still on when he got

back from borrowing two gallons. And it was Saturday *night*, midnight or later, right about the time someone was snuffing Stuck. You were in here, which explains how he got past the security system."

"What security? Uncle Walt installed it to appease the insurance man. He never activated it. Whole town knows that." Walt used to chortle about the pointlessness of a security system. *Who's going to walk in and steal a vintage car? They're like Old Masters. Each one has a provenance. You can't fence them or part them out. Chassis and engine numbers stamped all over the place.*

"You don't have a security system?"

"We don't use it."

"That's the dumbest thing I ever heard. But it don't mean it wasn't an inside job. Stuck was a rival, you were in the building at the right time and you lied about it. You're starting to smell worse than the body. I'm thinking about hauling you in."

"Not yet, Sheriff. I believe I'll call my lawyer." Rebecca pirouetted and returned to the office.

The situation was getting out of control. She had nothing to do with Graham Stuck's death. In life she'd avoided him as much as possible, which was difficult. Since she'd taken over her uncle's business, they hung out with the same monied enthusiasts. Graham preferred owners with overpowered cars and overdeveloped egos. The combination made it easy to overcharge them, he'd confided to Rebecca with an oily leer he used on the fairer sex. A few people found him delightfully naughty. Just shaking hands with Graham Stuck made Rebecca want to scrub all over with Gojo—the industrial kind with pumice. Dead, Stuck was proving harder to wash off.

Rebecca punched in Joachim Delacroix's number. Miraculously he himself answered. As she requested immediate counsel, Rebecca sat half on the edge of the desk with one eye on the lunchroom. Frank had entered it from the shop, closed the door behind him. He stood quietly, holding a greasy, foot-long wrench at his side. Lounging on alert, like a longtime security guard in charge of a psychopath. Which was probably the way Frank felt. He didn't speak. Didn't have to. Sheriff Zimmer understood what he was saying. Rebecca was touched to see Frank in the role of protector. Though his stance probably had more to do with testosterone, and the natural antipathy of criminals for the police, than with chivalry.

Had Frank overhead the sheriff's accusation and understood the implication? Would Frank buy into the scenario—that his boss had discovered Stuck in the shop and eliminated the competition with one swat of a hammer? She couldn't blame him. It was starting to sound plausible even to her.

She reentered the lunchroom, crossing between the men to sit at the table. She smiled at Frank.

"Jo Delacroix is on his way over. Thank you, Frank."

Frank nodded. Walking slowly, he exited the room, taking his spanner and aggression with him. Minutes later he was replaced by the lawyer carrying a waxed pastry sack.

"Morning, Sheriff." Joachim nodded to Zimmer, set the bag on the table where Moe could sniff it. "I've been in contact with Judge Wagner. Tomorrow morning we'll have an injunction to release the Bentley. If you wish to go over the car again, you'd better do it today."

That was fabulous news. Rebecca hoped Jo wasn't grandstanding just to annoy the sheriff.

"But that's not why you're here so early, is it, Brad?" Delacroix gripped Rebecca's arm, hauled her to her feet. "I'm sure you'll excuse us. I'd like to have a word with my client. Help yourself to a blueberry muffin and that wonderful-smelling coffee. Kenyan?" Jo propelled Rebecca out of the kitchen and into the office.

"Good nose. Paulie would be proud of you." She broke from his grip.

"Let's hope I'll be proud of you. What, pray tell, has riled the sheriff on this fine morning?"

Rebecca sat. She confessed she'd stopped in at the shop Saturday night around the time of the murder. After a few hours trying to relax at Tony's, she gave up on dancing with the locals and drove to the shop before going home. She had neglected to inform the sheriff of that small fact. An out-of-gas witness had done it for her.

Delacroix shook his head. Did Rebecca use the front door? *Yes.* Did she lock up? *Yes.* Did she activate the security system? *What security system?* Did she see anyone else around? *Not a soul.* Anything unusual? *A station wagon in front of the drugstore having car trouble. Hood up.* Any other cars? *Could have been one behind it. A van parked in front of Henry's.* Did she think the witness could have gone in after her and killed Graham? *Not unless Jo knew something suspicious about the seventy-year-old, one-armed deliveryman for the* Blue Marsh Gazette.

"Why didn't you tell Zimmer you were here?"

"I didn't know there was a witness."

"Such a silly lie, Rebecca."

"An omission."

"Brad isn't MENSA material, but he's listened to more tall tales than you've written about. Why not just paint a scarlet *G* on your chest for guilty? What was your reasoning?"

Rebecca raked her hair away from her face. "Zimmer would ask why I was in the building. I was reluctant to tell him."

"Ashamed to say you were here to pick up financial records? Is that worth lying about?"

"That I needed to go through those papers because the shop is in financial trouble—to me that's worth keeping quiet about. Yes. Among other business shortcomings, Uncle Walt didn't pay taxes as regularly as the IRS expects. Our accountant has broken an entire box of No. 2 pencils trying to figure the least costly way out of the mess. Any way out is going to take money the shop doesn't have. I sold my laptop to make payroll last month. But that's my concern, not this town's. Call me arrogant, but I refuse to have the shop's financial ruin—or Walt's poor judgment—as the next hot topic served up at Flo's."

"Is it better that Flo's customers suspect you of murder?" he asked, dropping his eyeglasses on the desk.

"They do anyway. I take comfort in knowing it's a lie."

Ten

Mick slid behind the wheel of the Jeep. He pulled a cell phone out of his pocket and punched the digits with his thumb. Sergeant Sal Bastisto answered on the second ring.

"Hey, *compadre*. How goes it down south?" Mick heard Sal spit out a hunk of pistachio shell, then crack another with his incisor. "Met any good lookers?"

Not the one you mean. Mick recalled Moore's face the previous day as she bounded up the porch steps to the house next door. Big white clapboard place, pointed roof in the center, wide porch on three sides, six steep steps down to a brick walk which petered out at a flower bed. Easy to imagine kids squealing with laughter racing up and down those stairs. Norman Rockwell, alive and well in rural Maryland. Moore was clutching a paper bag in one hand, tugging her shirt free from the waistband of her jeans with the other. Mick had snapped the shutter as she glanced over her shoulder at a noise imagined. Full face shot: good bones, expressive eyes, no makeup. More vulnerable than the black and white glossy in the police jacket. Way less cocky.

"Yeah, you ol' lech. Nothing but beauties. I've found one just your style—independent businesswoman with a deep laugh and ample meat on her bones. Send me your snapshot, I'll see if she's interested."

"She should be so lucky." Sal cracked another nut. "What you're saying is that you're not getting any. How's the weather? Tell me you're not calling from the beach."

"I didn't call to discuss the weather, Sal. Need you to do me a favor."

"You're on vacation, boy. Let it go. You did what you could."

"Not that. I need background checks on a handful of suspects. A couple with known priors. I'll fax photos and prints if we've got them."

"Who's we? What are you messing in? I thought you were taking time off, looking for, what's the word the shrinks use?"

"Closure. Sure thing. But while I'm waiting around for closure to happen, the local sheriff needs some pointers on a murder that may not be as simple as he'd like."

"Mick, what's going on? Clear the air with her, then get back up here while you still got a job."

"Right, Sal." Mick disconnected. He started the car and pulled a U-turn into the traffic heading west.

He could have talked with Moore last night at the bar. Should have. She was sitting at a corner table opposite a tall mulatto in a suit and school tie. Even money said he was a lawyer. Which was a good move, since if the sheriff had his way, someone from her shop was going to need legal help. Moore was a regular Scheherazade, leaning toward the suit, real intent on whatever tale she was spinning. The lawyer sat upright like a commemorative statue, absorbing every word. Maybe it made sense to him. To Mick, things didn't add up.

He fished in the ashtray for a wrapped toothpick. He'd let the department therapist convince him that if he talked with Moore face-to-face he could accept her role in David Semple's death, put the mess behind him. Reconcile his contradictory feelings toward her. Part of him continued to blame her for David's suicide; another part cast her as the victim in the affair. Both parts found her more attractive than he was comfortable with.

Particularly in the half-light of an out-of-town bar. Moore's drinking outfit suited her—short gray skirt, paler silk top. The neckline skimmed her collarbone. More good bones. Very classy. Definitely DC material, not Hicksville, Maryland.

But seeing her *in situ* only clouded the picture. Moore was from a prosperous New England family. She was well educated, a respected city reporter and a looker. Why would she dump a soaring career and bolt for the sticks to run a car shop staffed with criminals?

Sal called it conscience—remorse over the investor's death. Mick wasn't buying it. If she was capable of feeling anything so noble, Semple might still be alive. So what if she'd inherited her uncle's business? Why not sell it, invest the money? Keep doing what she was good at. Why would she care about old cars, or ex-cons? Heck, Mick was male and he didn't care much about old cars. The only use for an ex-con was as an informant.

And now there was a murder in her shop. Mick turned up the radio.

A few miles west of the old town center, suburbia reared its ugly head—clusters of two-story houses with vinyl siding and stone facades across the front, three-car garages. Communities named Westmont Village and The Gables at Back Cove. Harbingers of more progress to come.

When he turned south, the cookie-cutter homes petered out, replaced by almost-green fields. A smattering of horse farms with acres of whitewashed fencing. Day was nearly perfect: clear skies, full sun, less humidity than yesterday. Mick lowered the car window and breathed deeply. No just-mowed smell. Too bad, freshly cut grass was one of the only good things about the country.

A couple of miles farther Mick spied the sign for Hassan Field Road. He took a left and followed it until he saw a square mint-green house opposite a man-made pond. Lewes's home was just as Zimmer had described it: *One and a half, maybe two storys with them dormer windows, front porch in bad need of paint.*

Mick drove past it to a cluster of evergreens, where he stashed the Jeep. From the rear seat he lifted out a black sports bag with every toy a would-be housebreaker could want. In the tree line opposite the back porch he squatted on pine needles to scan the neighborhood. Two squirrels chased each other through last fall's oak leaves. A crow complained to no one in particular about life in general. He could smell rubbish being burned somewhere close by. Lonely stretch of road. No people in sight. Mick crossed to the back door. He knelt down, ready to work the lock. No point. When he rested his hand on the handle, it turned, the door swung open on oiled hinges. Careless criminal: Doesn't lock his car, doesn't lock his house. Country living had made him soft. Or Frank Lewes had nothing left to care about.

Eleven

Rebecca shut the door behind her lawyer and escaped to the garage. She was checking air pressure in the Hisso's spare tire when she was startled by rapping on the window. The face of Hal Lindeman rose into view over the sill like a harvest moon. He grinned, crossed his eyes, stuck out his tongue and slipped back out of sight. She unlatched the door and let him in.

"Rebecca, sweetie." Lindeman kissed her on both cheeks and smothered her in a bear hug. He was tall and wide, with a voice that preceded him the way trumpets announce a king. He owned the 1927 Hispano Suiza that Frank was prepping up front. A longtime customer of Walt's, Lindeman had been truly saddened by his death. He'd been equally amused by a slip of a lass taking over a car restoration shop. He trusted Rebecca, sort of. She trusted him less.

"What were you doing out there, Hal?"

"Glimpsed Stuck's car and wanted a word with him." Lindeman's voice dropped to what passed for a whisper. "Is he here?"

"In spirit only."

Lindeman frowned, moved on to a more pressing subject. "You didn't return my call, Rebecca. Very naughty. I know why. How could you agree to restore Shelley's Bentley?"

"Just a quick rewire, Hal."

"I feel betrayed."

"Don't." She tried to grin. "We're only working on Todd's car to help you."

"Help me? How?"

"Your victory would be hollow without a decent competitor. Todd's the only one with a chance of beating you. Right?"

"Bull. I'd be as relaxed as a purring kitten knowing victory's around the next bend. No, I don't approve of your shop preparing both the Hisso and the Bentley." Hal gripped Rebecca at arm's length and cocked his head: a puppy looking for approval, or a tender spot to chew on. "Can I convince you to do an imperfect rewire?"

"Not even if you paid me."

"Low blow, Rebecca." He bellied past her to coo over Moe lounging in the in basket "Then I insist you send the Bentley back to Graham. Make that pompous sod finish it himself."

"Guess you haven't heard." Rebecca headed for the lunchroom.

Lindeman and Shelley had spent Memorial Day wining and dining themselves in the nation's capital. They claimed to be blissfully ignorant of Stuck's demise. Over coffee, Rebecca filled Lindeman in. She could envision Hal later at the motel, pacing the length of the room with the phone glued to his ear and a glass of single malt in his hand, dialing everyone who'd ever heard of Graham Stuck. His version of the murder would be less gory than the one passing tables at Flo's, but it would travel faster, farther, and in much classier circles.

Lindeman begged to see the murder scene. *Please.* Then he could concentrate on the H6.

Rebecca led him into the machine shop. The corner of the room was dim near the glass beader. The odor of death mingled with whatever cologne Paulie had spritzed in the air.

The outline of a hammer was taped on the gray floor. A few drops of blood. No gore. Nothing to indicate that a life had been brutally terminated in the room. The British racing-green Bentley stood roped off in the center. After Billy Lee had driven the car over on Friday night, Rebecca had steered it through the car shop into the one bay in the machine area where it would be convenient for rewiring. If she'd left it beside the Hisso they'd be working on it now.

Hal's real object in visiting the murder scene, of course, was to gloat over the incapacitated Bentley. He needed to reassure himself that the 3-Litre was less well prepared than his Hisso. He grinned broadly at seeing the Bentley looped with crime-scene tape like crepe paper left over from the prom. The black fenders showed traces of fingerprint powder. The top was folded down. The tonneau covering for the back seat was unsnapped and stashed on the floor next to a cardboard box. Lindeman leaned carefully over the edge of the Bentley's door. "What's the petrol capacity?"

"Eleven gallons. You want the mpg rating?"

"Already know it: twenty-two miles per gallon at thirty-miles per hour. Hisso gets nineteen, but the tank's bigger. What spares has he got on board?"

"None. Graham hadn't outfitted the car."

"Good. What's in the carton?"

"Bits the cops found in the Bentley." Rebecca read from the list attached to the box. " 'Part qt. of oil, 2 CDs, 3 rags, spare fuse wire, 1 map of So. Cal., 8 gas receipts, sunglasses (missing bow), chewed pencil and a sticky dime.' Sheriff had every item fingerprinted, which was a waste of ink. He had an officer box it, tape it shut and leave it here, since he couldn't think of a reason to confiscate it and clutter up the station."

"What an inspiring sight." Hal sighed. "There sits my rival's car: unfinished and untouchable. Bless his heart. Graham Stuck has done me an unexpected favor. About time. Who could have scripted this?"

When the phone rang, Lindeman was trailing behind

Frank like an attentive Beagle. He listened respectfully as Frank opened the hood and pointed out the modifications and the new overdrive unit. When Frank pushed the starter button and the 6597cc, V-12 engine purred to life, Lindeman darn near purred himself. The Hisso gleamed. Hal glowed. To Rebecca, his joy looked like money in the bank—please. She suspected Lindeman was seeing glossy four-color photographs in *AutoWeek* recording his triumph. *American entrepreneur Hal Lindeman and his 1927 Hispano-Suiza H6 in front of the Eiffel Tower; Lindeman haggling in a Turkish bazaar; resting in the shadow of the Great Wall and, of course, in the winner's circle accepting the silver trophy and obligatory champagne.* Lindeman stroked the length of the drophead's hood with his massive hand, a lover caressing an ivory thigh.

Rebecca left the men discussing gear ratios and torque. She took the call in the office.

Edna, Delacroix's secretary, apologized for the lawyer not calling himself. "Mr. Delacroix wanted you to have this information right away. He said to tell you that 'the man'—he said you'd know who—is Lieutenant Michael Hagan, a detective from Washington, Second District. Not, underlined twice, not a serial killer. You can relax. Did you get that?"

"Yes, Edna. I get the message. But why is a DC detective trailing me?"

"That's precisely what Mr. Delacroix wants to know. What should I tell him?"

Todd Shelley, owner of the 3-Litre, was the next person through the door. He arrived at the shop before Lindeman could wipe the smirk from his face.

Shelley took vintage racing seriously. He'd flown in from Los Angeles on Friday, shown up at Capitol Chassis for a surprise visit to oversee final preparations on the car he'd entered in the Paris-to-Peking Rally. Graham Stuck wasn't at his shop, he'd already left for the weekend. That didn't stop Shelley from throwing a hissy fit when he examined the car.

Poking under the dashboard, Todd had found frayed wires leading to the dynamo, and plastic crimp-on connectors. More than enough to set his thin blue-blooded pressure soaring. Screaming lawsuit at Graham's assistant, Shelley got as far as the end of the driveway before he phoned Vintage & Classics. He groveled, in effete, pseudo-British fashion.

"Might be fine for a bloody Sunday drive in the country, but not for a race across Allah-forsaken Turkey, for Christ's sake. Rebecca, darling, friend that you are, you've got to help."

Reluctantly, she had agreed—bonus upon timely completion.

Now Todd Shelley listened with a mixture of feigned horror and vulgar curiosity while Rebecca repeated the details of the murder. He clucked along with Lindeman, enjoying the drama until she reached the punch line that the Bentley was sitting idle. Hal roared with laughter. Shelley blanched.

"What do you mean, off limits? It simply can't be." Todd's narrow face was mauve en route to purple. "It ships next week. You must be working on the car. I insist. I won't stand for this. Do you hear? I'll sue. You, and the effing police. I'll sue."

Twelve

At two-thirty in the afternoon, Mick had to wait five minutes for a table at *Flo's*. He couldn't believe that the Tuesday special was packing them in. Magic Marker sign boasted "Chipped Beef on Toast." The SOS of World War II: thick gray gravy flecked with dead beef sliding over the edge of the plates as the cute Hispanic dropped them in front of hungry customers. Only in rural America could they sell stuff that looked and smelled that bad.

Mick requested a menu. He watched the locals over the top edge. A one-diner town might have advantages. A cop could loiter all day, eat homemade pie, talk to his neighbors and never do a lick of legwork. Leads would come through the door, be handed to him like after-dinner mints. All he'd have to do was unwrap 'em.

As expected, there was a single topic of conversation— Graham Stuck, who'd done it and why. Most of the locals were maligning the ex-cons and their woman boss. Sentiment ran high against Moore, about seven to three, though no one had a real motive. Other than a woman like that ought to be married, raising her kids, not trying to boss a bunch of mechanics.

Flo defended her. "Rebecca didn't kill him. No way. Too small."

"Didn't take no strength to smack him. You ask Brad."

"Next you'll be telling me even his missus could have done it."

"Why not? Vera Stuck looks like a stay-at-home, mind-your-manners kind of wife, but who knows? Wife's always number one suspect. Might be that Graham stepped out on her once too often." Heads bobbed in agreement.

"Yeah. Like with Sissy over at the *Blue Goose*." Titters sprang up throughout the room.

Flo squashed their amusement. "Shoot, that's been over more than a year. Sissy's shacked up with the guy runs the bowling alley on the way to Waldorf."

Mick braced the menu against the napkin dispenser. His gut told him that the murder was too bizarre for the usual you'll-never-cheat-on-me-again retaliation. Still, if he was going to help out the sheriff, Mick would have to take a look at the wife, Sissy and any other girlfriends who surfaced. And their partners.

Of course, the woman he was most curious about was Moore. Could she have been another of Stuck's conquests? Or his partner in a business scheme gone bust? Drugs, maybe? Bet they could smuggle illegal substances around the world in those fancy cars without attracting attention. Or maybe Moore was researching another exposé, never quit her job at all, just went underground. Lured another unsuspecting sap to do her bidding.

Zimmer entered the diner just as Mick's corned beef on rye came out of the kitchen. The sheriff strode over, pulled out the chair opposite. One nod toward Flo and a piece of lemon meringue pie and two glasses of milk arrived at the table.

"Spoke to Moore," the sheriff said. "Claims to have gone into her building to pick up financial papers. Wanted to read over them on Sunday. 'Peruse' them, she said. Weak, if you ask me. She's hiding something. You heard anything from your Washington contacts?"

"Not yet. Got a good look at Lewes's place, though."

"Don't tell me you've been breaking and entering? No, don't. Just tell me you found something points to his guilt."

"Guilty conscience, definitely."

Frank Lewes's bedroom had been the most revealing room in his house, and it was real sparse. Second floor back, facing the field across the road. Hazy sun made rectangles on a braided rug in front of the dresser. Two bookcases ran along under the window, double-layered with used paperbacks bought for a quarter at library sales: *The Spy Who Came in from the Cold, Checkers for Winners, Mysteries of the Solar System, How to Fix Everything in Your House*. On the top shelf were two eight-by-ten photographs in handmade pewter frames. They were positioned to be seen from the double bed with its blue coverlet. One pictured a lovely dark-eyed woman, promise twinkling in her smile. The other held the swaggering face of a youth who resembled Lewes through the cheekbones.

If Mick were a betting man, he'd wager those were daily reminders of the mechanic's fall from grace. Portraits of the wife he'd throttled and the brother who drove him to do it. Zimmer's file said the man had done more than a decade for voluntary manslaughter. Frank Lewes may have paid his debt, but he hadn't forgotten the crime. Or forgiven himself for it.

"Hell, Hagan, conscience won't convict a man if he keeps his mouth shut. What I need is evidence."

"Lewes's house is too clean for that."

"Didn't think it could be that easy."

Mick bit into his sandwich. "Never is. Glad it's your case, Sheriff."

"Me, too." Zimmer was practically humming. He dabbed milk off his upper lip with a wad of paper napkins. "This is some week. First a juicy murder. Then you breeze into town to give me a hand. And just now I get a visit from a federal judge. Head Tide is a happening place. And I'm the man in charge."

"Federal? You saying Stuck was involved in something more creative than changing tires?"

"Nah." Zimmer drained one glass. "Judge says he's a friend of the family. Wanted to know if he could pick up the deceased's effects. I say, 'Hell, no.' He says, 'Graham's widow is concerned about papers that might have been found with the body. She has suffered a great shock, Sheriff Zimmer, and is looking for answers.' I told him if I have answers in my property drawer that might shed light on Stuck's murder, I'm keeping them."

Mick inclined his head at the chattering patrons. "For a married businessman with no priors, Stuck's death isn't generating much sympathy."

"Ain't that the truth. He wasn't from here. Got a real prize when he married Vera Murdock, come to settle in Blue Marsh. He worked with Walter Moore in his snooty car shop for a short spell. Got uppity one day and quit. Or got fired. Heard it both ways. A month later he opened a business in direct competition with Moore. Father-in-law financed him, folks said. Cocky little snot. Stuck, not Murdock, though he was a piece of work I wouldn't hang on my wall."

Zimmer stared into his milk. "Stuck was a bantam rooster, too full of himself. Started cheating on Vera right off. Vera's always been a bit sad. Got sadder after her marriage. Deserved better." Zimmer mashed the last piece of crust with his fork and used it to wipe the plate. "You get a chance, you go talk to her. She might be more open with an outsider. Okay, Deputy? Told her you'd stop by."

"Don't mind if I do, Sheriff."

Thirteen

Mick bought a *Washington Post* at the newsstand. He cruised by Vintage & Classics to make sure his suspects were accounted for, then drove to Blue Marsh, through town and toward the coast. At the sign for the Sunset Marina & Boatyard, he turned north, away from the water, and took the first left onto Crow's Nest Lane. Parked on the berm of the road where he could watch Stuck's house through a bank of overgrown shrubs.

He waited almost two hours for a gaggle of well-wishers to leave their casseroles and depart. Long enough to finish the crossword. He dropped it onto the passenger seat as the last car exited the driveway. Before Mick could turn the key in the ignition, the widow wobbled her way across the gravel. Dark glasses covered her eyes, bright scarf at her throat. Vera slid into a silver Jaguar, pulled out of the drive and purred down the highway toward the waterfront.

Mick followed.

He was too close when the Jag turned down the narrow road leading to the marina. He couldn't back off, the pickup behind him was playing bumper tag. Like circus elephants, the three cars wound through a cluster of faded two-room cottages with tin roofs, mended screens and no yards. At the last bend, the shacks on the right side gave way to a sand

parking lot for the boatyard. "Wet & Lift Slips." Whatever
that meant. Mick jerked the Jeep into the boatyard lot. Vera
Stuck and the pickup continued on past a sign that said
"Parking for Restaurant Only." The silver car disappeared
behind a wall of shrubbery. She could be there to grab a bite
to eat, or have a drink in public. Or to meet the undertaker.
Or someone else. He'd give her a few minutes to settle in,
then satisfy his curiosity.

Mick wedged the Jeep into a half space between a BMW
and a Dodge Ram. There were almost as many cars in the lot
as there were boats in the narrow inlet, but few people
milling about. A two-story dilapidated house from the last
century blocked the view of open water. It looked ready to
topple into the bay. It could have been the office for the marina, or someone's idea of rustic decoration. Or a relic too
stubborn to fall down and not worth the expense of a wreck-
ing ball.

He locked the Jeep and strolled toward the harbor. Slick
gray docks hugged both sides of the shoreline, sailboats and
yachts strung bumper close. An occasional fishing boat with
more antennae than a cable station was thrown in for variety.
Sailboats outnumbered powerboats two to one. Scenic on
postcards, they struck Mick as inefficient and unnerving.
With motorboats you were in control. You could direct the
speed and change the course. Sailboats were too chancy. At
the mercy of winds and currents and such.

A raised walkway spanned the shallow water connecting
the two wings. At the midpoint, Mick leaned on the railing,
looked beyond the hedge for Vera's car. It was prominently
displayed near the entrance, the metallic silver paint con-
trasting prettily with the pink tea roses. Valet-approved set
of wheels. The waning sun reflected off the plate-glass windows of the restaurant. It was a large rectangular building,
half of it perched over the water on weathered pilings: defy-
ing gravity, raging seas and strong winds. Two levels of
maybe twelve motel rooms harnessed it to land. From the
dining room, patrons could gaze out to sea or keep an eye on

their investments next door. Or watch weekenders try to tie up without scraping their bows.

Mick heard voices, two men approaching from the far dock. One was a big guy with a rusty beard flecked with gray. The other was a David Niven look-alike, complete with sandy mustache. Unless they separated they couldn't get by Mick. They stopped to natter. The large man addressed Mick. "Glorious day for a sail."

"I guess. Why aren't you at sea?"

"Touché." The fat guy laughed. "I don't have a boat. Here, that is. In Maryland my interest is automobiles."

"Vintage & Classics?" It wasn't much of a guess.

"*Et tu, Brute?* Tell me they're not prepping your car for the Paris-to-Peking? I can't stand more competition."

"They're not," Mick obliged. "What's a Paris-to-wherever?"

The guy beamed and stuck out a paw. "Hal Lindeman here. Delighted to meet a noncontestant. My friend, and main competitor, is Todd Shelley. Are you a reporter sniffing around the murder? No. With the local gestapo? Innocent tourist? No matter. Let us buy you a drink. I'll enlighten you about the Paris-to-Peking Rally. Then we can speculate about V&C and their tasty little murder. We crave diversion, don't we, Todd?"

Shelley grunted and led the others across the parking lot. On the far side, they ducked through an arch in the hedge and followed the flagstone walk to the restaurant and lounge. Shelley pulled ahead, sandals flapping, intent on reaching the bar. Type-A businessman, wound much too tight. Someone who makes bundles of money but has no fun spending it. Probably a couple of ex-wives who enjoy it, though. Of course, his tension could have been caused by the current events. Shelley was the poor sap whose Bentley was stuck in quarantine because of the murder. Shelley's bad luck accounted for much of Lindeman's mirth. The fat man jiggled all over with good humor. He'd just returned from "exercising the Hispano-Suiza." The name melted on his tongue like crème caramel. He glowed with assurance that Mick was drooling with envy.

"Make 'em in Detroit, do they?"

The big guy roared. Even Shelley tittered. Wasn't hard to amuse these yokels. Be nice if they'd amuse him in return with tales of Rebecca Moore and her car-fixing cronies.

The Half Shell Lounge at the marina was a scenic place to drink. Long mahogany bar with traditional brass rail, high-backed swivel seats and an unobstructed view of the bay. Drinkers gazed at the sparkling blue water at a distance, green and gold reeds sprouting from rocky clefts up close. A few circling gulls in between. Very conducive to getting very mellow.

Shelley led the way around the front curve of the bar to the end farthest from the dining area. Mick perched on the corner stool where he could keep an eye on the back of Vera Stuck's head. So far, she was alone at a table near the window, sipping. Working on the mellow part. Lindeman ordered scotch all around. Not Mick's drink, but hey, when in Blue Marsh, you go with the flow. The big guy swirled the brown liquid in his glass, set it down without tasting it.

"So tell us, Michael Hagan, what's your connection with Vintage & Classics?" Clearly Lindeman had dismissed the possibility that Mick was a customer. Shelley nursed his drink, nose first.

"Who says there is one?"

"Saw you casing the joint this afternoon when I returned from my drive."

Mick grinned at the observant bastard. "You could say I'm helping out with the investigation."

"PI?"

Mick took a sip. Lindeman took Mick's lack of response as a definite maybe. "Helping whom? Oh, right, you can't tell. Client confidentiality."

"Good of you to understand. You know the victim?"

"The late, hardly lamented Graham Stuck? Did we know him, Todd?" He winked at his friend. "Certainly. I've known—did know—knew Graham for more than twenty years."

"They fought like bloody cats and canines," Todd said.

Lindeman pretended not to notice. "Started out at his shop. With a Cord Cabriolet, L-29. Gorgeous car. Never got it to accelerate smoothly, but you should have heard her roar on the highway." Hal sighed, wagged his finger at the bartender for another round.

"Now you take your cars to Vintage. Why?" Not a hard question, but Lindeman thought about it a beat too long.

Todd prodded. "Yeah, Hal, tell him why you left Graham."

"You could say that Graham pushed his price too high for my taste. Graham tended to be pushy, didn't he, Todd?"

"Graham Stuck was a whore-mongering asshole. I'm surprised someone didn't kill the pretentious little shit before now."

Lindeman raised an eyebrow. "My, my. How do you really feel, Todd, old friend?"

"Yet you took your Bentley to him for work. How come?" Mick leaned over the bar and snatched a cube of lemon stuck on a toothpick. He dumped the lemon in the ashtray. Across the room, Vera was staring at her reflection in the plate-glass window. She raised a hand and held the palm against the glass as if to gauge the temperature or blot out the fading sun. Or her face.

"Let's say that Graham encouraged my patronage. Excuse me." Shelley slipped off the stool and headed for the men's room.

Lindeman watched his friend leave. "Yes, do excuse Todd. He's had a rough few days. Being screwed by Graham every which way. Bad enough that work on the Bentley was behind schedule. Then he pulls the car and takes it to V&C and what happens? Graham gets killed there. Now they're not allowed to work on the car, you know. It's a veritable curse." Lindeman's raised glass couldn't hide his smirk. "And, of course, there's Lily."

"Lily?" Over the big man's shoulder, Mick watched Vera fish in her purse. She pulled out a blue leather wallet and walked primly to the pay phones near the coat check.

"The lovely, vacuous Lily. Todd's current wife. Number three, or is it four? Several years ago rumors circulated that Lily and Graham were overly cozy at various functions. We waited for Todd to blow his top and take his Bentley elsewhere. When he didn't, more rumors emerged. My personal favorite involves business secrets Lily might have divulged to Graham. Pillow talk of the most damaging kind."

"Secrets Graham might have leveraged to ensure Shelley's continued patronage? A.k.a. blackmail?"

"That's the rumor." Hal nodded.

"This rumor mention what these business secrets might have been?"

"No. But Todd makes indecent profits on his overseas ventures. So it was assumed . . ." Lindeman lifted his glass to his lips as Shelley remounted his stool.

"Amusing Mr. Hagan with tales of infidelity, Hal? Hard for you to keep your trap shut, isn't it?" Lindeman flushed like a naughty, though unrepentant, child. Shelley picked up his drink. "Mr. Hagan, don't be offended if I tell that it's none of your business. Unlike Hal, I have an alibi for Saturday night. Her name is Denise Spotelli. She lives in Arlington. You, or the law, or the fecking *National Enquirer* may have her address, phone number and bra size *if* it becomes necessary. My dear wife can hardly complain if our liaison becomes public." Todd bobbed ice cubes with his little finger, then licked it.

Liaison, close bond, interrelationship, communication between parts of an armed force, and the ever-popular *illicit love affair.* Mick enjoyed fraternizing with educated people. Better vocabularies than the druggies in the District.

Fourteen

Ten of five. Rebecca couldn't put off the accountant any longer. She blew dust from her old leather briefcase, emptied it and crammed in a sheaf of company spreadsheets. She dropped it by the front door and headed into the car shop. Frank hissed like a radiator when she announced she was leaving for a couple of hours. She told him to lock up when he left. He flung an oily rag at the workbench, where it settled with an effete flutter. "Sure. Go. Get out of here. We can do the work by ourselves. Don't need you."

"That I know. Why bring it up now? Are you still annoyed because I called Jo?"

"That's nothing compared with what else you done." Frank grabbed for a screwdriver. "One thing for you to lie to the sheriff. No one going fault you for that. But why lie to us? What you doing hanging around the shop late at night when there's murder going on?"

"What do you think I was doing—killing Graham Stuck?"

Frank snorted. "No, little lady. I seen plenty of killers. You ain't one. You'd be so busy fretting about the outcome you'd never get it done. I know you wasn't killing Stuck. What I don't know is what you was up to that you won't tell us." Frank's glare was a red flag to a bull, but Rebecca refused to charge. He turned back to the car to tighten a bolt that was already snug.

Why not tell Frank that she was picking up financial spreadsheets Saturday night? Level with him that Walt had been too generous in giving his money to the needy; too lenient about collecting payments from the rich. Show him the overdue invoices, the thousands of dollars owed to Walt. The shop had been busy constantly catering to some of the wealthiest car enthusiasts in the country, yet it was in danger of going under. It's how the rich stay rich, someone once quipped. They don't pay their debts.

Rebecca leaned her hip against the workbench. Frank was too keyed up for her comfort. If he didn't think she killed Stuck, why did he care that she was at the shop at the time of his murder? Was Frank fishing? What for? His agitation was making her nervous, and angry.

She yanked Frank around to face her. "I thought we had an understanding about prying into each other's business. If you don't trust me to do what's best for this shop, you better start looking for other employment." It was a nasty crack. Frank wouldn't find another niche like working at V&C, or want to. Hurt flickered in his eyes. She softened her tone. "Frank, there's nothing for you to worry about, other than finishing the cars. I'll try to keep the sheriff at bay. You keep Val and Paulie working. Deal?"

"I know my job."

Rebecca wished she had such confidence.

She had the front door open when the phone rang. She grabbed it on the second ring. "Vintage & Classics."

There was no response.

She was about to dismiss it as a random computer call, then she heard voices and laughter in the background. "Hello. Who is it? Who's there?"

"Rebecca Moore? Is that you?" Vera Stuck's voice sounded far away, slurred.

"Vera, where are you?"

"I need your help."

Help driving, for sure. Why wasn't she home mourning in private? "Tell me where you are. I'll come for you."

"No, not here. Not now." A canned version of "Misty" played in the background. Someone said, "Excuse me." Vera's voice dropped a notch. "Maybe you can't help. Maybe no one can." She hiccoughed.

"Let me try, Vera. What do you need?"

Vera's earring scraped against the receiver. "Advice?" She made it a question. She could have been questioning her need for it, or Rebecca's ability to give it.

Rebecca pulled a pad of paper closer and reached for a pen. "What kind of advice?"

Vera was whispering now. "Graham said you used to be an investigator. You've dealt with the police?"

Too many cops, too often. Especially in the last year. "Some. As an investigative reporter, Vera, not an investigator."

"Autopsy?" Vera whispered.

"It's standard procedure in cases of violent death."

"Drugs? Will they test for drugs?"

Graham Stuck as a drug user? Conceivable, given his obsession with the lifestyles of the rich. Was Vera implying that Graham was killed over drugs? A deal gone bad? Had he hidden drugs in the Bentley, then come to fetch them after the car had been moved?

She kept her voice neutral. "Drug testing's pretty routine these days, Vera. Why?"

"Arsenic?" The word slid out as a hiss.

Arsenic? The chemical was used in chrome plating, but Graham couldn't have been exposed to enough of it over the years to matter. Was Vera planning to sue the plater? How could she? Graham had been bludgeoned, not poisoned. "Vera, are you concerned about the coroner finding traces of arsenic?"

She started to giggle. "Oh, yes. Poisoned cherries. Don't you love it?" Her giggles grew louder.

"Vera, what are you talking about?" Following the widow was like trying to trap a flying ping-pong ball.

As suddenly as they commenced, Vera's hysterics ceased. She hiccoughed into the phone. "Excuse me, Rebecca. I have to go. My white knight has arrived."

Vera hung up.

Fifteen

The widow returned to her table. Bracing one hand on the back of the chair, she tried to arrange her face into a smile for a man who'd just entered the bar. He spotted her and crossed the room. He was on the tall side of average, tennis player build, around sixty, with shocking white hair and matching mustache. Costumed in khakis, white polo shirt and navy blazer, all he lacked was the yachter's sun-creased complexion.

Vera tottered forward to embrace him. The man grimaced, held her at arm's length, guided her into her seat before taking the one opposite. Too dispassionate for Mick's idea of an undertaker. He had Nordic blue eyes which fastened on Vera like laser beams. He looked vaguely familiar, and totally unamused by Vera's conversation.

"Like I was saying, Mick, the Paris-to-Peking has only been run a handful of times since the first challenge in 1907. It's a two-month, ten-thousand-mile test of the endurance of man and machine. A kidney-busting trek through the primitive countryside of Turkey, Russia, China. It's the ultimate challenge of a driver's abilities and his stamina." Lindeman slammed his double Old-Fashioned glass onto the bar. The bartender got the message. Another round appeared.

"It's also a hefty drain on the old pocketbook. In addition

to the cost of preparing the car, shipping it and taking the journey yourself, Todd and I and two other fellows—who don't have a prayer, but don't tell them that—have a small side wager on the outcome. What's it up to, Todd?"

"You know perfectly well. Forty thousand." Shelley was becoming more morose with every swallow. He was also excusing himself more frequently. Weak kidneys must be a nuisance during a bumpy race.

With Shelley's departure, Lindeman leaned in close. "Let you in on my secret, Mick. I've got a sweet deal going with little Becca, owner of the car shop. After her uncle died, I agreed to let V&C finish the Hisso, on one condition. I pay for parts, but not for labor. Oh, I will. *If* the car's ready on time and to my satisfaction. I'll pay in full before shipping out. If it's not, I don't pay a cent for labor."

"Moore agreed to that?" Mick broke a toothpick in half and dropped it beside the lemon in the ashtray.

"No choice. If I'd pulled the car, it could have ruined her. Other customers would start to wonder if she could handle the shop. Send their cars elsewhere. Some chauvinists have anyway."

"If Moore's been working just on your car and you're not paying, how's she keeping the business afloat?"

"I've been pondering that question myself, Mick. No wonder she was so willing to take in the Bentley. Shame she can't work on it. She must be getting desperate." Hal Lindeman didn't look a bit concerned.

Mick filled another ten minutes listening to the car nuts talk about the upcoming rally. Really more of an endurance run, so having a car that stayed together until the end might be the ticket. Would it be worth killing a competitor's mechanic? Mick didn't think so. But then, Mick couldn't imagine that winning would be worth the expense or the hassle. Some people definitely have too much time, and way too much money.

At Vera's table, the white-haired gent looked uncomfortable when Vera pulled a twenty from her billfold and handed it to him. He shook his head, reached for his wallet and signaled the waitress. He'd pick up the tab. Not a gigolo, then. *What?* The couple pushed back from the table and prepared to leave the restaurant.

It was time for him to go as well. Mick thanked Lindeman and Shelley for the drinks. They were off to dinner at some place out of town. They were gentlemen enough to invite him. He was gentleman enough to say no thanks. The boys had provided him with two hours' worth of information he could report back to the sheriff. He didn't have a handle on Lindeman's game. Nor did he expect Stuck's affair with Shelley's wife to be germane, but they might be leads worth exploring. He probably should run the racers by Sal for background checks.

Outside, the air had cooled. The valet tucked Vera into the Jag, while the white-haired gent slid into the driver's seat. They left the lot at a discreet crawl. Mick gazed out toward the bay. Stars like he hadn't seen since summer camp dotted the sky above the dark expanse of water. Some were fuzzy. Or maybe he was. Slow waves slapped the rocks. A wisp of cloud drifted in front of the oval moon. Pleasant change from the city. Maybe he could get used to country living, if it weren't so quiet. He cut back through the gap in the hedge to the shipyard's parking lot.

Then again, what did people do around here to keep from going stir crazy? Eating at *Flo's* alone had no appeal. He'd already had enough to drink, so bar-hugging at *Tony's* was out. Now that Vera had company, interviewing her would have to wait until tomorrow.

He unlocked the Jeep and climbed in. He could check out the murder site—out of fairness to the sheriff. Moore would have to let him in. She was probably at home, cooking up a tasty dinner in a bright, warm kitchen. Something with pasta and a spicy sauce. Or was that asking too much? Did former newspaper reporters turned auto mechanics also cook? He might find out if he gave her a call. Maybe get to inspect the murder scene *and* get a home-cooked meal. For dessert, he could confess to Moore what he was doing in Head Tide.

Sixteen

Rebecca was working in the back room. She heard the remote chime of the doorbell over the motor of the milling machine. Loud and clear. She chose to ignore it. It was eight o'clock. The shop was closed. She was alone, trying to make up for the time lost to the sheriff's investigation.

She reached for a length of aluminum stock, positioned it under the hold-down on the bed of the mill. Slowly, she lowered the spinning cutter. It was a ball-nosed end mill used to cut the slot in each of the block clips.

The doorbell sounded again. Longer, more insistent. When it rang for the third time, she gave up. Leaving the machine running, Rebecca strode into the front office and yanked the door open.

The man lolling against the doorframe was the character who had tailed her to *Tony's* the night before. The one who had been taking pictures of the shop and her employees in the afternoon. The one her lawyer claimed was a DC cop.

"Yes?"

"Rebecca Moore?" He fumbled in his jacket pocket to produce a leather identification case. "Detective Michael Hagan, DC police."

"Out of your jurisdiction, aren't you?"

She reached for his badge. It looked real. So did he. How

had Flo described the stranger? *Hunk of a man, with an edge a gal could cut herself on if she's not careful.* Michael Hagan was a hunk with an attitude, but it didn't explain his interest in her, or her shop. She returned the badge.

"What do you want?"

He blinked thick lashes over too-blue eyes. Even money that his answer would be a lie. "I'm working with Sheriff Zimmer on the Stuck homicide. Thought I'd take a look at the crime scene if that's okay with you."

"Are you auditioning for the deputy's job? Last one was stupid and greedy. What are your credentials?" She regretted the crack the moment it was out of her mouth. The guy was being polite, hanging back until invited in, not pressuring her. He had to be more impartial than Zimmer. Getting to know him might be a prudent move. "Sorry about that. The killing has taken its toll on my manners. Come on in. The scene's out back."

Leading the way from the office to the machine shop, Rebecca felt the detective's eyes on her. She doubted he was impressed. Her hair was yanked back with a coated elastic. There was a smudge of grease on her cheekbone. She was clad in one-piece coveralls snapped shut at cuffs and throat and wearing laced-up boots. Fetching. She smelled of cutting fluid.

"I'm just finishing up. Beader's over near the fire doors." Rebecca indicated the far corner.

Hagan stopped halfway there to stare. Rebecca humored him. "That's chassis number 946. It's a 1925, 3-Litre Bentley. Four cylinders, 2996cc, overhead cam, twin magnetos. It will cruise at seventy on the highway. Touring body by Park Ward."

Hagan whistled.

Admittedly, even without garish yellow tape, the Bentley attracted the eye like a magnet pulls iron filings. Something about the massive hood—bonnet to the Brits—the upright windscreen and wire wheels epitomized freedom. It conjured up images of wind-tossed hair, winding roads and glamorous destinations. You could almost hear the tires squeal as the racer hugged curves en route to the casinos at Monte Carlo.

"You may drool," Rebecca said. "It's the standard male response."

The cop grinned, "That's quite a machine. It's like mobile history. Very essence of the between-the-wars spirit."

"Perceptive. That's a big part of their appeal. Vintage cars are much more than machinery. Look around all you want."

The room was vast, maybe forty feet square with sixteen-foot ceilings. Standard cinder-block construction, walls painted bright white, concrete floor painted gray. A cluster of tools—he recognized a wire wheel and a grinder, both bolted to pedestals—were plugged into outlets attached to the support beams. Workbenches lined two walls and a couple more sat in the center of the room parallel to the Bentley. Next to one, Mick knelt, checked out the hammer's outline on the floor.

The glass beading machine was tucked into the corner near the double fire doors. He peered into the machine through the frosted window. Plenty of room inside for a body, if you bent the knees. Waist-high door, about three feet square for easy loading. Hoisting the corpse up to the door would have taken strength, or perseverance. Or an overhead tackle and chain, like the one suspended from the I beam directly above him. Handy location; the beam ran the width of the building. Would move a body as easily as an engine. He'd have the sheriff check the body for bruises that could have been caused by a chain.

Moore had put on safety glasses. She stood in front of a giant machine labeled "Bridgeport" in fancy script, doing something to inch-long pieces made from a bar of metal. Mick wandered closer to peer over her shoulder. She moved levers and turned the wheels of the mill with the swiftness of long practice.

"You know what you're doing?" Mick asked over the whir of the electric motor.

"Can't you tell?"

"Not me. Loading film in a camera is my mechanical level. What are you making?"

"Block clips. They secure the wires which run down length of the car's frame. The wiring in the Bentley is pretty primitive. All black wires, unwrapped, no conduit. The clips fasten to the chassis rails with small bolts through the center. Spare originals don't exist. Replacements aren't available. New ones have to be made by hand." Moore inspected the clip in the beam from a magnetic lamp stuck to the bed of the mill. She removed metal shavings with a brush, then held it up for Mick's approval. "Where'd you learn to load a camera?"

"RISD. I spent three years throwing paint at canvases. Might have been an architect if I'd studied math harder. Mother would have settled for photographer, English teacher, anything but cop. Where'd you learn to run a mill?"

She reached up and flicked the lever to off. Using a wrench, she loosened the draw bar and removed the ball-nosed mill. "Right here. When I was twelve. I have younger brothers, identical twins, hellions from birth. Once they got to be taller than the kitchen counter, my mother lost all control. To minimize confusion, Dad shipped me off to Uncle Walt's for summer vacation." She replaced the end mill with a nasty-looking fly cutter bigger around than a bratwurst. Locked it into place. "I loved it. So I kept coming back. Every year until I graduated from college."

"Your parents sent a kid, a girl, to a place staffed by ex-cons?"

"They didn't know about the cons. Walt figured they wouldn't understand. He was right." She snapped off the work light.

"You hold that against your parents?"

"I think individuals should be given a chance. Not labeled or prejudged." She released the clip from the hold-down and tossed it onto the pile. "Seen enough?" Mick nodded. "Good. Over coffee you can tell me why you really came."

* * *

Without asking if he wanted it, Moore handed him a mug. She sat at the lunch table. He stood. They both sipped.

"Anytime you want to come clean, Hagan, I'll listen."

"What do you want to hear?"

"Let's start with why you're in town claiming to help the sheriff."

Mick held the mug with both hands. Why was it so hard to start? He had taken a few days' leave to drive to Maryland to face Rebecca Moore. The department shrink, the chief, Sal and his mother all agreed he should do it. Get some closure. Stop the wound from festering so he could get on with life. Now he was alone with her. No distractions. She was begging to hear why he'd come. There wouldn't be a better time and place. But he couldn't spit out the words.

He pulled out a chair at the end of the table. "Seems peculiar: two antique car restoration shops just a few miles apart."

Moore shook her head. "Okay, Hagan. Have it your way. Small talk."

She pulled the elastic band from her hair, releasing waves of auburn to frame her face, classic heart-shaped. "It's quite common. Restoration shops often cluster, like artist's communities. Walt settled here because its rural. Winding, two-lane roads with little traffic. Which is important when you're road-testing cars worth more than the town collects annually in taxes. Commercial real estate is cheap, zoning less stringent than in more populated areas. And there are good local machinists, which is a plus. Cars are transported in from all over the country and from abroad. Location isn't an issue. Reputation is."

"Shop has a good one?"

"It did. Before Graham Stuck died here. You have to love the irony. Walt fired him fifteen years ago to protect the shop's reputation. Stuck may yet have the last laugh." She stood to get a refill. "Am I allowed to ask if you or the sheriff have learned anything?"

Mick considered his position. To Zimmer, talking to

Moore would be fraternizing with the enemy. Still, if she was innocent, she had a legitimate need to see which way the investigation was heading. He hedged.

"I'm just feeling my way around town. Spent the last couple of hours with customers of yours: big guy with a reddish beard and—"

"The boy racers, Hal Lindeman and Todd Shelley. Hope they didn't stick you with the bar bill."

Mick replayed his discussion with Lindeman. Moore looked more bored than surprised.

"So, Graham hit on the wife of a customer. Tacky, but not news."

"The affair, no. But Lindeman claims that Stuck was 'blackmailing' Shelley into remaining a customer despite Stuck's dalliance with the wife. If that's true, you can bet Shelley wasn't the first victim. Blackmailers have a hard time breaking the habit. Most don't stop till they're dead."

"Pity that Shelley has an alibi for the murder. Are you sure he does?"

"Not yet. Sheriff's talking to Arlington."

"That's all you've uncovered?"

"Cut me some slack, lady. I just arrived. You should be pleased about the blackmail angle. It's unlikely Stuck was sucking the life out of your guys. Whole town knows they're criminals. Don't imagine they have enough money or clout to interest a blackmailer."

"Exonerated by proven bad character? Is that how detectives eliminate suspects in DC?"

"My point is that I like blackmail as a motive. Better than a wronged lover or irate husband. You knew Stuck. Does blackmail fit?"

"Like a surgical glove. Graham was manipulative, the lazy sort who adored having power over anyone."

A black cat appeared from the other room. He leapt onto the table, flopped down between them and began purring. Mick stroked the cat under his chin. "Sociable fellow."

Moore's face softened. "He came with the shop. Maurice,

say hi to Michael Hagan." The cat raised his head in greeting, bammed Mick's hand for more attention. Moore frowned and glanced at the round wall clock advertising Bijur Lubricating Systems. "What about the widow? Have you met her yet?"

Mick shook his head. Seen, but not talked to.

"Vera's proper, from a prosperous local family. Why was she married to a creature like Stuck? There might have been something between them years ago. But now? Why had she stayed with him, knowing what he was?"

"Another type of blackmail? Emotional, maybe?"

"Could be. There's a promising line to follow, Hagan. Check out the widow. Or her story: She thinks Stuck was seeing someone in Annapolis."

"Why there?"

"Fantasizing, probably. It's where she'd like to have an affair. Oh, while you're at it, add another name to your list: Stewart Thornton Reiske. Judge Reiske, of the Superior Court of DC. Zimmer told my lawyer that the judge is in town asking about Stuck's personal effects."

The name clicked like a coin dropping in an out-of-the-way pay phone. Mick swore under his breath. Judge S. Thornton Reiske was Zimmer's federal judge, the friend of the family who'd breezed into town. *And* the man who'd joined Vera at the marina bar. No wonder he looked familiar. The judge's face was often plastered in the *Post*. By bizarre coincidence, Reiske was scheduled to hear *United States v. Alonso,* the case Mick had worked undercover on for the past year. The case in which he would have to testify in just a few weeks. Man, Mick really hated coincidences. He picked up the elastic hair band and stretched it between his fingers.

"Think the judge is just a friend, come to console the widow?"

"Looks that way." Moore buried her face in the black cat's belly. The purring vibrated the table. "Though he could be here in a legal capacity."

"A superior court judge is overkill for a probating a will."

"What if Vera murdered her husband?"

"A prim matron? With a hammer, no less?"

"Why not? Looks are often deceiving."

"You mean you're not as smart and desirable as you look?" It sort of slipped out. Mick had consumed way too much scotch.

Moore raised her head. A lopsided smile twitched the left side of her mouth; her eyes twinkled with mischief. The animation was seductive. "Do you plan to find out?"

Mick planned to reach over and caress her cheek, slide his hand under that polished mass of hair. Maybe pull her face closer until—

The blast of an explosion shook the building.

Seventeen

Moe leapt to his paws and jumped from the table. Rebecca bolted from the room as Hagan shoved back his chair. She led the way, running through the semi-dark machine shop toward the red exit sign over the back door. As she reached to open it, Hagan yanked her wrist away. He stretched the sleeve of his jacket to cover his palm. Tentatively, he placed his hand on the knob, then gripped it firmly.

Hagan eased the door open just as a second explosion erupted. The door slammed into him, flattening him against the wall. The blast caught Rebecca full force. She flew backward, landed hard, skidded to a stop when her shoulder rammed into a crankshaft sitting on the floor. Hagan crossed quickly and pulled her to her feet. Together they turned.

Framed by the doorway, orange flames dissolved into billows of sooty smoke as Stuck's station wagon was reduced to toast—well-charred toast.

Rebecca freed herself from Hagan's side and ran to the office to call 911.

When she returned, Hagan was outside, holding a fire extinguisher which he'd snatched from the wall but hadn't discharged. The car was beyond help. The building wasn't in danger. The scrub pines were out of reach of the flames.

Side by side, they leaned against the stucco wall watching

the bonfire. The Subaru glowed, sputtered and sizzled. Paint melted. Occasionally some component would pop from the heat. Tires dissolved, poisoning the air with the acrid smell of burned rubber. The car's drive train settled in the dirt. Then sparks from the fire ignited grease-covered towels in a nearby rubbish bin. Dancing flames leapt toward the low branches of a blue spruce, threatening to add the entire tree to the barbecue.

Sirens first. Then a fire truck careened around the side of the building, stopping short on the tight turn around the barn. Seconds later, the sheriff's car appeared on the other side.

Fire Chief Charlie Crawford wandered over to check on Rebecca while his guys went to work. He introduced himself to Hagan. "Heck of a campfire, guys. Who brought the marshmallows?" Crawford was psyched. Claimed there hadn't been a colorful blaze since the Christmas decorations came down.

Sheriff Zimmer, on the other hand, was irked. Now that it was burned beyond recognition he was positive that the Subaru had been a prime piece of evidence. He slapped the wafting soot away from his trouser leg like he was fanning at gnats. Zimmer lashed out at Boeski, his still-wet-behind-the-ears patrol officer. "You sure you cleared everything out of that car like I told you?"

"Honest, Sheriff. Cleaned out the trunk and the glove box. Removed the seats. Picked up every scrap of debris, just like you said. There wasn't anything explosive in the car. I swear. Other than the gas tank, I mean."

"I didn't think there was a bomb in it. But there was something, sure as death and taxes. Else why destroy a harmless, ownerless car? You miss prints anywhere?"

"No, sir. Olson and me got 'em all. Sent the whole batch over to the state lab."

"Terrific. So, you got any ideas of what you didn't get?"

Hagan jumped in to deflect Zimmer away from the young officer. "You have a problem with vandals, Sheriff? How about high school kids experimenting with recipes off the Internet?"

"You're joking, right? Vandals? Tonight? Isn't the timing a mite suspicious, this happening to Stuck's auto right after he was killed?"

"It certainly is, Sheriff," Rebecca said. "It might not have happened at all if you'd removed the car from my property."

"Why's that? Your head mechanic can't resist blowing things up? Stuck's car was just a mite too tempting?"

"You see any of my guys here?"

"I see you." The sheriff turned to Hagan. "You positive she was inside when this thing went off?" Hagan nodded. "You frisk her for a triggering device?"

"Didn't have the opportunity."

Zimmer grunted. He walked away to join Crawford, who was brandishing a hunk of something charred trailing a melted cord. The sheriff considered it for a minute, then yelled over his shoulder to Hagan. "You know anything about detonators, Hagan? What does this look like to you?" The sheriff held up a chunk of melted plastic, metal and wires. Hagan reached out and took the mass, rotating it in his hand.

"To me, Sheriff, this looks like the remains of a transformer. The kind they use to run model trains. Though I guess it could be a timer. Better ask your bomb squad."

"What bomb squad?"

Wednesday

Faulty Wiring

Eighteen

Mick had slept poorly, which was unusual. He could sleep anywhere, under any conditions, and wake up good to go. The guys on his stakeout crews hated him. Now, on a vacation of sorts in a rural town, he wasn't sleeping. Firm mattress, soft pillow. Lu Chan hadn't lied about the creature comforts of the room over the restaurant. Little street noise. Nothing external was bugging him.

Mick recognized the problem for what it was. He was procrastinating. Latin, wasn't it? *Pro* plus "belonging to the morrow." Yeah. Like tomorrow and tomorrow and tomorrow creeping in its petty pace. He needed to get this over with. *Need* was another word he hated when it applied to him. He could respect others' needs, be the first one to help out. He wasn't comfortable acknowledging his own. Or doing something about them. Mick stared at a paint crack in the ceiling. So far, the sheriff thought he was a savior who arrived in town at an auspicious moment. His mother thought he was making peace with Rebecca Moore. Sal thought he was messing on another lawman's turf when he should be relaxing. What the hell did he think he was doing?

At the moment—lolling in a double bed, ignoring the mustard-yellow walls and stewing about Moore. He could empathize with David's falling for Moore. If she smiled and hooked her finger, most men would trot along behind. It wasn't just looks—he'd been a fool over better lookers—but there was an intelligent composure that begged to be shattered, a tinge of vulnerability that a man wanted to protect. Dust that with a barely camouflaged sensuality, and you have the ideal Venus flytrap. That was another cliché that irked Mick. There's no ideal anything. Particularly anything female.

Weak sunlight filtered in through the curtained window. A small spider used the corner of the frame to harness a delicate web. From left to right she spun a gossamer thread, dropped down, swung back, and began again. Apt. It seemed like someone was weaving a sticky web, big enough to cover Blue Marsh County. If Mick didn't watch his step, he'd be the one wriggling in the center of it.

An hour later Mick was downstairs in the Great Wall Chinese Restaurant fortifying himself on stale doughnuts before wading through the notes on David Semple. Sal had overnighted the file to the sheriff's station and Sergeant Olson had delivered it to the restaurant on her way to *Flo's,* along with the message that an Arlington officer had spoken to Denise Spotelli. She confirmed that Todd Shelley had been with her Saturday night, all night. Spotelli was so strung out, she didn't know what day yesterday was, but she was standing by her man. Olsen also handed Mick a note saying that the autopsy had been moved up to eleven A.M.

From behind the screaming orange counter Lu Chan bobbed in greeting, white apron folded around his skinny hips. Chatting with Mick, Chan chopped carrots, cabbage, celery, scallions into dainty morsels all the same size, without looking at the cutting board. Mick couldn't take his eyes off the blur of the fat-bladed knife.

"Of course, I fix you tea. You sit. Anywhere you like. I bring. How is room? Very comfortable, yes? Good bed. You like?"

The room was great, if you didn't mind the smell of fried

egg rolls at five A.M. Lu Chan finished chopping, stacked the bowls in the walk-in refrigerator and moved to the other counter to steep the pungent green tea. Mick slipped a manila folder from the envelope. There was a coffee ring on the cover and a Post-It from Sal: *Open at your own risk.*

He should have heeded it. The high-contrast photographs made his hands go clammy. Head wounds inflicted by guns at close range are too vivid to gloss over, particularly when you know the vic. Thanks to a Smith & Wesson .38 Special fired into his mouth, David Semple's boyish face was as vacant as the top of his head was missing. Bone had dissolved to a puddle of blood and tissue.

Semple had been a financial advisor with Burton, Findlay and Wilde in Alexandria. Thirty-five, an ambitious hotshot who didn't want to wait for the good things in life. Easier to con his clients into paying for his lifestyle up front. The scam had worked until he met Rebecca Moore: thirty-seven, ambitious hotshot reporter who couldn't leave a story alone.

Mick bit into a glazed doughnut. Flakes of frosting drifted onto the table. Stale. Man, three f'ing days stale. There ought to be a law. Cops worldwide would enforce that one. He dropped the doughnut back into the paper sack and squeezed it into a ball. Tomorrow morning he'd eat at *Flo's*. As Mick tossed the bag into the trash, Sheriff Zimmer pulled his patrol car to the curb out front and honked the horn. Mick waved through the window.

"Hey, Lu Chan, make that tea to go."

Nineteen

By eight o'clock Rebecca had already hung up on two scum-sucking reporters.

At five past eight, the first visitor arrived. Edna, Delacroix's secretary, came bearing gifts. Which was a good thing considering the way Rebecca felt after the explosion, Zimmer's interrogation, and only four hours' sleep. Edna stopped on her way to work to deliver a half dozen corn muffins and Judge Wagner's signed release for the Bentley.

"Mr. Delacroix received this late yesterday. He asked that I drop it off first thing. Judge said it didn't make sense to keep the car from being repaired. It had been dusted for fingerprints—none. And searched through for evidence—nothing. The loose items have been boxed. Samples have been taken of the blood on the door. Sheriff couldn't come up with one valid reason for keeping the car tied up."

Bless you, Judge Wagner. The guys still had three full days to attack the Bentley. It might just make the boat to Paris after all.

Edna didn't linger. She was sure Miss Moore had lots to do besides socialize. Rebecca blessed Edna as well as they walked to the door. Not another soul in greater Blue Marsh would have passed up a chance to pump Rebecca for the juicy details about a grisly murder *and* a car explosion two days apart at the same address.

Zimmer was the next one through the door, Hagan in tow. Said he'd return in daylight to poke through the remains of what had been one ugly car. Might have been reason enough to bomb it. If he didn't find anything he wouldn't stay long.

"Do you know how the explosion was triggered?" Rebecca fiddled with a stack of pink phone messages.

"Not yet. Inside of the car had been doused with gasoline. Cans left on the seat. They caused the second blast. Car's gas tank went first."

"Those were our cans. Paulie drained the old gas from the Bentley's tank on Monday afternoon. Set it out back."

"Charlie's betting the arsonist nicked the fuel line, then rigged something that would spark and start a fire. Piled it with paper, rags, whatever from the trash. Could have set it off by remote. Then again, we found a transformer or timer, so he could have plugged it into the side of building, set it to go off, and beat feet. Could have. *How* doesn't matter so much. I'm still fretting over *why* the car was destroyed."

"Either way the perpetrator was right outside the shop?"

"Sure was. With you inside working late." Zimmer's grin was snide. "If you're not nervous already, Moore, this'd be a good time to start. When you're ready to tell me what's going on here, you give me a call." Zimmer snapped on latex gloves and exited out back to poke through the rubble. Hagan glanced her way, tried on a smile. She returned it with a tentative one of her own. He followed Zimmer out back.

They didn't stay long. The sheriff had discarded the gloves and was on the way to his car when Frank arrived for work. Frank slammed the front door on Hagan's heels. "You got a thing going with that redneck cop? Or maybe his sidekick?"

"Hot and heavy. And I keep coming up with inventive ways to get his attention."

"Like what?"

"Like last night's excitement. Someone blew up Graham Stuck's station wagon."

Frank frowned. "What? You mean his car that was sitting out back?"

Frank was moving through the shop before Rebecca could nod. He left the back door open in his wake. Rebecca lingered at the threshold. When she asked, Frank confirmed that he'd stayed after Val and Paulie left, locking up around six-thirty, before she'd returned from the accountant's. He hadn't heard anyone, any noise out back.

Frank stared at the burned rubble, shook his head from side to side. "Good thing the fire didn't hurt the building. Who'd do a thing like that? Why?"

"Those questions were asked a lot last night by everyone putting out the blaze. The only clue is a congealed blob of black plastic with wires. Sheriff thinks it's a transformer, the kind used to run a model train."

"Shit." Frank pushed past Rebecca, returning to the building without further comment.

Minutes later, Val and Paulie arrived. Hearing the news of the Bentley's release, Val slapped Paulie a high five and turned to do the same to Frank. Glowering, Frank ignored him and exited into the machine shop.

"What's eating him?" Val asked.

"Small matter of an explosion out back. Go look."

Paulie stayed behind to make coffee, grinding beans from a waxed bag marked "Ceylon."

"Bodies and bombs. Murders and mayhem. I never thought working here would be so film noir. And Mother says the life of a working man is dull." He measured out seven scoops of ground coffee, mouth moving as he counted. "And now the Bentley is all ours. How wonderful. As soon as we remove the old harness, I'll cut the wires to length." Paulie set the carafe on the burner and slowly poured water through the mesh opening. "What should we do with the carton?"

"Carton?"

"You know, the 'stuff' Officer Boeski pulled out of the Bentley."

"Drop it on my desk, Paulie. I'll ask the lawyer."

At ten-thirty Juanita breezed in with a casserole.

Juanita's youth and size cried out for coddling that she wouldn't tolerate. The girl had become pregnant, run away from her home in Richmond, and lost the baby at an age when most teens' biggest worry was which shade of lipstick to shoplift. She found her way to Uncle Walt like stray dogs sniff out neighborhood handouts. He took care of her medical expenses and she clung to him like the lifeline he was. She cooked, she cleaned, she answered phones at the shop. At Uncle Walt's insistence she'd reentered school last September. Her marks were decent. It looked like she would live up to her promise and graduate from high school.

Juanita was unflinchingly female in her belief that food is essential to the spirit as well as the body. Sort of a young, Hispanic version of Mrs. Bellotti. For her there was an appropriate dish for every calamity, and as the eldest of eight children it was often her job to create it. In Juanita's cookbook the death of a spouse rated a casserole smelling of corn and cheese with a hint of cumin.

"I make it for Mrs. Stuck. It will keep warm at the diner. I take it to her after my shift if I may use the pickup, yes?"

Twenty

An autopsy's not most people's idea of a fun way to spend a spring morning, but it was necessary to police work. *Autopsy,* Greek: the act of seeing with one's own eyes. Mick suspected that the sheriff had invited him along to see how tough a city cop was in the morgue. The autopsy room in the county hospital was smaller than Mick was used to, only two tables, but it smelled the same. Same sterile coldness, same forlorn finality.

Mick could stomach the procedure as long as he concentrated on the implied puzzles. Like how hard would someone have to swing a dead blow hammer to smash cranial bone? How could Tolland tell from the wound that it was inflicted by a right-hander swinging backhand, not by a left-handed killer? Where did Stuck's left ear disappear to? And why did his privates look like they suffered from rug burn? Despite the general tissue swelling and discoloration, even a casual observer could see the raw, inflamed condition of Stuck's genitals.

"You want my best guess?" Harry Tolland scratched under his chin with a gloved finger, leaving behind a bloody smear. "I'd say the killer tried to remove Stuck's genitalia in the beading machine. Or rough it up a bit anyway, with predictably poor results. The clowns down at *Flo's* might be right about that fantasy. Probably heaved the body in on top of the engine block and started blasting. When it didn't have the desired effect, he quit."

"I thought the body was behind the block."

"Was when we found it. Gravity pulled it down as the fluids settled. He started out on top of the block."

"Any indications of chain marks?"

"Nope. Body wasn't bruised until it landed on the cylinder head studs. They left the indentations in the flesh of his rib cage and flanks."

Tolland put down the scalpel and eased out the stomach. He placed it on the scales. "I'd say that helps exonerate the ex-cons. They'd know the beader won't make headway—pardon the pun—on anything soft. Skin on a flaccid penis is about as soft as it gets, isn't it, fellas?" The coroner grinned like sin. "You know, I feel more kindly towards Stuck dead than I did when he was alive. Not hung as well as commonly assumed. Pretty ordinary. I've carved up enough men to know." He pressed the tip of the scalpel against the stomach casing. "Any bets on his last meal?"

Zimmer was still fretting about the genitals. "This look like a sex crime to you, Harry?"

"Yes and no. Being naked and bound suggests it. But it could have been made to look sex-related to mislead law officers."

"That's what I'm thinking." Zimmer poked the coroner on the arm with a rubber-encased finger. "In which case, the cons could have blasted him with glass beads just to throw us off the track. What do you say about that?"

"I say you better make an arrest soon, or the Staties will move into your spanking-clean office and bill you for the pleasure." Humming, the coroner reached back into the body cavity for the small intestines. Nice to see a man enjoy his work.

Outside the examination room, the buzzards were waiting—reporters and lawyers. Mick skirted the crowd to lean against the tiled wall, away from the media spotlight. Zimmer faced the handful of reporters with a stern yet kindly expression. He promised them a typed statement within the hour. They could pick up copies at the station house. He allowed a scrawny kid with a press card from the *Blue Marsh Gazette* to snap his photo in front of a wall of community service plaques. Then asked the lawyers to step into the coroner's office for an update.

Delacroix, the legal type Mick had spotted at the bar with Moore, was there, representing the employees at Vintage & Classics—no one in particular. Judge Reiske said he was present as *amicus curiae*. Hoping that the sheriff's information would relieve some of Mrs. Stuck's anguish over her husband's death.

Zimmer grunted. He read the notes jotted on the back of an electric company bill: " 'Inflamed genitals, recent sex, wrists bound after death, stripped after death, dead from one blow, delivered from behind back-handed.' Those sound like words to make a recent widow sleep tight and wake up rested?"

Mick returned to the station with Zimmer. The sheriff lowered himself behind his desk like he was bone-tired. The chair creaked.

"What bothers me, Hagan, is the setup. Wife knifes her husband in the kitchen. We find him on the linoleum in a pool of blood. That's natural. Here we got somebody smashing Stuck in the head with a hammer. If we stop there, I'm okay. It plays." Zimmer leaned back. He opened the top drawer for a pencil. "Could have been someone's already in the shop—like Lewes—up to no good. Graham surprises him. The guy grabs up the hammer, and smack. He leaves us one dead body."

"A murder of opportunity."

"Right. But our murderer had to go and get fancy. He undresses Stuck, binds his wrists with a necktie—Stuck's own, Vera identified it—loads him into the beader, tries to blast off his manhood, then leaves the body for Moore to find. That sound as wacko to you as it does to me?"

"Wacko. And purposeful. Can't help feeling there's a message there."

The sheriff started flicking the pencil on the desk, trying to find a rhythm with the eraser end. "Got to be a warning to someone at the shop."

"Not an urgent one. The shop was closed. No one was likely to discover the body over the weekend. No one expected to see Stuck before late Monday, except the friend he was going to visit. You find her yet?"

"Not a whisper, which is mighty queer. Why didn't she report him missing?" Zimmer's tapping picked up tempo.

Mick shrugged. "Married and doesn't want to get involved? Maybe she arranged to see him only Friday night? Or they had a fight? Maybe Stuck lied to his wife and never had out-of-town plans for the weekend. Or she lied to you. Vera Stuck have an alibi?"

"Hell, no. No one in town has an alibi, near as I can figure. Me included. I'm betting there was a Friday night gal, all right. Graham didn't go long without a new conquest. I'll find her. She'll tell me something."

"Maybe." Mick wiggled two fingers in the watch pocket of his jeans, hunting for a toothpick. "Or maybe she's the murderer and won't tell you the time of day."

Zimmer's tapping emerged as "The Star Spangled Banner." "I like that, Hagan. If the Friday night gal was the murderer, and the murder took place at Vintage & Classics, then I've still got Rebecca Moore as my most likely suspect." The sheriff paused after "so proudly we hail." "Doesn't that make my day."

Twenty-one

The law office of Joachim Delacroix, Esquire, occupied a narrow, three-story Federal brick house with glossy black shutters. It was about a quarter mile west of V&C around the curve on Main Street. The last building before the spit of water that gave the town its name. At high tide, seawater ran under the bridge and through the side yard like a misplaced brook. When it receded you could watch the well-nourished weeds start to grow.

The shiny front door was closed but unlatched. Edna's chair was vacant. Rebecca crossed to the inner office and knocked. Jo bade her enter. As she closed the door behind her, Jo beamed. As usual.

"Ah, Rebecca. You have come to ask me to lunch."

"I've come for a restraining order against the sheriff's whipping boy, your Lieutenant Hagan." Rebecca leaned into the front of the desk. "I didn't like him photographing the guys on Monday. Now he's invading their homes. Mrs. Bunting, a fluffy matron who owns the trailer next to Val's, just called. Someone—who is the spitting image of Hagan— was rooting around Val's place, pretending to be a gas meter reader." Rebecca straightened, tucked hair behind both ears. "Frank overheard the story and compounded it. He swears that someone had messed around with his train layout yesterday. Engines weren't where he left them."

"No detective would risk breaking and entering charges to snoop on a suspect. He'd obtain a warrant."

"Wouldn't be an offense. Frank never locks his house."

"Perhaps he should start." Jo removed his glasses and rubbed his eyes. "Hagan's investigation of your employees is not illegal. It's unorthodox for Zimmer to bring in a rogue detective, but he's empowered to deputize whomever he sees fit."

She dropped into the chair facing the desk. "Granted. But why Hagan? Have you ever heard of him? How does Zimmer know him? How did he happen to materialize in Head Tide the day the murder was discovered? Or was he already in town?"

"Excellent point. We'll ask around. No stranger goes unnoticed for long."

"Is he really a stranger? I have an uneasy feeling about him." Rebecca stood and walked to the window. "Last night he shows up at the shop around eight P.M. Asks to see the murder site. He noses around, but seems more interested in what I'm doing. Asks personal questions." Rebecca crossed her arms, hugging her elbows. "He peers at me like he knows me, Jo. Watches like he's waiting for me to reveal something. I don't know what. Maybe I'm totally paranoid."

"Could you have crossed paths with him before? In Washington?"

Rebecca shrugged and returned to her seat. She had flipped through her mental file of cops a dozen times—those she'd used as sources for stories, those she'd faced after David's death. She always came up blank.

"See if this helps." Jo handed her a two-page synopsis Edna had typed up.

Michael Patrick Hagan was in caps at the top of the page. He was forty-three, raised in the Crestwood section of DC. He'd been a cop for eighteen years. Went to college in Rhode

Island as he'd claimed. He'd had a couple of civilian jobs after college: assistant to an architect, a stint teaching high school English. One marriage to Loretta Tagye, ending in divorce four years back. No children. Son of a cop, Patrick Francis Hagan, who was killed on the job. His mother, Kathleen Connelly, remarried. Edna had highlighted the next bit: *Hagan's been working undercover for the last eighteen months (on loan to the Feds) building a case against reputed crime boss, Anthony Alonso. Same Alonso who's appearing before Reiske in court starting tomorrow!*

Jo watched her read the page. When she looked up, his expression was almost serious. "Your uncle was very proud of your investigative abilities, you know."

"Really? Well, it's a good thing he died when he did."

"Rebecca, we don't have an investigator on our side. Even if you could afford one, no one local is any good. After the explosion last night you should realize that we need one, quickly."

"You don't think Zimmer can handle it?"

"Neither do you. And by the time he calls in the state police it may be too late to save the shop's reputation. Which seems to be your main concern."

"You're implying that I care more about the business than my employees?"

Jo leaned back. "I think your response to this situation mimics your writing style: tense, factual, engrossing, but lacks heart."

"Thank you for the literary critique." Rebecca grabbed her shoulder bag from the floor. "Why don't you investigate this mess, then? With feeling."

"I'm but a country lawyer, Rebecca. Research is not my forte."

"Methinks you doth protest too much."

"Not about that." He redonned his glasses. "You, on the other hand, were trained to investigate. You're familiar with how to access records, ferret out contacts. You have a well-honed intuition."

Rebecca stood. "Anyone can do it. See what Edna's already uncovered about Hagan? You'll be amazed at what she can dig up on ordinary citizens—pasts and present circumstances."

"With whom should she start?"

"How about with my current customers? Shelley was in the area over the weekend, supposedly with a woman friend, but she could be covering. Check his alibi. Lindeman confessed to flying in on Friday to get a cheaper airfare. Which is uncharacteristically frugal of him. Perhaps he came early to see Graham. If not, what was he up to over the weekend? If he was hanging around here, someone will have seen him."

"Who will show Edna where to look? I can't." Jo spread his hands in appeal.

"Why do I feel like a fish staring at the end of a hook?"

"You don't have to nibble the worm, Rebecca. Though it's tasty and to your liking, isn't it?"

"Joachim, that phase of my life is over."

Grinning, he stood. "Let's talk about it over lunch."

Twenty-two

Lindeman and Shelley were in the machine shop when Rebecca and Jo returned from Flo's. The tables had turned. Todd Shelley was the one sighing with contentment as he watched Paulie string wires down the Bentley's frame rail, connecting the taillights to the distribution box. Val was barely visible inside the car, rubbing Lexol into the leather seats. Frank was fine-tuning twin S.U. carburetors under the bonnet. When Rebecca introduced him to Delacroix, Lindeman perked up. Aroused by a new audience to impress, Hal dragged the lawyer outside to admire the Hispano-Suiza.

With reluctance, Shelley allowed Rebecca to pull him away from the 3-Litre and into the office. She lifted a cardboard carton onto the desk, cut the sealing tape and slid it across toward him. Then handed him the sheriff's checklist.

"The effects collected from the Bentley. Sheriff asks that you check off each item you take and initial it on the list."

"Fine, fine. Most of it's junk. Hadn't cleaned the car lately, couldn't you tell?"

Shelley gingerly opened the flaps and began extracting items. "Broken pencil, sunglasses minus a bow. I don't think so." He tossed both into the wastebasket, then ticked them off the list. He pawed deeper in the carton. "Can always use the map, I guess. What are these?" He held up CDs of *Pi-*

rates of Penzance and *The Mikado*. "Belong to you? They're not mine."

Rebecca shook her head.

"Wouldn't have thought so. They must be Graham's. He loved this vaudeville stuff. Always had it playing at the shop—background caterwauling, Hal calls it."

"How did they get in the Bentley?" Rebecca picked up *The Mikado* and broke open the jewel case. " 'Sir Charles Mackerras; Orchestra & Chorus of the Welsh National Opera. Act One—Courtyard of Ko-Ko's Official Residence.' "

"Who would guess that Wales had a national opera?" Shelley continued going through the box. "Maybe Graham dropped the CDs on the seat while the Bentley was still at his shop? Keep them away from the grease and grit, perhaps? I didn't notice them on Friday, but then, I was pretty steamed. Could have been in the back, under the tonneau." He bowed as he handed them to her. "Keep them as a souvenir, I insist."

"Gracious of you, but I'd better return them to Vera. She may like light opera as well."

"Don't forget to sign for them." Todd handed her the sheriff's list. With a finger wave he returned to supervising the work on his car.

Rebecca held a CD in each hand. Vera might be a fan of Gilbert & Sullivan. It was equally possible that she didn't care a fig about anything that had been Graham's, light opera included. If Vera was having trouble coping, as last night's phone call indicated, this might send her over the edge. She could misconstrue Rebecca's returning Graham's favorite music. Assume that Rebecca had had a relationship with her late husband and that he had given her the CDs. Or they had shared them together.

Rebecca fought back the impulse to pitch the recordings into the trash. She didn't have the energy to deal with the blasted things. As a compromise, she penned *Return to Vera* on a Post-It note and stuck it to the top jewel case. She placed the CDs on the desk close to Moe's head, where they became an impromptu pillow.

Twenty-three

"Detective Hagan. I assumed you'd be sniffing around the sheriff's station."

Mick paused with his hand on the Jeep's door handle. A light breeze carried the squeals of children playing on the park swings. The voice he sought was closer at hand. Delacroix, Moore's lawyer, was sitting on a bench facing into the town square, suit jacket unbuttoned, long legs stretched out in the dirt in front of the bench. He was shelling peanuts, tossing them to a pair of interested squirrels. One sat up chattering, twitching his tail.

Delacroix turned his head. "You know who I am?"

Mick nodded. He had confirmed the lawyer's identity after seeing him at Tony's and at the autopsy. Zimmer described Delacroix as congenial, sharp and caring. In short, a better attorney than Head Tide deserved. Just dead wrong about Moore and her cons. Mick dropped onto the bench beside the attorney. Delacroix grinned. Behind thin tortoiseshell glasses, his eyes were the amber of inferior sherry, mellow like his voice. Until you noticed the glint. What was the kid's rhyme—" 'Welcome to my parlor,' said the spider to the fly?" Delacroix's demeanor was almost as inviting. "Excellent. I believe it's time we talked about your investigation."

Mick reached into the grease-stained paper bag and

helped himself to a peanut. "It's Zimmer's investigation. I'm only assisting. Still, I can't discuss an active case with a civilian."

The lawyer made clucking noises to get a squirrel's attention, then lobbed a peanut. Or maybe it was a *tsk*ing sound in response to Mick's objection. "You're not on the county's payroll, so you're not bound by such restraints. Nor am I, strictly speaking, a civilian in this case."

"No? Which criminal are you representing?"

"Whom are you accusing?"

"Checkmate." Mick snatched another nut. He cracked the shell, then tossed the peanut. Pieces flew, the squirrels scurried after. The smaller rodent snatched a chunk and raced up the nearby maple. Held it in both paws while he nibbled, tail snapping as if he were annoyed by Mick's paltry offering.

Delacroix laid his arm along the back of the bench. Relaxed pose, but there was tension in his voice. "I hoped you would be an asset, Hagan. Zimmer needs help—a skilled investigator, one who's not emotionally involved. You see, I once made the mistake of thinking I could be both lawyer and investigator. I refused to recognize that my passion had obscured the truth, until it was too late for my client. I don't want that mistake repeated." A bell in one of the church towers tolled four. Delacroix turned toward the sound. "Perhaps I have made a different one: mistaking you for a dedicated investigator."

"I investigate where the leads take me. In this case, to Vintage & Classics."

"Yet you have no damning evidence, do you? No motive. No smoking gun. Nothing incriminating against anyone at V&C. It's little wonder Rebecca suspects you have a personal stake in this matter." He rummaged in the bag for a nut. "Do you?"

"I just happened to be in town."

"How? Why did you happen to be in this place, at this time?"

Mick stretched forward. "Lawyer Delacroix, you're not

sounding neighborly towards a stranger in town. Should I report you to the Chamber of Commerce? Their offices ought to be near the courthouse somewhere."

"Few strangers come to stalk one of our most upstanding citizens."

"Moore is no more upstanding that I am a stalker." Mick resented Delacroix's accusation. After David's death, okay—the term might have fit, at a stretch. Mick had occasionally snuck a break from undercover work to troll past the loft where Moore had lived. First time, he'd seen her lug broken picture frames from the apartment and throw them into the dumpster in the alley. A week later, huddled in a doorway across the street, he'd watched her leave for a professional meeting or court, decked out in a designer suit and leather briefcase. One damp night he trained binoculars on her through a rain-streaked window. Stared for hours while she sat curled in an overstuffed chair and did nothing, tears on her cheeks glistening in the lamplight. He'd been hard at work the day the moving van showed up and took her out of the range of his surveillance.

"No? Then humor me, Hagan. What is Rebecca Moore's fascination for you?"

"You're not blind, Delacroix. You can answer that one yourself."

"Certainly the lady is attractive. Very. But I don't think that's your game, Hagan. If it is, you go about it badly. Besides, you hardly have a sporting chance. Unlike you, I shall have the leisure and the proximity to discover all of Rebecca Moore's attractions long after you've left town." Those damn golden eyes were smiling.

Mick cracked a single peanut, flipped it into the air and caught it between his front teeth. He crunched. The squirrels chattered. "Lucky you. But I'm not leaving just yet."

"So, you are intrigued by our local crime. Investigate it, then. Do something more constructive than harass Rebecca. Uncover the truth, Hagan. If you're capable of it." Delacroix crumpled the empty bag of peanuts.

Mick swung toward the lawyer. "The truth is that Rebecca Moore's not what she pretends to be."

Delacroix pitched the last peanut, sending the squirrels scattering. "Few of us are."

Twenty-four

The cheering stopped as abruptly as the Bentley's engine. Rebecca leaned into the topless car and pushed the starter button again. Nothing. She climbed into the car through the passenger-side door, adjusted the throttle control and gave it another go. Same result: the effete grinding of an engine that won't catch. The car had started fine in the garage. It purred out through the back doors and around the corner, with Shelley, Frank, Val and Paulie jogging alongside like the Secret Service on parade. When it reached the apron in front of the building the 3-Litre died and coasted to a stop.

"I tested every connection with the voltmeter. Honest. Val and I did. They all checked out." There was panic in Paulie's whine.

"Sure you did, Paulie. Nothing wrong with the wiring." Frank opened the left side of the bonnet. "Mr. Shelley, did Stuck overhaul the magnetos when the car was with him? Bench-test them, maybe?"

"He didn't bill me for it, that I remember. So, I guess the answer's no. Is that what's wrong?" Todd peered into the engine compartment, then backed up as if one or both of the magnetos would reach up and bite him. He bumped into Hal.

"Could be." Frank disconnected a high-tension lead from the spark plug and held it close to the engine block. "Okay,

Reb, crank her over." Rebecca did—no spark. Frank lowered the bonnet. He walked around to the right, unlatched the hinges on that side and lifted the bonnet to repeat the procedure. Again, no spark. "Doesn't look good for the mags."

"Tough break, Todd. Well, magnetos are legendary for failing. Better that it happened here with mechanics on hand than beside a cow path in Uzbekistan. Maybe tomorrow the auto gods will be with you and the car will run." Hal slapped his competitor on the back. "Let's leave the magneto resuscitation to the professionals. There's a stool at the Half Shell with my name on it." He winked at Rebecca over Todd's shoulder, then bust into song, bemoaning that when felons weren't employed, a policeman's life was not a happy lot.

"Oh, Frank. What do we do now? Both magnetos are bad?" Paulie was wringing his hands à la Lady Macbeth.

"Car's probably been limping along on one mag for who knows how long. Rewired and ready to run was too much for the baby. It will be okay, Paulie. Let's push her inside. Get those mags to the workbench."

Rebecca climbed out. "Not tonight. It's been a full day. We'll start on them tomorrow when we're fresh. Anybody up for pizza?"

Frank bent over the right rear with hands on the tire, ready to roll the car forward. He glanced at Paulie, then Val. He grinned at Rebecca. "You buying?"

"You bet. Start pushing."

"Personally, I think Mr. Lindeman did it." Paulie dabbed tomato sauce from the corner of his mouth. "He's much too cheerful all the time. Probably has a terrible temper."

"What's his motive?" Jo Delacroix separated off a slice of pepperoni with mushrooms.

"Revenge," Val said, chewing. "Stuck stuck it to everyone. Happy Hal decided to get even."

"Those two did have a major rift, but it was several years ago. Uncle Walt assumed it was over inadequate car repairs or an inflated bill. Why retaliate now? Besides, Hal would view besting Stuck as a personal challenge, something to add spice to their negotiations. His style is to stay right in your face and push."

"Ah, so. The Sumo wrestler approach." The lawyer bowed to the room.

"Unless there was major money involved." Rebecca swigged some diet Pepsi, then stood to fetch another slice of pizza. "If Lindeman did it, it was a killing for profit."

"Can you find out?"

Rebecca ignored him, though his question hit its mark. As the others continued speculating about possible suspects, Rebecca concentrated on Lindeman.

What did she know about him outside his interest in classic cars? She wasn't sure how he made his money—something to do with leasing, but specifics had never been discussed. Another peculiarity of the very rich. They rarely spoke of where their wealth came from. Those who toiled for it were almost embarrassed to admit it. Those who inherited it assumed everyone knew. Lindeman seemed to have plenty of spending cash. He must have, if he could afford to take part in the Paris-to-Peking.

Or did he? He was stalling on paying her for the work on the Hisso. Apparently he had flown to town early to get the Saturday stay-over rate. Plus he had finagled Shelley and two others into an ever-escalating side wager. Taken together, they could indicate that Lindeman wasn't as flush as he made you believe. Could he and Stuck have been partners in a business venture gone sour? Their apparent animosity was a cover to deflect suspicion? A clandestine, somewhat shady business venture would suit both men. Had anyone checked out survivor's insurance in connection with Stuck's death? She'd have to ask Jo.

When she tuned back in, Val was tipped back in his chair insisting that none of Graham's honeys had killed him. "It's not a woman's kind of crime, you know, like poisoning."

Juanita punched his arm. "Why you men always think

women poison you? I never once poisoned nobody in my family. I could have many times. They deserve it."

Poison. Vera's "poisoned cherries"—what had she meant? Recalling the widow's tinkling, drunk laughter during last night's phone call made Rebecca edgy. She had intended to call Vera first thing this morning before she got distracted. She would do it as soon as dinner was over. She took a final bite, discarding the crust in the trash.

"What about a male honey?" Paulie turned away from the group to pop the top on a soda can. Val tittered. Delacroix considered Paulie's question in earnest. The lawyer had shown up at the shop before they'd finished chewing the first slices. When invited to join them, Jo had removed his jacket, rolled up his shirtsleeves, but left the tie firmly knotted. After a few minutes of awkward silence, the guys resumed eating and talking.

"Do you have a reason for suspecting that Stuck had a male lover, Paulson?"

"No. It's possible, isn't it, Mr. Delacroix? Some men just like sex. They're not fussy about the gender of their partners."

Delacroix raised an eyebrow in Rebecca's direction. She shrugged. "No rumors about Graham and men, but it would account for the contradictions of his murder—a violent death laced with sexual overtones. I like it, Paulie, I really like it."

"And whom do you like for the murderer?" Jo asked.

"Hagan." Rebecca smirked at Jo, who laughed. "I'm serious. What do we know about him? He could have signed on with the police to throw them off the track."

"You talking about that guy in lockstep with the sheriff?" Frank lobbed a napkin at the wastebasket. "That'd be real cool. County pays him to investigate the crime he committed. No wonder he's checking us out. He's looking for some sap to pin it on. Like pin the tail on the donkey, only he ain't blindfolded. Hey, Janie girl, what's in the fancy tin?"

Juanita shifted a round red metal tin from the counter to the center of the table. It had once held the ubiquitous holiday fruitcake. Someone had spruced it up with a gold mesh ribbon securing the lid with a massive bow. "Maybe dessert? Mrs. Stuck says I am to give it to Miss Rebecca and no one else. She thank me so nice for the casserole. And the CDs. She is a lady. But she begs me to take the tin and for us to go. I think she is close to crying. So sad."

The girl's observation reminded the group that the local tragedy wouldn't go away as quickly as the cars that were nearing completion. It also reminded Rebecca that she'd forgotten about Stuck's Gilbert & Sullivan recordings.

"You gave her the CDs?"

"When Frank drives me over to Mrs. Stuck's. I find them on the desk, next to the truck keys and the note. I thought you meant for me to take them. It is okay?"

"I'm glad you did, Juanita." Rebecca folded a napkin into quarters. "I'm glad Frank found time to drive you." She tore the corner from the napkin.

Frank twirled a soda can, watched it go around. "Seemed like the thing to do. Gal's little feet hardly reach the pedals."

Rebecca let it go. "I'll call Vera. Explain about the recordings and thank her for the treats. Only Miss Rebecca is stuffed right now. Let's save them for tomorrow."

Frank pushed away from the table. "If we ain't having dessert, I'm going. I got special plans tonight." He started gathering the soiled paper plates.

Paulie jumped up. "Let me help. Mother has the monthly bridge club at the house—it's a good time to be absent. I'm going shopping. We need anything?"

Frank clapped him on the shoulder. "If you go near an auto parts store, get us a plastic gas can or two. Replace the ones used for the Subaru barbeque."

Twenty-five

Mick was not spying on Vintage & Classics.

He was sitting in his car at a parking meter in front of Henry's rereading yesterday's *Washington Post* and watching the evening fog melt to moisture on the windshield. Any thicker and it would become rain. From his perch he happened to see Frank Lewes drive off at five past seven. Paul Antrim came out just after. He left his car in the lot and walked down the street past the fabric store and the realtor to the Rite Aid, pausing to pick a leaf from the hood edge of a shiny black Bimmer parked opposite the door. Val and Juanita exited the building ten minutes later. They donned helmets and straddled a polished Yamaha. Val cranked it to life just as Mick's cell phone rang. "Yeah."

"Yeah to you, too. This is your research slave, Sal. Remember me? What's the racket?"

"I'm on the street."

"You got to get a home, boy."

"What you got, Sal?"

"Aren't we in fine humor. Where you want me to start?"

"Just start."

"First, you got the file?" Sal lowered his voice. "Did it help? Or depress?"

"The latter. But that's okay, I needed to see it. Tell me

about the mug shots. You uncover anything?" The fog had succumbed. Rain streaked the windows, drummed softly on the roof.

"Skimpy on the cons. Probably what you already know." Sal described Frank Lewes's time in prison as exemplary. That was the term used decades earlier for any con who avoided fights, was obedient to the guards and didn't get himself shivved. Lewes had worked at the auto shop ever since he was released. No backsliding. Val Kearney was a typical juvenile offender. Doing just enough drugs to think he's smarter than he is. Got caught on a electronics heist because he was too polluted to run away, unlike his buddies. "Put money on seeing him back inside in a few years. But as of now, nothing. Not a whisper on Antrim."

"What about Lindeman and Shelley?"

"Carole says she don't do business types, just lowlifes. You want info on them, come do it yourself."

"What about Stuck?"

"Who?"

"Don't get cute, Sal."

"I'm adorable." He chuckled. "Your stiff ain't who he said he was."

"What? Graham Stuck . . ."

"Ain't Graham Stuck. Not always. Which, along with hick incompetence, explains why your new buddies couldn't find squat about him. He was born Clarence Small. Legally changed his name in his twenties. Who could blame him for getting rid of 'Clarence'?"

"Not me. Could have been sensitive about the Small part, too. He was shorter than average." Mick flashed back to the photo of Stuck's naked form wedged in the beading machine. He pulled a notepad from over the visor and jotted down the name. "Where'd the alias come from?"

"Danny's betting he was a race fan—Graham for Graham Hill, Stuck for Hans Stuck. Both prizewinning drivers in Formula One in the sixties, seventies, thereabouts."

"Ambitious little bastard. Planned to make a mark in the

automotive world from an early age. Should the name change excite me?" Mick flipped on the wipers.

"Nope. Another hallway leading to a locked door. All I can tell you is he was born in Cincinnati and that he ended up in NYC as a teen, probably a runaway. And he has a juvie record. Sealed. Albany's not playing nice. Carole promises to get what she can—city, court jurisdiction, etc., etc., but may take a day or two."

"Okay. What else did she dig up?" Mick could hear hollering in the background.

Sal sounded distracted. "Hey, give me five minutes, pal. I'll ring you back."

Sal clicked off. Mick ditto. He checked his watch: 7:42. Antrim was returning for his car, carrying a sack from the Rite Aid. Sprinting to avoid the first splats that heralded a sudden squall.

Neither Delacroix nor his client had left the building. They must be working hard on a defensible position.

Twenty-six

"Rebecca, pull your head out of the sand. The sheriff's lariat is looped around this shop and tightening. Circumstantial evidence can convict, I know."

The image of a roundup of panicked ostriches flashed into her mind, but Rebecca refrained from sniggering. Jo looked tired. They were still in the lunchroom. He was slouched in a chair pushed back from the table. Moe sat on the seat next to him, washing his whiskers.

"First, there's motive. Your business needs money. Thanks to Graham's death, you've already inherited one customer. Others should follow."

"I inherited Todd Shelley *before* Graham was murdered." Rebecca reached for the cookie tin Vera sent over, hesitated, then pushed it away. She didn't need a sugar high.

"Second, there's access. There was no sign of forced entry. The only fingerprints belong to you and the boys. Third, knowledge. The murderer had to understand glass beading machines, at least how to turn one on. And blowing up the car required basic understanding of fuel systems. You are all mechanics." He leaned forward. "Then there's the transformer."

"You're as dense as Zimmer. Each point is easily refuted." Rebecca held up her index finger. "One: With Graham out of business, there's no guarantee that we'll get his customers.

Vintage car enthusiasts ship their cars all over the world for service. I'm still handicapped—a woman trying to compete in a rich man's hobby. Two: As for the fingerprints, the killer could have worn gloves, or picked them up here. There's a box of disposables on each workbench. As for access: You know Walt handed out shop keys all over town like Halloween candy. Graham may have had one for years. And you're wrong about the glass beading machine." She stood up, kicking the chair away from the table. "The killer wasn't familiar with it. Come on. I'll prove it."

Rebecca opened the door to the machine shop and strode to the far corner, to the glass beader. She reached it well ahead of Jo. Moe brought up the rear. Without disturbing the police tape, she slammed the door shut and yanked the lever to lock it. "Turn it on."

Jo started to ask how, then saw the clearly marked red plastic on/off switch above the window. A monkey could operate it. Point one to Rebecca. He flipped the switch. The motor whirred to life.

"Now watch." Rebecca moved him aside, thrust her arms fully into the gloves. She stepped on the foot pedal to activate the 'gun' and pointed the trigger—a light dusting of beads spurted out, then nothing. "No pressure. You have to turn on the compressor in the circuit breaker panel in order to operate the machine. The killer didn't know that. Leftover pressure will work for a few seconds before it fizzles out, but that's all. Highly frustrating if the murderer thought he could somehow damage the body. My guys know better. Believe me."

He did. He also believed that Rebecca was in denial about Frank Lewes's involvement. Jo stepped back from the machine, laid his hand on her arm. "Again, Rebecca, what about the transformer? Frank has a passion for trains, you know."

Of course she did. She'd spent a rainy Sunday forming rolling hills from flour, salt and water. She and Walt had streaked them green and brown with water colors, glued dwarf trees in the valleys. Frank had sat beside her admiring their handiwork as they licked orange sherbet from sugar cones. She remembered the trains and that day with clarity. She refused to connect them to the melted blob discovered at the car fire.

"He has no motive, Jo."

Delacroix's grip tightened. "Rebecca, is it possible you don't know?"

"You'd better tell me."

Jo perched on a workbench, hands pressed together between his knees. "You are aware that Frank and Graham were never friends, not from the first years ago when they both worked for your uncle. Publicly, Graham insisted that Frank was the reason he left V&C. He refused to work with a degenerate black. Walt's version of Stuck's departure had more to do with his lack of abilities and inclination to take shortcuts."

"That's ancient history."

"Recent history is darker." Last October, Jo explained, Frank had joined fellow checker players at the Blue Goose for a celebration. Vera was there, alone. Had been for hours. She was drunk and maudlin. Frank, a man capable of nursing one beer for three hours, took his mug to her table. He sat with her until closing, listening. Then drove her home in his car. She wasn't safe behind the wheel. Next morning, Frank and Walt returned Vera's car to her house and went to breakfast at Flo's. Before they were served, Graham Stuck arrived. Red-faced, he accused Frank of improprieties with his wife. Threatened to have him put back in jail before he assaulted her again, or worse. Frank remained stoic until Stuck called Vera a whore. He lunged for Stuck's throat. Walt and others broke it up before anything more than a few plates were broken.

"No charges were filed. The locals figured it was the pot calling the kettle black. If Vera was stepping out on Graham, no one was going to blame her, though they might have questioned her taste in men. Now, of course—"

Rebecca turned and walked away.

Jo saw himself out. Rebecca stretched her back against the doorjamb to the office and considered her options. A more pleasant subject than Frank's temper—but not by much. The guys had two days to fix the mags, road-test and prep both cars. If no one from the shop was arrested, they might do it. With the cars crated and ready to sail, Lindeman and Shelley would have to pay up. Part of the money would go to the accountant to accompany the revised tax forms he recommended sending to the IRS. "Good-faith payment," he called it. Enough money to convince the tax men that she would pay the last four years' back taxes and fines, in time. Then she'd pay the guys a bonus. Then reimburse herself, maybe buy a new laptop.

That done, she'd think about the rest of her life—which was starting to read like a filler article in the Sunday supplements. "The Life and Times of Rebecca Moore" contained a colorful pastiche of events: a crooked lover who commits suicide, a self-mutilated career, a murdered body found in her shop, a car bombed in her back yard, ex-cons and suspects as her only friends. She was being manipulated by a laid-back lawyer, at the mercy of an arrogant city cop, and the confidante of a recent widow with a drinking problem. Speaking of whom . . .

Rebecca switched off the lights and entered the office in search of the phone.

Twenty-seven

Waiting for Sal to call back, Mick tuned the radio to the local oldies station. It was playing Bobby Vee's "Suspicion." Mick mumbled off-key along with the refrain, feeling like a teenager with a crush on the girl next door. He swiped a circle of moisture from the side window. The lawyer was leaving V&C. Standing in the doorway, silhouetted in the pool of light from the security flood, Delacroix turned up the collar of his suit coat before heading south on Main Street toward his office. No sign of Moore. No peck on the cheek to send him off into the lousy night. Mick grinned. Good. The coast was clear. As soon as Sal phoned, Mick would go have it out with Moore. Then hit Tony's for fish & chips washed down with a Miller or two. Tomorrow he'd head out of town, with a relatively clear conscience.

As he'd promised the sheriff, Mick had run background checks, and done the local legwork on Moore's employees. He'd checked out Antrim, the last of them, that afternoon. Driven out to Sylvia Antrim's tasteful manse, which she shared with her only child, Paulson III. Stone manor house and spacious lawns seeded with greenbacks and acres of old, well-pruned foliage. Not a neighborhood easily canvassed, but a groundskeeper across the street was friendly and fond of the kid. Gave him high marks for working when he sure didn't have to. To thoroughly exonerate the dapper Mr. Antrim, Mick would have to watch the guy for a couple of days. Follow him after work, see where he went, who he hung out with. But instinct told Mick that Antrim wasn't guilty of anything worse than being a little light in his Cole Hahn loafers.

The phone rang. Mick snatched it on the first peal. "Sal. Everything cool?"

"Sure, just one heroin-happy felon thinking he's superman. Oh, yes, and one irate commander. Remember him? He wants me to relay a message: 'What the hell are you doing messing around in someone else's crimes? If you're so bored, get your ass back up here to the people who pay you.' I think that's a direct quote."

"Message received."

"Good, where was I?" Sal shuffled papers. "Becca Moore, your lady friend, it's good enough to gag on. Bosses thought she was Pulitzer material. Journalistic review boards couldn't give out blue ribbons or whatever without handing her one. Late nineties she was recognized for a multipart series on car bombings, terrorist-style stuff. You writing this down? I'm not repeating it." Mick grunted. "A year later she gets mentioned for 'Rehabilitated Criminals: an Oxymoron?' Included a sidebar on your pal Reiske. Guy gets around, doesn't he? Another gold medal or something for 'When Wires Start Fires Who's to Blame?' about the Glenside Park Apartments, the complex in Arlington that burned to the ground, killing six. Lot of finger-pointing on that one."

"Unhealthy interest in crime."

"You were expecting reviews of bake-offs at the county fair? She investigated injustices for a major metropolitan paper, just like Clark Kent."

"You siding with the lady, Sal?"

"What's with taking sides? Mick, she was exonerated in Semple's death. You may not like her ethics, but she's not guilty of anything."

"Fax copies to the sheriff's station, will you?"

"Your wish, my command."

"And Sal, add Judge Reiske to the pile. See if you can connect him with Stuck."

"Righteous Reiske? What gives? This to do with *Alonso*? That case's a no-brainer. You got it sewed up tight. A blind judge could see that. Someone like Reiske'll put him away for five, ten lifetimes."

"When the mob's on trial, you never know."

"You nervous about testifying? That's not like you, Mickey."

"Reiske showed up yesterday in this backwater town, Sal. You know how I feel about coincidences."

"Like an itch under a plaster cast. Okay, I'll give it a shot. I suppose you want this tomorrow?"

"Yesterday. I'll call you at home tonight." Mick turned off the car, dropped the toothpick in the ashtray. It was time to have a heart-to-heart chat with Rebecca Moore. He'd put it off long enough.

He almost made it. Hand on the door handle, Mick glanced through the cleared side window. A tall figure in a hooded raincoat splashed through puddles, heading for the front door of Vintage & Classics. *Christ.* Mick dropped back into the driver's seat, flipped the ignition to accessory. The radio blared to life. Otis Redding moaned about sitting on the dock of the bay, wasting time. *You said it, Otis. Moore's busier than the deli counter at Wegman's. Looks like I forgot to take a number.*

Twenty-eight

Rebecca let the phone ring twenty times, then dropped it on the desk. Vera wasn't home, or didn't feel like talking. Which was understandable. Or had drunk herself into a stupor. Equally understandable. Rebecca considered driving over to the widow's house to check on her, until she looked outside. The afternoon's thick clouds had developed into a Class 6 storm. Wind and rain lashed against the building. Branches on the maple dipped down to kiss the ground, then arced up higher than the building. The power lines sagged and swayed. The security light was a dim glow obscured by a nimbus of mist.

She blinked as a figure emerged from the shadows. He scurried toward the front door, skipping to avoid puddles. The figure paused under the overhang, slapping rain from his coat. He craned his head as if listening to the whoosh of rain running through the gutters, or the fire siren wailing in the distance.

Rebecca sighed. It could be her lawyer returning with another theory to consider. Or the sheriff looking for answers she didn't have. Frank not able to sleep until he adjusted the carb on the Hisso one more time. The accountant in search of one more deduction. Or Hagan come to harass her with unspoken criticisms. So much for the men in her life. She shut down the computer as the doorbell sounded.

She twisted the deadbolt, then smiled to herself—*none of the above*. Stewart Reiske was standing in the doorway, appropriately judgelike: neat, trim and somber. She remembered using those exact words in a filler piece she'd written on his impressive conviction record. It had accompanied an article on the effects of prisons in rehabilitating criminals. Reiske belonged to the lock-'em-up-and-throw-away-the-key school. Unless, of course, there was sufficient cause to execute.

"Judge Reiske. This is a surprise. Come in out of the weather."

"You know who I am, Miss Moore. Should I be flattered?" The judge lowered the hood of his slicker to reveal sugar-white hair swept off a high forehead and matching bushy eyebrows over blue eyes.

"Only if you think newspaper photographs do you justice. Your face is often in the DC news."

"Too often for an officer of the court. Still, it's gratifying when an attractive woman takes notice." He dipped his head in a mock bow, his thin smile tight enough to pass for a grimace. His eyes flitted around the office taking in the ledger sheets and stacked invoices. "I hope I'm not intruding?"

"Catching up on accounting." Rebecca dismissed the clutter. "What can I do for you?"

Reiske unsnapped the raincoat as he entered the room. "Two things, really. I learned this afternoon that you are Becca Moore, the reporter who penned such insightful articles for the *Post*. Your absence from the paper has been noted. So, on one hand, I came to express amazement that you've left a promising career. On the other hand . . ." He idly fingered strewn computer disks awaiting labels. "Well, frankly, I came to elicit information you may have uncovered regarding Graham Stuck's death."

"You think I'm investigating Stuck's killing?"

"Aren't you? As a former reporter, surely it was your first instinct?"

So everyone kept insisting. "As a federal judge, your first instinct was to rush to the widow's aid?"

"Graham was an acquaintance."

"And the widow needs representation?"

This time he smiled broadly. "Wishful thinking, Miss Moore. Vera doesn't need my services, just friendly support. I return to Washington tomorrow."

"But first you want to know what I know?" He nodded. "That won't take long."

"Long enough for a cup of tea, perhaps?"

Rebecca didn't offer to take his coat. Her handful of facts could be related in about five minutes, if she were inclined to share them with the Judge. At the moment, her only inclination was to go home to bed and sleep. The long day had drained her.

She lead the way into the lunchroom. Reiske pulled out a chair at the table. He brushed at the ubiquitous cat hairs. Once settled, he interlaced his fingers on the surface. "Vera thinks Graham was involved in a potentially lucrative financial scheme. Would you know anything about that?"

Rebecca almost laughed. "If he was, the scheme had nothing to do with vintage car restorations. This is not a get-rich-quick kind of business." She poured steaming water into a mug with a tea bag in place. "But perhaps you knew that. Are you a car enthusiast?"

"Hardly." The Judge confessed that he only drove to escape town on a dull weekend. He had known Graham years ago. When Reiske moved, they'd lost touch. They'd met again fairly recently at a fund-raiser—a carnival event in Bethesda: tents, amateur polo and vintage cars on display for charity—autism, or some other cause. Graham had been there with a customer's car.

"And you were there with—"

"A fellow jurist, Stephanie Newel, if it's any of your business."

"Sorry. Habitually nosy."

"And what does your nose tell you about this?" Reiske blew on the tea, rippling the brown liquid.

"That Graham was killed by person or persons unknown, for reasons unknown.

"Disappointingly vague. You must be the only person in town who doesn't think someone who works here is guilty." The judge sounded positively testy. He started to raise his mug of tea, then set it back down. There were bright patches of color on his cheeks. His eyes wandered, darting down and sideways. They lit on Rebecca, dragonflies landing on a lily pad.

"Would you by chance have something to nibble on? I'm feeling a bit faint. Blood sugar must be low."

"Muffin?"

"Something sweeter? Cookie? Cake, perhaps?" His wry smile apologized for imposing.

Rebecca, hostess-trained by Mrs. Bellotti, retrieved the fruitcake tin from the top shelf of the cupboard where she'd stashed it. Better than an even chance it contained something sweet and caloric enough to cheer a grieving widow, or fortify a fainting judge. She was peeling off the gift card and bow as the doorbell sounded. She shrugged and asked the judge to excuse her.

She had pried the lid from the tin and was inhaling the aroma of rich baked chocolate as she opened the front door. Hagan stood there, dripping. His eyes lively and arrogant.

"Hope it's not too late for another look at the murder scene?"

Without waiting for a response, he pushed his way into the foyer, shedding puddles on the hall floor, forcing Rebecca to back up. "Refreshments?" He reached into the open tin. "Brownies, my favorites."

She replaced the lid. "They're for the judge."

"You've got company? Great. We'll have a party."

Hagan broke a brownie in two, popped a piece in his mouth and chewed his way past her into the lunchroom. He swallowed enough to address the judge. "Evening, Your Honor. We didn't have the chance to shake hands at the autopsy."

Stewart Reiske rose. "Should I know you?"

"Not yet. I'm—"

Hagan's cell phone sounded. He frowned. Flipped the phone open with one hand, holding a chunk of brownie in the other.

"Yeah. What's up? What? . . . Damn it to hell." Mick pitched the brownie. "What happened? When? Okay, I got you covered. Yeah, looking at her. At her shop, entertaining Judge Reiske. I'm on my way. Right." Mick snapped the case closed and looked at the wall clock.

"Okay, Moore. It's eight fifty-five, do you know where your workers are?"

"Why? What's going on?"

"That was the sheriff. Vera Stuck's house is vanishing in a blaze of glory. A three-alarm blaze. The fire chief suspects a gas leak, maybe faulty wiring. Zimmer swears it's arson. He's trying to track down the logical suspects—your employees."

"That's insane. They'd never do anything like that. Has he flipped?" She didn't wait for an answer but headed for the front office. "They'll be home. Bet on it. I'm calling them."

Mick tossed her his cell phone. She caught it left-handed. "Do it on the way. Come along, Judge. Sheriff may need you to identify the body."

Rebecca froze as she wrestled her raincoat from the hat rack next to the door. "Oh, God. Not Vera?"

"Her car's there. Neighbor says upstairs lights were on before the house went poof. It doesn't look good."

Twenty-nine

"Paulie's at home. Sylvia roped him into playing the fourth at bridge. He just made five no trump. Mother's so proud." Moore dropped the cell phone onto the seat.

"Grand for her." Mick was unimpressed.

The windshield wipers were going full tilt, but they couldn't keep up with the downpour. Mick wondered if the deluge would put out the fire, or at least slow it.

"You reach Lewes?"

Moore shook her head. Her hair fell forward, caressing her cheek. Even in the half-light inside the truck, Mick could see she was defeated. "But you found Juanita?"

"With Val. Not where I wanted to find her, but no surprise either. They're both old enough to vote."

"Right. And you're their boss, not their mother."

He looked back at the highway in time to brake hard for one of three stoplights between Head Tide and the north side of Blue Marsh. The tail end of the Jeep swerved, then snapped back in line, bouncing Reiske off the back of the seat. Mick eyed the judge in the rearview mirror.

"You okay, Judge? My driving bothering you?"

"Just keep your eyes on the road."

The judge's tone sounded appropriately critical. *Critic,* from the Greek, able to discern or judge. Funny how all the synonyms—*hypercritical, fault-finding, captious, carping, censorious*—had negative connotations. Curious how well they all applied to Judge S. Thornton Reiske. Born to be a critic. Mick didn't relish being stared down by him in the courtroom.

Moore was huddled against the car door. A single strand of hair had snagged on the mole on her left cheek. He wanted to smooth it away, lighten the worry in her eyes. He tightened his grip on the wheel.

"Moore, just so you can't accuse me of bias, let's check on the boy racers. They should be snug as bugs in the lounge at the marina."

She sat up. "Or they could be lurking in the bushes at the fire. From the marina it's an easy walk inland to Vera's, just follow the bridal path." Moore pushed buttons on the cell phone, reciting the number under her breath.

"Are you saying that even the fat man could saunter over to the Stucks' place, light a match, and return to his barstool without breaking much of a sweat?"

She nodded, at the same time she asked to speak with Hal Lindeman. "Try the Half Shell Lounge, will you? Thanks."

Crawford's crew had a swarm of company. The two closest counties had responded to help fight the blaze. Red fire trucks, yellow and white rescue vans were angled in every direction on the Stucks' once-manicured lawn. Onlookers huddled in the dark fringes, oblivious to the rain. Harsh spotlights planted in the flower beds lit up men in rubber suits controlling hoses that pulsed gallons of water toward the house.

Behind a tower of billowing smoke, a portion of the second floor closest to the chimney was still standing. The rest had collapsed into a mound of charred rubble. Most of the first floor had been eaten away. At the edge of the property, the garages housing Capitol Chassis appeared untouched. The scene was washed in shades of white and gray, mist and smoke; only a few low flames remained. Beside Mick,

Moore shivered inside her slicker. The sheriff looked up from talking to one of his men, saw Mick and waved. He stood and loped over toward the group waiting in the harbor of a bank of rhododendrons.

"You bring me my prime arson suspect, Hagan?" Zimmer glowered at Moore.

She snapped back, "I've been at the shop all evening, Sheriff. I have a slew of witnesses."

"So you say."

"Sure it was arson?" Mick stepped between Moore and Zimmer.

"It will be. The storm stopped everything from becoming ash, so Charlie'll find evidence. You'll see. No way this fire wasn't set. Which makes it homicide as well."

Mick cursed.

"You can say that again. They found Vera in her bedroom when the second floor came down. She didn't stand a chance. Oh, hell. Sorry, Judge. Didn't see you there." Zimmer pulled off his hat and took a step closer to Reiske. "I'm afraid Mrs. Stuck—"

"Vera?" It was a gentle question. Reiske's right hand fluttered as if looking for support or casting a benediction. Moore reached out, but stopped short of touching him. Her arm remained suspended as if in a tableau. Trickles of rain streamed down her sleeve before cascading to earth. Reiske nodded. His head kept moving like a man with palsy. "Was she . . . was she . . . oh, dear . . . recognizable?"

Zimmer looked embarrassed for the older man. "Don't fret, Judge. It was her. Wasn't burned bad. Probably went quick, smoke inhalation."

"Both of them. This is too tragic, so like a Greek curse." The judge stifled what might have been a sob and straightened. "You can't really think it was murder? Isn't it more likely that she started the fire herself?"

"On purpose?" Suicide by burning was not something Zimmer considered likely.

"She was despondent without Graham, of course. But, I

meant unintentionally. Vera had been drinking lately. Quite a lot, really. Downing her sorrow, I suspect. Her tragic flaw."

"Accidental-like? A cigarette in bed—that sort of thing? We'll check out all possibilities. But, man, coming on the heels of her husband's death and the car explosion and all, it's hard to accept this was an accident." Zimmer shot Mick a conspiratorial glance which clearly said, *Accident, my ass.*

Though he sided with the sheriff, Mick hoped the judge was right. It would make him feel a lot less guilty.

Moore finally brought her arm back in to cradle her body. As if released, Reiske rocked back, shrinking within himself, and moaned. "It's unthinkable that her death was murder as well as Graham's."

"To you, maybe. Not to the killer."

Not to the killer, indeed. Mick faced Moore. She looked like a drowned rat, stranded on the banks of a stream, bereft and soggy beyond saturation. Not the portrait of a killer enthralled by the fruits of her labor. But what did he know? Where Moore was concerned, Mick wasn't his normal, perceptive self.

At the end of the drive the attendants from Rescue Truck No. 8 lifted a thin black body bag onto a stretcher, collapsed the legs and slid it into the ambulance bound for the morgue. The knot of spectators stood numb as it pulled away. One fireman removed his helmet until the truck was out of sight. When he redonned his helmet, Rebecca broke from Hagan and the sheriff.

Kneeling in the mud behind where the van had been parked was Billy Lee—keening and cursing. He alone seemed to mourn Vera. Billy Lee was a figure from Uncle Walt's past. There was a time he'd worked for Walt, a time when they had been close friends. Then there had been a falling out—over what, Rebecca didn't remember, if she ever knew. Billy Lee had left Vintage and gone to work for Stuck. Gossip said he stayed with him because of Vera—cared for her like a daughter. Walt freely admitted Billy Lee was a good mechanic, and conscientious. Without him, Stuck couldn't have kept his business open for five minutes. That was all Walt would say on the subject. Now, with Graham and Vera gone, there was no business for Billy Lee to sustain, no one to claim his devotion or give him direction.

Rebecca was halfway to Billy Lee when Hagan's hand clamped down on her forearm. His rasp sounded in her ear. "Where do you think you're going? You can't run away this time, Moore. It's too close to home."

"It wouldn't be if Stuck hadn't died in my shop. I've done nothing. Nothing." She wrenched her arm free and kept walking.

Hagan trotted beside her, hissing close to her face. "That so? That how you rationalized it when Semple blew his brains out because of you? 'Just doing my job?' "

Rebecca stopped as if she had taken a blow to the stomach. "What do you know about David Semple?"

"Enough to advise Zimmer to contact the DC police about the real reason you skipped town."

"Who the hell are you, Hagan? Why are you hounding me?"

His eyes flashed with frustration. "This shouldn't have happened. Vera Stuck shouldn't have died. Suspicious deaths follow you like footprints in snow, don't they? A regular Typhoid Mary. Why is that?"

Rebecca's cheek twitched. She could feel anger and tears clashing, like gears out of mesh, each grinding for supremacy. She willed the anger to win. She backed away from the detective.

"Get out of my face, Hagan. Leave me alone. You're right. Vera should not have died. If you'd spent more time investigating her husband's murder and less time harassing my employees, her death might have been prevented. Live with that if you can."

She turned and ran the rest of the way to Billy Lee.

Mick remained standing in the drive, breathing through his mouth to control his mounting frustration. He watched

Moore reach the old man and kneel beside him. A volunteer, witnessing the tableau with Mick, commented that the old guy had worked for Stuck. He'd come running through the yard, full tilt into the house after the woman. Stupid move. A medic was trying to bandage the guy's face and hands. He was crying and gesturing toward a soggy flowering dogwood near the end of the garages. Moore nodded. She helped him stand and gave him a hug before the medic handed him up into a second ambulance reserved for the living.

Moore walked to the tree. She stretched out her hand to a Doberman tied there. He sniffed. She fondled his muzzle, then unfastened the leash. She turned, coaxed, but the dog stood fast. He wouldn't be coaxed away from where his master had disappeared. She knelt again in the oozing mud. Taking the dog's head in her hands Moore fingered his stubby ears. He cocked his head, studied her, then licked her nose. Seemed they had come to an understanding. The dog didn't have any trouble trusting her. Moore rose, looped the leash around her hand and headed off at a jog across the waterlogged meadow.

"Where's she going?" Zimmer slapped clumps of melted mud from his slicker.

"Not far, dragging a dog through the muck."

"She take Wonder?"

Mick nodded. "If that's the mutt's name."

"Then she's probably going by Billy Lee's for dog food. Better her than me. Don't like Dobermans. Sly, mean and always ready to pounce. Probably why it gets along with Moore." Zimmer chuckled. "Sent Boeski out to Frank Lewes's place. Be nice to know where the ex-murderer's been all evening."

"You better add Lindeman and Shelley to your list of suspects missing in action. Bartender at the marina hasn't seen them tonight, which is real unusual. Include any irate husbands or boyfriends of Stuck's conquests, or anybody else we might have dismissed. Somebody's playing fast, dirty and for keeps."

As he watched the firemen reel in the hoses, Mick admitted that Moore's accusation stung worse than the mental kicks he'd been administering since he heard about the fire. He'd screwed up big time. True, it wasn't his investigation, but he should have paid closer attention. Somehow he'd been blindsided. Correction. He'd blinded himself. He'd been so obsessed with Moore that he hadn't taken the murder of Graham Stuck seriously. Even when the victim's car exploded at the shop, Mick had ignored the emerging pattern. If Vera's death was murder as Zimmer suspected, everything had changed. These were not what Mick usually faced—white-collar killings for greed, or urban drug busts gone sour. These were crimes of passion, and power. Almost dares. Bold, flagrant, decisive murders carried out with no fear of being stopped.

Thirty

The rain petered out about halfway home. Rebecca's adrenaline quit just shy of two miles in front of Henry's. She stopped jogging abruptly, doubled over with hands on her knees, and tried to catch her breath. Wonder slipped his head under her arm and whimpered.

"Miserable night, boy, I know. We're almost there. Water, food, bed. In that order." She straightened, shifting the ten-pound bag of Purina to her right arm, leash to the left.

Across the street the shop looked quiet. A security light glowed over the front door, illuminating the Vintage & Classics sign. No cars in the lot. No strangers. No explosions. Moe would be curled asleep in the in basket. If there was a body keeping him company, she didn't want to know about it.

Rebecca urged Wonder across the street at a trot and started up the grade toward the house. It was then that the darkness registered. A double floodlight off the back side of the shop should have been shining this way. Instead, the walnut grove was blacker than pitch, ripe with the fetid smell of humus. Not a glimmer to distinguish shadows among the trees. She paused. Raindrops fell from branches to splat on the hardened ground of the path. Had the lights been on earlier? She couldn't recall. Moisture had shorted out the fixture before. Probably that's what happened tonight. Still, she was reassured by Wonder's taut body bumping into her leg.

"Come on, boy. Let's go in."

In unison, they bounded up the front steps. Rebecca braced the bag of dog food on the knob while she fished the keys from her pocket. The knob turned under the weight. The door swung inward. Wonder darted inside. Before Rebecca could reach for the light switch, the dog's momentum pulled her into the room. Her right foot collided with something heavy. She fell hard onto her knees. The bag of Purina flew from her arm.

"What the—"

Wonder's leash jerked her arm as the dog danced and whimpered. "Sit," Rebecca yelled, amazed when the Doberman complied.

She rolled on her side to feel for the object that had tripped her. It was a shallow drawer. Her fingers traced the edges, recognized oak handles carved like bunches of grapes. It was the drawer from the marble-topped chest that sat in the corner. The one that held key fobs, rubber bands, pesticide instructions—the detritus of everyday living you don't want to throw away but have no place for. Why was the drawer in front of the door? Who would—?

A frisson of fear raced up her neck. Someone had been in her house. *Shit*. Could still be in her house. Her heart pounded. Her fingers fled over the contents of the drawer, feeling for scissors, letter opener, anything resembling a weapon. The best she could find was a knitting needle.

Wonder whined. Rebecca held out her hand hoping to still him. In the dark she could make out the shadow of the dog's head cocked to one side. *You hear anyone, boy?* Minutes passed. She moved her tongue to moisten dry lips. Wonder continued to listen. All Rebecca could hear was the faint tick of the hanging clock in the hallway. Bored, Wonder lowered himself to the floor and scuttled forward until he could lick her face.

"You think the coast is clear, do you? Okay. Let's turn on a light."

Rebecca pushed back onto her haunches, listened, straightened to standing. She reached for the wall switch and flicked it on. She should have left it dark. The living room looked like Kansas after a tornado. Pillows from the sofa had been gutted and pitched. Books lay on their spines like fallen soldiers, pages spread wide. Her few CDs had been opened, thrown, crushed or all three. The company financial files she'd left on the coffee table had been shredded into a flurry of white confetti. The cherry-framed mirror listed— still on its hook, its glass shattered into a hundred shards. By the fireplace, a small Oriental rug was bunched up against the hearth where it had done noble service. Cradled in its folds was her grandmother's maybe-Ming-dynasty vase. It looked unbroken.

Straight ahead, through the wide arch, Rebecca could see that the kitchen had suffered the same fate. Jars, cans, boxes of crackers and cereal littered the floor. Most were mangled, their contents spewed. The earth-toned tiles were dusted like doughnuts with a coating of flour. Without getting up, she couldn't see into the dining room off the short hall to the right. She didn't want to see, afraid that the antique Haviland china service for ten was no longer displayed in the corner cabinet.

Rebecca set the knitting needle on the arm of the sofa. She untangled the dog's leash from her wrist and sank back on her heels. Wonder snuggled close.

Why?

She stared at the wreckage. What was the intruder looking for? This was not a burglary. The few items with street value were still accounted for. The CD player was open and the VCR had been thrown on the floor, but they hadn't been taken. Nor had the TV or 35mm camera. Rebecca wasn't sure anything had been taken, at least nothing within immediate sight.

And there was too much unnecessary destruction. The intruder hadn't been content to search, he wanted to destroy. Why mutilate the CDs, shred the papers? Was it frustration at not finding what he was looking for, or a personal attack? It had to be connected with Graham's and Vera's deaths. But how? Why were their deaths being dumped on her doorstep? They were only acquaintances. What linked her to their fates? Why was she being made to feel so guilty?

Rebecca bent down to take comfort from the Doberman's warmth and wet dog smell. "What have I done, boy, and to whom? Do you know? Do you?" The dog whimpered. Rebecca hugged his neck and let her tears come.

Thirty-one

Mick sat on the hood of the patrol car. Zimmer leaned against the fender. Both were drinking tepid coffee from Styrofoam cups that a considerate neighbor had brought over. Most of the fire trucks had secured their ladders and gone home. Only two floodlights remained. The crew from the No. 5 engine was hanging around in case some smoldering chunk of wood decided to flare up. One of Crawford's men walked back and forth, jabbing at the charred debris with what looked like a fireplace poker.

"Why is it I feel like everybody involved with this case has a hidden agenda?"

"That comment meant for me, Sheriff?" Mick pitched the dregs of the coffee.

"Don't see anyone else here. Do you? You going to tell me what you and Moore were screaming about?"

"If we'd been screaming, you would have heard." Mick leaned back against the windshield. The stench of burned wood was brutal. He breathed through his mouth to keep from gagging. "You shouldn't have to ask, Zimmer, I should've told you. Last fall, the body of a financial executive, David Semple, was found in Moore's apartment. Head blown off. It was ruled suicide."

Charlie Crawford started toward them from the far side of

the blackened rubble. Walking slowly; carrying something. Zimmer watched the man approach, then turned his attention back to Mick. "You have trouble with that ruling?"

"No. And yes. The evidence pointed to suicide, but they've been staged successfully before. Most likely she goaded him into it. However it went down, she has his blood on her hands."

"You investigate it?"

"Nope. Men I trust did."

Crawford was getting closer. He looked whipped. Sheriff watched him come; chewed at his bottom lip. "Yet you're sure she's to blame?"

Mick slipped off the car. "Semple was weak, greedy, emotionally involved with Moore. She used him, then betrayed him. If he killed himself—*if*—he did it on her bed as a statement of his pain. She was the cause."

"So, because of his death you like her for Stuck's killing? Kind of a stretch—much as I'd like it to be so." Sheriff half turned to face Crawford.

Mick persisted. "Look, I cruise into your lazy town and voilà, there's Rebecca Moore bending over a naked, dead man. Tell me that wouldn't have gotten you going."

Zimmer nodded to the fire chief as he answered Mick. "Enough to get any cop's juices flowing. What was Semple to you? You going to enlighten me?"

Mick didn't answer. Zimmer wasn't listening. The expression on Crawford's face had captured the sheriff's attention. The fire chief handed over a couple of sooty file folders, wiped his hand on his thigh, glad to be rid of them. Zimmer raised an eyebrow. Charlie stood mute. Zimmer rested the folders on the roof of the car and flipped back the cover of the top one to reveal a stack of eight-by-ten black and white glossies. The first few must have told the story. Zimmer didn't look at the rest.

"Sweet Jesus. What's going on in my town?" The sheriff slammed the folder shut and jumped into the car. Mick slid into the passenger's seat.

Thirty-two

"Don't touch anything if you can help it. Use a handkerchief to close and lock the door. You're certain the house is empty?" Jo Delacroix was speaking faster than Rebecca had ever heard him. His voice faded in and out on the other end of the line. She could hear coat hangers clang together, the jangle of keys.

"Pretty sure. I haven't been upstairs. Billy Lee's Doberman is right beside me. He's not spooked. Well, no more than I am."

"Good. Keep him close. I'm on my way. If you hear a noise, any noise at all, dial 911. Don't hesitate."

After he disconnected, Rebecca listened to the hum coming from the other end of the line, then set the phone in her lap. Cross-legged on one of the fallen pillows, she leaned against the front edge of the sofa. Wonder pinned her down, his head thrown over her thigh. She massaged his velvet stub of an ear. Rebecca liked dogs the same way she liked kids—in the abstract, and only if they were well behaved and belonged to someone who lived in the next state. She might have to reconsider her position. A dog could have its uses—like personal security.

"Would you attack to defend me, boy? Would you save me from the bogeyman?" Wonder stared at her intently. Or rather, he stared over her shoulder at the discarded bag of dog chow. She got the message. "Okay. Sure thing. How do you feel about a picnic right here?"

Jo found them still sitting in front of the sofa. Rebecca was feeding the dog out of her hand. Wonder was lapping it up, literally.

"Rebecca, I told you to lock the door." He squatted down in front of her. "Rebecca. Rebecca, look at me." Her hands were cold to the touch. So was her chin when Jo gently forced it up. Tears had etched streaks through the soot on her face. She was wearing a mud-covered slicker. The legs of her jeans were soaked, molded to her skin. She looked like a ten-year-old refugee. "Where do you keep blankets?"

"On a bed?"

"It's not a quiz, Rebecca. Where?"

"Why do you want a blanket?"

"I don't. You do." Jo sprinted for the steep stairs disappearing behind the floor-to-ceiling wall of bookshelves. He grabbed a chenille spread from the unmade bed in the first room he came to. He assumed it was Juanita's. There were garish rock posters on the pink walls and discarded clothes, shoes and jewelry everywhere. The room might have been tossed, or this might have been its normal teenage state.

Jo returned to the living room. He pulled Rebecca to her feet, unfastened the wet rain jacket, peeled it off stiff arms and let it drop. He wrapped the spread around her and eased her onto the one cushion remaining on the sofa.

"Rebecca. Talk to me. Focus, please."

Rebecca bent forward, dug into the bag of dog food and held out more pellets for Wonder. He wolfed them down, drooling.

Jo looked around frantically. She was scaring the hell out of him. Where was the animated combatant of the last few days? He wanted to shake the limp imposter in front of him and shout, *What have you done with the real Rebecca Moore?* Instead he headed for the dining room in search of brandy. In the bottom half of a corner cupboard, he found an unopened bottle of *Wild Turkey Bourbon, 101*. It seemed like a sacrilege, but this was an emergency. The top cabinet, containing good dishes and glassware, was locked. He ran into the kitchen, crunching Cheerios into powder as he searched for a glass.

The first shot went down without protest. The second one raised a sputter. The third shot caused Rebecca to grab Jo's wrist and ask, "Bourbon in a juice glass? A well-mannered Southern boy should know better."

"Raised in Jamaica, ma'am. All we had were juice glasses." He set the bottle down. He smiled and brushed a lock of hair from her cheek. His hand lingered, cradling her face. "Nice to see you again, Rebecca. Where have you been?"

"Train-wrecked." She removed his hand from her face, held on to it as he helped her stand. The spread slithered to the floor. "Have you called Zimmer? I didn't think to."

"From my office. Sandra Olson was the only one there. The rest are at the fire scene. She'll be over as soon as Boeski returns. You know about the fire and—"

"I was there when they brought her body out. What's going on, Jo? Zimmer claims the fire was set. Who would do that? Who would want both Graham and Vera dead? Their car and house destroyed. Why? Why ransack my home? What are they looking for? Who is doing this? Who? Why?"

"Stay calm, Rebecca. We will get to the bottom of it. I promise you. You and I will figure it out."

By the time Olson showed up, Jo had finished guiding Rebecca through the house to inspect for damage and missing items. Jo didn't care about what might have been taken. He was more concerned about what might have been left behind, like an incendiary device that would go boom in the night. He didn't have the foggiest notion of what to look for, or where. He sincerely hoped Rebecca was coherent enough to notice anything out of the ordinary. He'd ask Charlie

Crawford to check the premises as soon as he could. At the moment Charlie had his hands full.

Jo also wanted Rebecca to see the extent of the violation while she had company, to convince her that there were no trolls hiding under the beds. He couldn't make her feel emotionally safe in her home, but he could help her intellect understand that it was void of real-life enemies.

The rooms on the second floor had received the same ransacking as those below. Bedding ripped off, books tossed, lamps upended, alarm clocks thrown and smashed. Rebecca stayed in the hallway outside her bedroom, which spanned the back of the house, one hand clutching the doorframe. The quilt was in a lump, sheets half torn from the bed, pictures crooked on the pale apricot walls. Everything—hairbrush, gold earrings, a tube of mascara, the silver-framed photo of her paternal grandparents—had been swept from the top of her bureau and lay littered on the floor. She blanched. Then turned abruptly and went to Juanita's room.

Closer inspection revealed the damage overlaying the standard mess. Many of the girl's CDs had been crushed. Some of the artists Jo recognized, but most were foreign groups he'd never heard of. Alternative music, Rebecca called it. She knelt and gathered up the shattered cases, matching pieces of disks to the colorful covers. Tears were welling in her eyes when she asked him to fetch a bag to put them in.

"I don't want Juanita to see them. She limits herself to one new CD every two weeks. Orders them on-line. She pays for them out of her tips. If she doesn't have enough money, she adds the title to the list of wants and waits until she can afford it. I hope these can be replaced easily."

Jo had no idea. He took the bag from Rebecca. He would ask Edna to locate the music site on the Internet. Replacing them was one small thing he could do for the girl. For Rebecca.

Rebecca left Officer Olson upstairs and retreated to the kitchen. She rescued a can of tuna fish from the floor and shook crushed crackers from a metal mixing bowl. Mayonnaise, capers, dill weed, salt and pepper went into the bowl with the tuna. She retrieved four slices of white bread, squashed but whole. She cut the crusts from the bread and quartered each sandwich into triangles, arranging them on a platter.

"Tea sandwiches, Rebecca? Is this your upbringing showing? Or is it Paulson's influence?"

"Both, I guess. Don't you like tuna? There's not much else."

"I don't want food. I want to talk."

"I don't."

Jo removed his glasses. "We won't talk about the murders."

"What then? You? You want to tell me what you're doing wasting away in this nowhere land?"

Jo carried the plate of sandwiches to the table and sat. He wasn't going there. Instead he returned the conversation to her. "Tell me what you meant earlier. You said you'd been 'train-wrecked.'"

Rebecca pulled out a chair and joined him. A faint smile flitted across her face.

"My favorite Christmas present ever was from Uncle Walt when I was seven—a handmade train set. Shiny silver engine and four cars on fat wheels, red caboose. When I asked what the train was called, Uncle Walt said, 'Thought.' He called it my 'train of thought' because he said I was mulelike about following an idea through to its conclusion. Like a train with a full head of steam, hitching on cars along the way, never slowing. Just like him. He warned me against jumping tracks, or becoming derailed, or worst of all getting train-wrecked. It was our private joke."

She offered Jo the plate of sandwiches. She used to be proud of her tenacity. It helped her excel as a reporter. Others would float along the surface, occasionally dipping below. Rebecca would spy the tip of a ray as it bob in the trough of a wave and grab on, allowing herself to be pulled under, ride it to the end. The danger was getting caught up on a side trip, missing the intended journey. She shuddered. She always did at the thought of being pulled under icy waters. Jo laid his smooth hand on hers.

"Do you still have the train?"

"I did. Until tonight." Rebecca indicated upstairs. It had been among the debris on the floor of her bedroom. "I may not have crashed and burned, Jo, like the train, but I've been stuck at the station, wheels slipping on the rails and not moving an inch. I'm sorry. We have to take action quickly, don't we?"

Jo pulled her hand into both of his. "We do indeed."

Thursday

Cutting Tools

Thirty-three

A thin line of pink filtered through the gray clouds on the horizon behind Flo's Café. The diner looked smaller with no lights glowing in the windows, no pickups parked out front. Zimmer pulled the patrol car into the lot, shut it off and rolled down the car window. The air was heavy with dew and the smell of hot grease billowing from the diner's exhaust fan. A pleasant change from the stench of smoke saturating their clothes. Five minutes till opening.

Crawford's bombshell had lit a fire under the sheriff. He ordered Boeski to deliver Judge Reiske to the Sunset Marina, then he and Mick went on a manhunt for the sheriff's favorite suspects.

Antrim was at home, recapping the evening's bridge game over espresso and sugared pecans. The matriarch graciously offered them sandwiches. She promised to send flowers to the funeral if the sheriff would call her secretary with the details.

Val and Juanita were at his trailer, doing what hormonally charged young couples generally do in front of late-night television. Juanita burst into tears at the news of Vera's death and fled into the bathroom. They left Val to comfort her.

They located Lindeman and Shelley at about one A.M. By then, the racers were on last call in the Half Shell Lounge in the giggling company of Todd's friend Denise and her friend Glory. The four had been slumming at the Blue Goose earlier in the evening, from eight to eleven, and missed the excitement of the fire. The men were suitably shocked at hearing the news about Vera. They raised a glass to her memory.

It was almost two A.M. when they confronted Frank Lewes at the YMCA all-county checkers playoff marathon at the elementary school. He'd been disqualified in the previous round but was rooting for the half owner of the hardware store, Gary somebody. Fellow contestants swore Frank had arrived around nine o'clock for the opening round. He hadn't missed a match. Been home alone before that.

Mick dropped his head against the headrest and closed his eyes. "Couldn't the judge have been right, Sheriff? Vera accidently caused the fire herself? She was drinking enough to drown it."

"I guess. Hell, she could have set it intentionally. Decides to bug out, and take all traces of her sad life with her. I wouldn't have it in my heart to blame her. Well, not much." He cracked his neck, swiveling it from side to side. "I didn't have a chance to tell you earlier. Harry came over to the house after he scrubbed up. Confessed he was bothered by the color of Stuck's finger- and toenails. Called up some medical expert friend in Richmond, and guess what."

Mick opened his eyes. "What?"

"They suspect old Graham was being poisoned. Arsenic, or something like it. Dosed out a little at a time. It builds up in the system, Harry says. Doesn't always show in an autopsy 'less you're looking for it. Some folks develop a tolerance. Even so, if they ingest enough of it over time it'll get them. Wifely kind of crime, don't you think? Could be Vera was feeding it to him for months, waiting with the patience of Job to be free of the louse."

"Then what—she snaps? She decides she won't share another Memorial Day cookout with him? Bashes his brains in? Kills herself out of remorse?"

"Something like that. Or she came across those." Zimmer pointed a thumb toward the files on the back seat. "Take a look. Be better on an empty stomach."

Mick twisted over the seat back to retrieve the folders. Four manila files: "Health Insurance," "Fire Insurance," "House Insurance," "Life Insurance." The last file was empty. The others each contained multiple photographs of dozens of nubile women. Most were nude. Those who were clad wore what appeared to be the same garter belt, which struck Mick as unsanitary. The women were in flaunting poses generally considered erotic. Or captured in libidinous action with each other, which Mick did not consider erotic. No way was sex a spectator sport. The camera had been in a fixed position out of sight, so not all the photographs were in focus. The room was the same one in all the shots—standard-issue sleazy motel. Zimmer would know if it was local. Occasionally Stuck was pictured as well. He didn't look all that much better alive. Slimy leer on his face was a good match for the rent-by-the-hour decor.

Mick flicked through the stacks quickly, shaking his head. "Stuck liked watching. Or directing. Liked the control. You recognize the women?"

"Most of them. Local housewives. Girls too dumb or desperate to know better."

"Think he was blackmailing them?"

"For sexual favors, maybe. I guess I'll have to talk to them." Zimmer twisted sideways. "Look, Hagan, I only let you see the pictures so you'd know Vera might have had reason—if she did it. Can't imagine what that smut would do to a lady like her. As far as you're concerned, the files were empty. Get it?"

Mick returned the folders to the back seat, tucking them under the raincoats. "You really think Vera killed her husband, then herself? 'Cause if you do, Chief, then your case is closed and I'm out of here. We can celebrate over pancakes and grits."

The sheriff shrugged. "Breakfast sounds good. But don't hire the marching band just yet."

By the time Charlie Crawford joined them at Flo's, the table looked like the aftermath of a 4-H eating contest. So many plates were squeezed on the surface that he had trouble setting down his orange juice. A cynic might suspect that Flo kept bringing food in order to listen in on the sheriff's conversation. She insisted that the food was on the house, thanks for fighting the fire. Mick figured she was writing it off under the heading of "Entertainment." Flo had gleaned enough firsthand details to enthrall her customers for months.

Charlie swung a chair around and settled in. One at a time he scraped, then stacked, the dirty dishes. Zimmer sucked the last bit of pancake off his fork. He handed Charlie the plate.

"Charlie, you got something to tell us, or you moonlighting as a busboy?"

"No news. What I got is a hunch."

Zimmer signaled Priscilla to come clear the table. "Mighty fine breakfast, Priscilla. Please thank your mom."

"Uh-huh." Priscilla waddled away with the tray.

The sheriff prodded Charlie to begin. Crawford's story was more supposition than fact. He'd found concentrated traces of kerosene in the kitchen. Those could have been easily explained—lots of folks have radiator-type heaters that take kerosene. But volunteer fireman and local HVAC guy Tom Laughlin wasn't buying it. He claimed the Stucks had a state-of-the art furnace installed last year when he added air-conditioning. Zone control, whole bit. Tom was adamant that the Stucks wouldn't have needed a kerosene heater in the kitchen. Definitely not this time of the year.

Then, in searching the nearly untouched garages, Charlie had found a newish kerosene space heater, but no fuel. He admitted that they could have run out and Billy Lee hadn't bought any more, but then where did the kerosene in the kitchen come from?

"Instead, you're thinking someone could have carried a can of kerosene from the garage to the kitchen, and what?

Put a match to it? Not likely. Instant crispy critters—one fried-to-death arsonist." Zimmer wadded up his napkin, tossed it on the table and leaned back. "That leaves out Vera. Her body was upstairs, pretty much intact. So, you're talking arson, and you're talking a remote setup or timer. Again."

Charlie straightened the napkin dispenser. "One or the other. Don't know yet. But this sure feels, smells and tastes like a torch job to me. We'll keep sifting."

Flo edged her way toward their table. She slapped the check down between Zimmer and Mick. Mick reached first. Bill was for two coffees, period. Mick smiled up at her.

"Hey, gorgeous. You know your way around a kitchen. How would you set fire to it without taking out your customers?"

"If I knew how, you'd be eating at McDonald's. I'd be poolside in Aruba drinking Mai Tais with them paper umbrellas and working on my tan." Hand on her hip, Flo stuck a cover-girl pose and winked.

"It's a serious question, Flo," Charlie said. "Suppose you got a can of kerosene. What's handy in the kitchen you could set to spark? You know, heat up the oil at some time later, like after you close up and go home. Something that'd look accidental?"

Flo borrowed a chair from the next table and plopped her amble rear onto the seat. "Timers on everything in a kitchen these days, hon. Ovens, microwaves, fryers. They wouldn't spark enough to set off a fire, would they?"

Charlie shook his head, took a small sip of orange juice.

"You're wondering about Vera Stuck's kitchen going up, aren't you? She wouldn't have so many gadgets. The gal didn't cook. Real proud of her new coffeemaker, though. Kind you put the grounds in the night before. Coffee's brewed by the time you roll out of bed. Me, I don't let water sit overnight. It gets stale. Folks around—"

"Hold your horses there." Zimmer leaned forward, almost touching noses with Flo. "Vera Stuck had one of those programmable coffeemakers?" Flo nodded, chins creasing.

"There's your answer, Charlie. A timer sitting right on the counter."

"Or on the stove. If the coffeemaker was black plastic, could be the blob melted into the cook top." He gave Flo a thumbs up. "I believe I've been looking at this backwards. The arsonist didn't spark the fuel. The fuel hit the flame. Flo, darling, this calls for a slice of pie."

"Pecan—why do I ask? But you're not getting it until you explain what you just said."

"Simple as an everyday accident. Vera's stove was electric. Let's say someone left a burner turned on. That same someone fills the carafe with kerosene instead of water and sets the timer for whatever time he—"

"Or she."

"—has an alibi. He places the coffeemaker on the stove, plugs it in, removes the carafe. And walks away from the house. Hours later the coffeemaker comes to life, starts dripping out kerosene. Kerosene runs over the cook top, where it hits the hot burner. Sizzle, pop. More kerosene runs out. Poof, flames spring up, hungry, licking for fuel like napkins, newspapers, whatever. Shoot up, get at the exhaust fan grease overhead. Then the flames move on to the wood cabinets, cookbooks, curtains, anything flammable. Vera's kitchen was at the back of the house. Fire could get a mighty good start before a neighbor would take notice."

Through the screen door, Mick spied Harry Tolland struggling to extricate himself from his car. He held on to the door while he caught his breath. Backlit by the sunrise, the stocky coroner yanked open the loose door to the diner and marched into the artificial light like a man on a mission. The wild-ass speculating about the fire ceased. Tolland looked scrubbed, hair damp from the shower, but the expression on his face said he felt a whole heap dirtier than the soot-covered men gathered around the table. Mick could sympathize. Given enough water and manpower, fires can be put out. Houses can be rebuilt. Coroners, on the other hand, confront daily the sick things human beings do to their own kind. With no power to stop it. No way to make people whole again.

Tolland snagged a mug from a nearby table. He reached over Crawford's shoulder for the carafe. "Charlie, don't mean to tell you your job, but the fire wasn't an accident, or suicide, or anything Vera could have had a hand in. She was dead before the blaze broke out. Killed closer to seven than nine."

"What the hell?" Rising, Zimmer tipped over his chair. Mick caught it before it toppled.

"Vera suffocated all right, but she didn't die from smoke inhalation. She was smothered by someone determined enough to crack her nose and most of the vertebrae in her neck when she struggled. Someone who figured her body wasn't going to be around to tell tales."

Charlie shook his head. "I was praying she was drunk enough to breathe smoke in her sleep. Go easy."

"She didn't go easy. Shortly before death her wrists and ankles had been tied, probably with her own scarves. General abrasion was present. She was naked. That sick bastard had been torturing her. Nipples burned off, but not from the fire. Take my word for it. Death was a blessing." Tolland drained his cup and banged it down on the table. "You keep that news to yourself, Flo McNalley, or I'll make you wish you'd died in the fire." With that, Harry Tolland stomped out of the restaurant.

Zimmer trailed close behind.

Thirty-four

"Because I said so. It may not seem logical to you, little lady, but it sure makes sense to me."

Zimmer was pissed. Hagan, lounging just inside the door, looked equally annoyed. Wonder swiveled his head, keeping an eye on them both.

Rebecca kicked a fallen pillow toward the sofa. "Shutting down the shop *now* makes sense to you? Vera wasn't killed there."

"Her husband was. And his car was destroyed out back. And your house was ransacked. Look at this mess." Zimmer waved his arm in disgust. "And just so you keep this in perspective, Vera didn't die in the fire, she was murdered first. Someone's not playing nice."

"My God, Sheriff." Jo moved closer to Rebecca. "Are you sure?"

"Harry is. You can see his report once it's typed up." Zimmer snorted. "In my book that's sufficient reason to close down the damn business. And confiscate every last key. If you wouldn't clutter up the station house, I'd take the whole bunch of you into protective custody where I could keep an eye on you. You included."

The last remark was directed at Jo. Sometime after three A.M. Rebecca had fallen asleep in his arms. Well, not in his arms, exactly. Jo had a started a fire in the fireplace and propped her in front of it. As he prodded her memory about the events of the last two days, he pulled her into the harbor of his legs and began massaging her neck, shoulders and spine. After a while, Rebecca stopped talking. The silken quality of Jo's voice and the magic of his long fingers melted her against him. For a few hours they'd dozed on the floor. Jo supported by the reading chair, Rebecca curled between his legs, her head on his chest, aware of nothing except the even cadence of his breathing.

Too bad if they presented a suggestive picture to the sheriff and Hagan as they peered through the front window when no one except Wonder responded to their pounding. Rebecca didn't give a damn. For a few hours she'd felt safe. Facing the sheriff, she still felt protected. Jo stood close behind her, his hands resting on her shoulders. He was the first kindred spirit she had discovered in the county. A friend, like those she'd left behind on the paper. A quick-witted, slow-talking intellectual, more inclined to analyze issues than gossip about people, though he was good at both.

"I sympathize with your desire to control the situation, Sheriff, but what do you think you'll accomplish by preventing my client from earning a living?" Jo sounded alert and lawyerly. Either he'd slept more than she had or he could function without his brain in gear.

"With everyone out of the way I can tear that car shop apart in my own sweet time. Maybe I'll find what's causing all the fuss. If not, then the state police get a shot." Zimmer raked back his hair with both hands. "So first I'll get a search warrant for the shop and another one for the fancy sports car. If that don't work, I'll get warrants for this house and the homes of your employees. Till I'm done, Boeski's going to guard the shop, Olson will stay here."

Rebecca eased away from Jo. "You don't need a warrant, Sheriff."

For a second her eyes locked with Zimmer's. He blinked, then nodded almost imperceptibly. He was willing to concede that they were in agreement, on this one point. The mystery centered around the Bentley's arrival at the shop. That was the trigger that had set everything in motion and kept it escalating. Solving Stuck's death was linked to uncovering what lured him to it. The sheriff had shared the note he'd found—the one Billy Lee left in Graham's study telling him where the Bentley had gone. The one Graham must have read before driving to the shop in Head Tide. Rebecca earnestly hoped that whatever the killer was hunting for was in the shop, if not in the Bentley. And that the sheriff would find it before anyone else was harmed.

She tossed Zimmer his hat. "Wait while I change. I'm going with you."

Arms folded on her chest, Rebecca glared at Zimmer. "I said you could search the shop. I did not say you could take the Bentley apart—not without a mechanic who knows what he's doing."

She stood protectively in front of the 3-Litre's bonnet, Jo at her side. Zimmer had ordered Boeski to open the hood. He tried twice. Neither one knew how to unlatch it. Rebecca wasn't about to show them.

"Sam from the Texaco can't change the oil in a Taurus. Do you have a spare quarter of a million dollars in your petty cash drawer? You'll need it if you damage that car. Frank, Val and Paulie will be here at eight. Leave the engine alone until then or go hunt up your search warrant."

The sheriff tugged at the belt on his trousers and exchanged glances with Hagan, who shrugged his shoulders. For Rebecca, that was the last straw. "I realize the department needs a detective, Sheriff, but you can't be that hard up. Hagan breezes into town and you clutch him like a life preserver. Have you ever questioned why he's here? What do you know about him?"

"I know enough. Lieutenant Hagan has been real useful. Like filling me in on your run-in with the law. Not the first time you've come home to find a dead man, is it, Moore? You're a regular femme fatal."

"Fatale."

"Rebecca?" Jo tossed her a quizzical look.

"Fatale. It's 'femme fatale.' He mispronounced it."

That amused Hagan. Grinning, he plopped down on a stool by the workbench, leaning back on his elbows, ready to enjoy the show. Zimmer closed in on Rebecca.

"What if I did? I can say 'murder one' just fine."

"David wasn't murdered. He committed suicide. Or didn't your snitch tell you that?"

"Rebecca, please, be quiet. You don't have to explain." Jo's words were confident, but his eyes were full of questions.

"What happened in Washington has nothing to do with this." She laid a hand on Jo's arm. "If it had, I would have told you." She walked to the end of Frank's workbench, putting distance between herself and her audience. Gazing over their heads, seeing neither them nor the machinery that defined her current life, Rebecca began.

"Last summer, I was investigating financial scams for a series for the *Post*. The kind of insider data-fiddling that starts out small but costs innocent investors their life savings. I began hanging out at *Le Bar* and the *Eye Street Grille*, where the wunderkind from Merrill Lynch exchange war stories over glasses of single malt. After a week or so I moved downscale to *Bottom Line*, chatting up the lunch crowd not glued to ESPN. There I met David Semple, a broker with Burton, Findlay and Wilde. He was easy to talk to, fun company. I told him I was researching the investment community. He was eager to provide the background information. He liked the role of co-conspirator. We had drinks a couple of times, then dinner." Rebecca started to pace. "After a month of dinners, we became lovers. I hadn't told him the slant I was taking with the article because I wasn't sure where it would lead. I kept researching, interviewing other players until I'd found—"

"Enough, Rebecca." Jo's voice was soft. He stepped toward her. His hand brushed her wrist to stop her from walking back and forth. She halted, but her delivery sped up.

"Exactly—enough. I found enough damaging information to confirm my thesis, Jo. Proof that someone within the Arlington office was bilking investors for thousands of dollars. I went to the SEC and convinced them to investigate. They organized a raid on the firm. The evening before it was scheduled to go down, David and I ate in at my apartment. He cooked his one speciality, Cioppino."

"Cioppino," Hagan echoed *sotto voce*.

"We were on our second bottle of wine. I was euphoric about the impending bust. Everything was going so well, I didn't want David to be surprised, or annoyed with me for keeping him in the dark. So I told him what I'd uncovered. Not the details, but enough to spell out what was about to happen."

She faced Jo. "I was such a simpleton. So wrapped up in my own cleverness that I never connected the sick look on David's face with what I was telling him. I blamed it on the clams."

"The next minute we're fighting, trading insults about the importance of our respective jobs versus our relationship. He's exploding over my obsession with another sensational story. I'd never seen him angry. I didn't defend myself. I didn't know how. David snatched up his keys and stormed out."

Rebecca walked over to the Bentley and sank down onto the running board, knees pressed together like a girl in Sunday school.

"I downed another glass of merlot and rationalized it as our first lovers' squabble. I was sure he'd cool off, come back. But David didn't return that night. Over breakfast, I convinced myself that I'd see him after the bust. We'd talk, everything would work out. The pressure of the story would be lifted. I'd have more time for him. I thought he'd be proud of me once he read the story."

"It never occurred to you that he was involved." Jo kept his tone neutral.

Rebecca hooked a lock of hair behind her ear as she shook her head. "He wasn't in his office. I didn't have time to hunt for him. The SEC officers arrived and all hell broke loose. Of course, we were too late. Computer files had been altered. Some deleted entirely. Most of the pathways linking transactions had been corrupted. Passwords no longer worked. The SEC guys were furious."

"Yeah, those government pricks hate wild goose chases. They accuse you of setting them up?" Hagan was sucking on a toothpick.

"Not then. They did later." She wrapped her arms around her legs, hugging them to her.

"You found him." From Hagan it didn't sound like a question.

She stared at a splotch of transmission fluid on the floor. "I raced home hoping to confront David. I don't know why I assumed he'd go back to my apartment. Maybe wishful thinking. I was so furious and humiliated and angry and scared that I couldn't see to drive. How could I not have realized he was in the thick of it? How could I have compromised the operation by telling him about it? What was going to happen to my career? I couldn't wait to get my hands on him. I wanted to throttle him."

"Guess you didn't get the chance."

"The front door was locked. There were no sounds coming from the apartment. I let myself in, assuming I was too late, that I'd find that all traces of David Semple had been wiped out of my life."

Hagan was up and crouching over her. "Instead you found traces of David Semple's brains splattered on the bedroom walls. Where did he get the gun, Moore? You keep it in the nightstand for protection? Carry it on dangerous assignments?"

Into the tense silence filtered the sound of the front door

opening and closing, snatches of conversation as the guys arrived for work.

Rebecca stood up to face Hagan squarely. He refused to step back. She could feel his breath on her face, but she held her ground, met his stare. "David had the gun. I don't know where he got it. I keep thinking that if it hadn't been so easy, he might not have killed himself. If you're so curious, Hagan, why don't you just check the police file?"

Behind Hagan she saw the office door open and Frank stop with his hand on the knob. Two cops, one lawyer and his boss arguing about a gun. No way Frank Lewes was walking in on that.

Hagan was too steamed to notice. "I have checked: make, model, that's it. No one followed up on where the gun came from."

She stepped around him. "Guess you're not much of an investigator, then, are you?"

Frank Lewes retreated, pulling the door closed behind him.

Thirty-five

Once Rebecca had set down the rules for searching through the Bentley, she agreed to accompany Jo to his office. Frank and Val promised to pick up behind the officers. Paulie would make coffee and keep Moe out of harm's way. No one—least of all the sheriff—had looked pleased at the arrangements.

For Rebecca, the stakes had changed. She needed time to regroup. Yesterday, she'd logged on to the Internet and typed: *phayes@washingtonpost.com*. Then stopped, fingers poised on the keys. What could she say? *Hey, guys, your favorite screwup is at it again.* With the botched sting and her lover's death, Rebecca had embarrassed herself by starring in headlines rather than writing them. One of the reasons she'd fled Washington was to avoid her former colleagues. She'd stayed out of contact for over six months. How could she just pop up on Peter Hayes's computer—begging for information—as if nothing had happened? Not that Peter would mind. He'd be thrilled. Rebecca Moore was a prime suspect in the death of another naked man and he'd be the first to know. Peter would be screaming along the highway toward Head Tide tomorrow before Flo stirred up the breakfast grits.

Rebecca had shut down the computer without connecting. Yesterday she couldn't stomach the idea of opening herself up to her fellow reporters' ridicule, or pity. Today was a different story. She punched in Peter Hayes's phone number.

He answered on the second ring, sounding more preoccupied than curious, until she asked for his help. Hayes lowered his voice. "What's up? Give."

Rebecca complied.

Receiver wedged against one ear, notepad in hand, she paced the width of Jo's office.

"Start with Hagan, Michael. Supposedly a police detective, Second District. But I wouldn't put money on anything he says. I don't think he worked the Semple case, though there's some connection. See if you can find out."

On the other end of the line, Peter Hayes chuckled as his fingers clicked across the keyboard. "Too cool, Becca. Sean and I guessed you'd fled south to go undercover for something mega-major."

"I fled south to get away from you guys and rest."

"No way you'd give up the hunt. You want results via phone, fax, e-mail, or in person?"

"Electronic is fine."

"Do I get a byline?

"Hayes, you get to run with whatever evolves. Ten inches, front page. Trust me."

"I do, Bec, baby, I do. You can sniff a scoop surer than a pig snorts truffles. After 'Hagan, comma, Michael' where do we go?"

Rebecca spent the next few minutes striding the width of the office, spelling names for Peter Hayes to run through the mill of media data banks. His attitude fueled her confidence. He wasn't treating her like a Jonah. He sounded pleased to hear from her. He assumed she'd landed on her feet and was still on the fast track, pursuing stories more interesting than those that came across his desk. Rebecca grinned. *Peter, boy, if you could see me now.* As usual, she'd been harder on herself than others were. She was so busy wallowing in guilt, she forgot that reporters are a self-centered bunch, concerned only with the immediate story. And only then if they got credit.

She instructed Peter to hunt out bios, backgrounds, run-ins with the law, everything. She gave him Graham and Vera Stuck, Todd and Lily Shelley and Hal Lindeman. Rebecca stopped short of including her employees. Hagan had checked them out for the sheriff. If he'd uncovered anything damaging, they'd be behind bars already. If any more digging was needed, she'd do it.

Nor did she include Joachim Delacroix. The man definitely had a past worth excavating, but instinct told her it had nothing to do with the murder. Besides, he was frankly listening to her conversation.

"On Lindeman, check on his financial solvency."

"Another sting in the works?"

"No. It's mostly personal. While you're at it, check Shelley's as well."

While she tossed out suggestions and fielded the questions coming through the line, Jo polished his glasses with a white handkerchief. When she hung up, he laid them carefully on the desk. "I'm impressed, Rebecca. You're finally acting like the journalist your uncle admired. You're a bit intimidating."

"I am?" She lowered herself into the side chair. "Or what you heard about Semple's death is?"

"As your lawyer, I would have preferred knowing about the incident before it became public. As a friend, I hope I understand why you kept it to yourself."

"It wasn't pertinent."

"If you say so."

"You don't believe me?"

Jo leaned forward, touched her lightly on the knee. "I always believe my clients."

"Good. Let me phone Juanita to warn her about the mess at the house. Then we'll play twenty questions."

It was Jo's turn to pace. He did it rocking in his desk chair, letting his mind stroll. "With your friend Mr. Hayes handling the background checks, we can skip the 'who' for the moment. We know the 'what': two murders, two fires, one burglary."

"Call it ransacking. Nothing's missing."

"The 'how' seems unnecessarily complicated. 'When' is not easy to establish, thanks to the possibility that the fires were started via timers, though the killer had to be in town Saturday at midnight and sometime Wednesday to commit the actual murders. And the 'why' remains tantalizingly elusive." Jo assumed a Buddha pose, interlaced fingers resting on the hint of a belly. He rocked. "So, we begin with Mr. Stuck's murder. What about it seems awry?"

"Other than its being committed in my shop?" Rebecca batted her eyelashes in mock innocence while she thought about it. "The flamboyant displaying of Graham's body. The killer wasn't simply eliminating him, he was humiliating him. Something voyeuristic about looking through the window and seeing a trussed body hugging an engine."

"Trying to mislead investigators? Staging the scene to make the sheriff think it's a sex crime? Or was the body left in your shop to appear business-related? When really it's neither."

"Possibly, though I vote for humiliation. The setup feels intensely personal."

Jo stopped rocking. "Rebecca, if this were a normal city, not a sleepy backwater town, what would have happened?"

"Media blitz. The homicide would have been plastered on the front page of both newspapers for two to three days. The press would have milked the sex angle first, then fleshed it out with the local business rivalry. Smearing suppositions on everyone involved."

She knew the technique too well, from both sides. During the weeks following David's death, Rebecca had scoured street corners collecting every city paper, even the advocacy freebies. She'd stacked them around the living room by date, unopened. She waited for the blessed numbness of shock to wear off, for her self-pity to reach its nadir, before searching through the papers. One Sunday morning, with the pigeons hunkering on the window ledge, she'd spread the papers open on the pine-board floor of her loft. With a black marker she'd circled the news columns, highlighted every accusatory phrase, every mention of David's name or her own. When she'd wallowed enough, she refolded the newspapers, reordered them by date and boxed them. Sealing the carton shut with electrical tape. The carton rode with her to Head Tide on the passenger's seat of the van.

Three months later, the first warm weekend in March, she'd gone to Tony's just to get out of the house. Half the county was there letting loose, lured by the balmy weather. She decided it was time to join them. She consumed enough vodka gimlets to enter and win a dance competition sponsored by the beltway Smirnoff distributor. Embarrassed, hugging her bottle-shaped trophy and more than a little drunk, Rebecca had let Frank drive her home. Then begged him for one more favor. Together they lugged the carton of newspapers from the basement to around back of the shop. She crammed it into the same metal rubbish container where the police found Stuck's clothing. Frank doused the box with gasoline and loaned Rebecca his lighter to ignite it. He didn't ask what they were burning, or why. People with pasts don't ask nosy questions. As they watched the flames, he looped his arm around her shoulders and complained: One of them should have brought hot dogs.

"Exactly. *If* there were any full-time reporters in town, *if* the county had a daily not a weekly paper, or *if* the sheriff were less stubborn about bringing in the state police, less stingy about revealing facts, the media would be all over this like yellow jackets on a honey-glazed ham." Jo swiveled his chair. "Do we have a killer who flaunts the body in order to get his crime noticed—"

"And isn't getting it. So, he commits additional crimes to assure headlines? The car bombing, Vera's murder, the house fire were simply attention-getters?"

"It's possible."

"That's revolting. I'd prefer a psychopath with a vendetta against the Stucks." Rebecca arched her back in a feline stretch, then stood. "Whatever his motive, Jo, something's missing. Literally. It's as annoying as the skip on a long-playing record. What's our current scenario?" She perched on the edge of the desk. "The killer wanted something that Graham wouldn't hand over. Step one: Killer murders Graham. Two: Killer searches car, comes up empty-handed. Burns car. Three: Killer questions Vera. Kills her. Four: Presumably he searched her house. Burns it. Five: Killer searches my home—here the chain starts to break down. Why would the killer think I have whatever it is that Graham wouldn't give him? Did Vera point him in my direction? Why? Out of spite? By mistake? Or did she think I have it?"

"Do you?" Jo leaned forward, eyes twinkling.

"Not that I know of." Rebecca hopped down, faced Jo across the desk. "Second anomaly: While the ransacking of my house follows the general pattern—searches, doesn't find it, so he destroys everything he touched—he didn't burn the place down. What, no matches?"

"Or, as in the case of the shop, you arrived home at the crucial moment."

She thought back. "No. The house was too quiet when I walked in. He was long gone."

"Then at the time he was violating it, you must have been next door at the shop. Perhaps he was aware of that? He had enough self-control to curb his destructive impulses to keep from being caught." Jo frowned. "You realize that you saved your business by going in after the financial records on Saturday?"

Rebecca played with a fat-barreled fountain pen on his desk, focused on it spinning around and around. "Jo, I heard a noise that night. A scraping, maybe—maybe the latch on the glass beader door—coming from the machine shop. I didn't check it out. I was tired, alone and in a hurry. I ignored it, turned out the lights and went home." Rebecca bit at her bottom lip. "Could I have saved Graham if I'd gone into the back room to investigate?"

Jo shook his head, stayed the pen in its rotation. "No, you'd be dead, too. And the shop would be in ashes."

Thirty-six

"Tell me we're not back at square one. Make me feel better—tell me we're not back at the beginning."

Mick spat out the broken end of a toothpick. "Zimmer, I don't know you well enough to lie to you. We're—no, make that *you're*—sitting on square one too whipped to stand up and move."

"Thanks, Hagan. I needed confirmation." The sheriff leaned across the sun-faded top of the patrol car. He stretched his arms, rotating his shoulders to ease the tension. "I've never seen so many unrecognizable tools and dirty car parts in my life. What I didn't see in that blasted building was anything that points to a motive for murder or arson. Lord, I'm tired. How about I write the mess up as a hate crime and close the file?"

"Yesterday you swore it was a crime of passion."

"You're feeling contradictory, aren't you?"

"I'm not contradicting you. I'm agreeing. You got jack shit. No evidence that means anything. A bunch of maybe suspects, not one of them with a DA-approved motive or an alibi. You got nada, zilch, zero." Mick opened the passenger side door and slid in. "I need a beer."

"So do I, but not yet." Zimmer reached into the glove box and extracted a notepad and pen. "Walk me through this, big-city detective. Saturday night—when Stuck got what he deserved—can we eliminate anyone? Moore admits to being on the scene. Kearney was probably in Richmond, though no one can vouch for him all night. Guess that's good for the little Mexican girl—he wasn't cheating with some biker babe while away from home. She, incidently, was in bed asleep. The maternal Moore checked on her before turning in. Antrim was out somewhere until after two. His mother doesn't pry—'After all, he is a grown man with normal interests.' Her quote, not mine. Lewes says it none of my business, but he was home alone, reading. Shelley has an alibi in Spotelli, but I'd want two independent witnesses before I'd take her word into court. Lindeman, the heavyweight, was drinking in the lounge at the marina. Waitress remembers him there from around nine to eleven. He claims he took a stroll along the coast after that, then to bed, regrettably alone. Who am I forgetting?"

"Other than half the husbands in the county?"

"Other than them." Zimmer tapped the pen against the steering wheel. The tune might have been 'When the Saints Come Marching In.' He gave up after the first stanza. "Nope, can't buy it. Maybe I can see one of my yokels following Stuck, fighting with him, bashing his brains out with a hammer for messing with the guy's wife. But the rest of it? Rigging the car to explode and the house to go up in flames? Torturing poor Vera, smashing up Moore's place? Doesn't set with me. Locals are too lazy for that much vengeance. And for what—girlie shots of their wives? Hell, half of them would frame the photos, get copies for their cousins and sell them on the Internet." Zimmer started the car. "I'm betting on one of the magnificent seven. Let's talk with Billy Lee. See who visited the widow on Wednesday."

The nurse said they could stay five minutes, not more.

Zimmer leaned over the old man sunk in the white bed. His voice was a cross between a whisper and a growl. "Hey, there, Billy." Billy stirred at the sound. He turned his head;

the tip of his tongue flicked between cracked lips. His throat moved, no sound escaped. The sheriff patted his shoulder.

"That was very brave, and foolish of you, Billy Lee. Rushing into the burning house like that. You always took real good care of Vera, didn't you?" Billy Lee's head moved a fraction. His face was the color of the bandages. A tear emerged at the corner of one eye and sat there swelling. Zimmer sounded a bit choked himself. "No one could have saved her. Harry says she was already dead when the fire broke out. Nothing you could have done." The tear broke free, trickled down the side of Billy Lee's nose.

Zimmer dragged a metal-legged chair up next to the bed. "Looks like someone who visited the house earlier in the day might have rigged the fire. Can you help me, Billy? You remember seeing cars that day? Vera have any visitors?"

Billy Lee squeezed both eyes shut. He could have been trying to envision Vera's last day, or holding back a flood of tears for the woman he'd helped for two decades. Or he could have been nodding off. The plastic chair creaked as Zimmer shifted his bulk. He looked over at Mick, shrugged, then turned back to the man in the bed.

"That's okay, Billy. We'll leave—"

"Minist . . ."

"Minister? Minister Anderson?" Billy Lee's chin bobbed. "Natural that he'd come by. Anyone else?"

"Truck." He licked his lips and hissed, "Shop . . ."

"Shop truck? You mean the pickup from Vintage?" Again Billy Lee's head nodded. "Who was driving. Did you see?" His head wagged. He didn't know.

"Okay, Billy. That's good. Anyone else?"

"Jeep."

Zimmer shot Mick a look. Mick nodded, then leaned against the radiator and rummaged in his jacket for a scrap of paper on which to take notes. He wouldn't have trouble remembering the handful of well-wishers who visited Vera Stuck on the day of the fire. The usual suspects, you might say. The boy racers came together; the minister; judge; two neighbors carrying casseroles; at least one employee from Vintage & Classics driving the pickup. Writing down the names was better than watching the old man's gullet bob in pain each time he tried to speak. It made Mick feel like he was finally paying attention.

In the hallway, Zimmer ran a finger around the rim of his cap to smooth the inside band before settling it on his head. "When did you interview Vera? And when were you planning to tell me?

Mick scowled. "I didn't get to. I showed up at her house around five-thirty yesterday, but she wasn't receiving. She opened the door wide-eyed, jumpy as a junkie coming down. Begged me to come back later."

"And you just walked away?"

"Well, I would have, but something caught in my throat, Sheriff. It started me coughing real bad. Vera Stuck was too much of a lady to deny me a glass of water."

Zimmer nodded in approval. "Okay. You see anything inside the house might explain her nerves or what happened?"

Mick replayed his brief trip through the house. "Signs that she'd been drinking: open decanter, half full glass. One high-heeled black pump discarded on the stairs. Small suitcase at the top of the flight."

Zimmer interrupted. "Charlie found three suitcases packed full. Looked like she was getting ready to run. Wish she'd made it."

Mick concurred. "She might have been listening to music—CD player was open; lights glowing on the amplifier. Computer was on, screen saver was active. Only clutter was in the kitchen. What you'd expect: baked goods wrapped in aluminum foil and too many flower arrangements.

"Did you see the coffeemaker? Was it on, carafe in place?"

"Didn't notice. Must have looked normal or I might have."

Zimmer sighed. "Don't suppose you saw anybody lurking in the shadows?"

"No visitors. No cars. One of the garage doors was up, but I didn't see or hear anyone."

"Too bad."

Mick agreed. Way too bad. He should have checked out the garages. He'd thought about it. Once outside, he'd even turned back toward the house to get Vera's permission to poke around. From the flagstone walk, through the window he saw the fragile, pale woman standing motionless in the dining room leaning against the front of the sideboard. She was staring into an ornate mirror. In the glass, framed by the sparkling bevel, her reflection was crying.

At that moment, Mick couldn't bring himself to intrude on her pain.

If he had, she might still be alive.

Zimmer strode down the beige corridor out of the hospital and into the sunshine with renewed purpose. "I sure do like Frank Lewes for it. Bet that was him in the shop truck. There's something about that guy. Spooky silent. Makes you think he's capable of anything."

"You subscribe to the still-waters-run-deep school of self-incrimination, do you?"

"Innocent people act innocent. Talk a lot, scream for their lawyers. That sort of thing. Lewes gives you one-word answers. Does what he's told. All the time looking straight through you and out the other side. Hint of a smile, like he knows something you don't. Kind of guy that might stash a body in a machine, or torture a proper lady just for kicks." Mick pushed open the double doors; Zimmer followed him through. "Got a temper. He's already spent half a lifetime in prison for murder."

"Voluntary manslaughter, Zimmer. I read the file. Lewes killed his straying wife in a fit of jealous rage. Discovered her doing the deed with his own brother. Shocked the hell out of his neighbors, who thought he was pretty passive. What's his motive in either of the Stucks' deaths?" Mick couldn't reconcile what he'd seen of Lewes's spartan home life with the flamboyance of the murders.

"You want motive, how about the widow? Whole town

knows he got her drunk one night, drove her home. Stuck wasn't there, so who knows what happened between them? Next day, he calls his wife a whore in front of God and everyone and would have beat the crap out of Lewes if Boeski hadn't stopped him."

"You think Vera Stuck was messing around with Lewes?"

"Hell, no. But Lewes might have wanted her to. Maybe he obsessed on her, approached her after he killed her husband, hoping she'd be desperate enough."

"A black mechanic and a prominent white woman?" Mick shook his head.

"What, Hagan, no mixed couples in the big city? Think there's no chemistry between the races, boy? What about Moore and her lawyer?"

"Delacroix? Are you saying—"

Reaching for the door handle, Zimmer smirked. "I'm not saying nothing, city boy. I'm not saying you're mighty interested in a woman you claim you never met before now. I wouldn't be so rude as to mention something like that, would I?" He plopped behind the wheel as Mick got in. "Remind me again—what's your personal business in our neck of the woods?"

Mick slammed the door shut and turned to face him. "You're so keen to hang Lewes, there's something else you might want to look into. Remember the melted transformer you found near Stuck's burned-out car?"

"What about it?"

"Lewes is a model train buff. Saw his setup when I checked out his house. One serious "N" gauge layout. Multiple transformers."

That hardly did it justice. Lewes's passion for trains took up almost the entire downstairs. Two eight-by-twelve-foot platforms of plywood resting on sawhorses, spanning what had been designed as adjoining living and dining rooms. Every inch of the surface was covered. Multiple sets of tracks rose on bridges spanning painted rivers, then disappeared into tunnels in plaster-of-paris mountains, past towns with storefront buildings, park benches and tiny townspeople. Lampposts just inches high lined the streets. There were golden fields dotted with farms. Strong men and boys haying. Industrial suburbs with a grain mill and working gravel yard. In a grove on the edge of town kids were necking in a Pontiac convertible. A passenger train paused at the platform waiting for commuters to board. A long-haired collie barked at the conductor.

Mick had stared in wonder. An entire community frozen in a gentler time. Every detail just right. Just like the hometown everyone wants to be from. He felt like a kid again. Better. He'd never had a train setup like this. The impulse to switch on a transformer had been too hard to resist.

Zimmer slammed the steering wheel. "Jesus, Mary and Joseph. You've known about this how long? Keeping clues to yourself is not friendly, Hagan. I guessed you was a maverick, but I expected better." He snatched up the handset. "You got more tidbits up your sleeve? I've embarrassed half the women in my graduating class waving bare-assed photographs in their faces—of them, or their daughters—while you're sitting on incriminating evidence against a real suspect. One who has done time for killing; plays with toy trains; has no alibi for either murder; could have driven the shop truck to Vera's house the day she died; could have killed Stuck for Vera, then killed Vera for rejecting him."

The sheriff snarled into the microphone. "Olson, you there? Olson, get Judge Wagner on the phone. I know it's his golf day. I want a search warrant for Frank Lewes's place out on Hassan Field Road. And I want it now. I don't care, Olson. Make it vague but all-inclusive. You know how."

He started to slam the handset back into its holder. Olson's voice stopped him. "Should I care? Oh, the Honorable Judge Reiske wanted me to know that he's returned to Washington but will be back to arrange the funerals. Hell, we can take care of that ourselves. She was one of us. One of the best." Zimmer hung up on Olson and started the patrol car.

Thirty-seven

Rebecca was curled up at the end of a hard tapestry divan. She watched the dark pink buds of a maple scratch against the window. Jo was in the outer office conferring with an elderly waterman who wanted to rewrite his will, again. Version number five would disinherit his middle son, again.

Hiding in Jo Delacroix's inner sanctum was seductive—a respite from worrying about the sheriff rifling through the shop, from puzzling about the murders, from dwelling on David's death. Rebecca let her mind drift as the sun faded on the glorious day that followed yesterday's storm. The county was awash in spring freshness. She could picture every part of it. Gulls circling the shore looking for hurt crabs. Inland mists hanging low over the river and marshes. Woods so still you could hear a summer tanager clawing for grubs under dry leaves. Vivid memories from her childhood in danger of being blotted out by the horrors of the last few days. Which was real? The innocence of her summers spent in the sleepy countryside, or the seething hatred that infiltrated every society bubbling over to bring death and destruction? If she were back in the District the question wouldn't have occurred to her. Her former job made her too accepting of the darker side of human nature. She relished exposing it. But that was there, where it was a given. Here, such darkness was an intruder.

When Jo returned to his office, Rebecca was balancing one of his storytelling dolls on her lap, fingering one of two sausagelike protuberances that represented infants. The figurine's mouth was an open O as if it were singing to the infants or keening at her own fate. Jo pitched a legal document on the desk and balanced one leg on the polished edge.

"If that doll represented Cyrus Borden's life it would have three boys held at arm's length with detachable heads. Timing will be everything with that brood. Which week the obstreperous curmudgeon dies will determine which son gets nothing. Of course, if he keeps paying me to change his will, there'll be nothing left for them to get." Jo nodded in the direction of the doll. "That's Helen, named after the potter. She's a Cochiti from the early 1960s. Her tales center on children, early life and growth."

Rebecca held the Indian doll up to the light from the window. The rough cream slip of the surface was embellished with fine lines of black and rust detailing the mother's dress and expression. It was not entirely blissful. "Did you know Vera Stuck as a child?"

"I did not. I doubt anyone did, but hand me Helen and I will tell you the tale I've heard of little Vera Murdock."

Rebecca passed the terra-cotta doll to Joachim. He held it in cupped hands as if it were a bird getting up the courage to fly. He concentrated his gaze on the small figurine and began to weave a story suited for a late-night campfire.

"Vera was the only child of Robert and Winifred Murdock. Murdock was an important commercial contractor in the Crystal City area. A builder of strip malls and office complexes that make suburbias everywhere look the same. He amassed endless amounts of money, but coveted the power that went with wealth even more. His wife, like many attached to powerful men, stayed in the background. Mrs. Murdock was rarely seen in public, other than on the arm of her husband, her free hand clutching that of their daughter. Like her mother, Vera Murdock was porcelain-fair, with delicate bones and silky hair, hers pulled back in a satin ribbon. If my memory is correct, she was often dressed in Laura Ashley outfits to match her mother's. She was a well-mannered, 'please, thank you' kind of child, speaking only when spoken to. And neat. Vera was tidy almost to the point of compulsion. She was a fair student through elementary grades, too shy in class to excel, but no trouble to her teachers.

"Instead of finishing at the local middle school where the town could watch how she turned out, Vera was sent to St. Mary's Academy. Neighbors shook their heads. 'Getting to be a handful,' they hissed in the grocery store aisles. Mrs. Murdock insisted that Vera would receive a better education at a private school. Perhaps. And it afforded the Murdocks increased status among their peers. If you believe my cousin Miranda, though, they sent Vera away as punishment for keeping company with the Bentmeyer twins, worldly black delinquents from Upper Marlborough. Whatever the reason, Vera was removed from local scrutiny for a number of years."

Pausing in his story, Jo rose. He replaced the Cochiti doll on a shelf with a half a dozen others, adjusting her to face his desk. From a higher shelf he retrieved a larger doll. Its design was more refined, in subtle shades of beige and gray. The storyteller was seated with eleven children crawling up her body or squatting on the flared pottery skirt. Jo balanced the doll on the arm of the sofa near Rebecca. She reached out to steady it. Their fingers brushed in passing. "Stella, she's Navajo," Jo said, making the introduction, then settled on the sofa next to Rebecca. He laced his fingers on his lap.

"Small-town folks love to gossip; I don't have to tell you that, do I? I used to think it was because there wasn't enough to do. Now I accept it's human nature. People will always find time to talk about each other. So, there were whispers about the teenage Vera Murdock. Wormlike, slithering whispers about how rapidly she'd changed. She became sullen.

Sassed her teachers. Failed eighth grade. Or would have if she hadn't been Robert Murdock's daughter. She was apprehended in *K mart* pilfering a paperback romance. Not much on today's scale of teenage offenses, but unexpected from a girl of her upbringing. When questioned, the local teens shrugged, guessed she was running with a wild crowd. The crones suspected much worse. They *tsk*ed, shook their heads and labeled her troubles 'closer to home.'"

"How close?"

"Closer than is approved of in the *Bible*. Cousin Miranda swears that before Vera developed breasts you could read the mistrust in her eyes and the lust in her father's." Jo lifted the prolific storyteller and reshelved it.

Rebecca sighed. "Sad. And provocative, but does it bring us any closer to explaining Vera's murder?"

"I doubt it. And only if you are comfortable with a lot of 'ifs.'"

"Such as?"

Jo walked to the window. He watched the sapling's branches sway as Rebecca had earlier. "Enter from the wings a young man of the town who always has been sweet on Vera, though she did not return his affection. For years, he hears whispers about the father's abuse. He's outraged, but too young, poor and powerless to combat Robert Murdock. Then Vera goes away. By the time she returns, she has a husband. The young man has grown to be respected in town. Outwardly, he honors her marriage. But what if eventually he hears rumors that the husband, too, is abusing Vera? Perhaps Vera even turns to him as an old friend, confides in him, begs for help. Might that not cause the man finally to avenge the woman he has loved all his life?"

"And the man's name is?"

Jo's answer was aborted by the phone ringing. He listened to Edna, nodded and passed the phone to Rebecca. "For you, a Mr. Shelley."

"Shit." Rebecca took the handset. Shelley had begun his tirade without her. When he paused for breath, she jumped in.

"Todd, I know that the car has to ship in two days, but there's not a thing I can do about it. The sheriff confiscated the keys to the building. He refuses to let anyone in the shop until he's—" Todd cut her off with a high-pitched whine. Rebecca shut her eyes, counted to ten. "I don't know how or when a 'hick, no-nothing' like Sheriff Zimmer expects to solve this murder, Todd. My only hope is that he'll calm down and let us back into the building tomorrow. If it's humanly possible, your car will be ready to ship in the same container with the Hisso. Promise. I'll keep you posted. Sure. Hoist one for me." Rebecca laid down the phone, shaking her head.

"A satisfied customer?" Jo chuckled.

"Mr. Shelley is a tad upset."

Jo was somewhat sympathetic. "It's his car they're tearing apart."

"But for what, and where is it hidden? The police have searched twice and we've had the whole car apart. While stringing the wires, Paulie scraped and repainted every inch of the frame rails and undercarriage. The under trays have been off and cleaned. The Bentley's running, so there's nothing extraneous banging around in the engine. Val removed the seats and scrubbed the interior. Even if they overlooked it, Frank would have spotted anything unusual."

Jo closed the distance between them. "Rebecca, isn't it just possible that Frank—"

"Don't say it, Jo."

"Think, Rebecca. You're all the family Frank Lewes has. All that's left of Walt, the one person willing to give Frank a second chance. The shop is his life. Maybe we're all wrong. Maybe there isn't anything hidden there. What if Stuck, in a rage, broke into the shop: to destroy the car, the building, the business, whatever. And Frank discovered him. Would Frank hesitate to—"

Rebecca jumped up, turned away from Jo. What had he just said? *Maybe we're all wrong. Maybe there isn't anything hidden.* "Jo, could that be it?"

"What?"

She began to pace. "We've been assuming that Stuck went to the shop to retrieve something from the Bentley. What if he went there to hide something in the car? Something he wanted to smuggle out of the country, that would ship with the Bentley. Or, more nefariously, to plant something that, if found, would get Shelley in trouble. Could Shelley have followed him there, guessing what he was up to; killed him and taken back the evidence?"

"Stuck and Shelley?"

"Why not? I've been toying with the idea that Lindeman and Stuck were in cahoots. But Shelley's known him almost as long. Maybe he had a stronger reason than shoddy wiring for taking the car away from Stuck."

Again, the phone interrupted. Edna couldn't identify the caller. "Somebody foreign and upset."

Jo put on his most soothing tone. He took in several broken sentences before he understood the gist of the panic on the other end. He snatched up his glasses as he hung up.

"Gather your purse, Rebecca. It's time I earn my retainer. That was Lu Chan. The sheriff just arrested Frank Lewis for the murders of Graham and Vera Stuck."

Rebecca blanched. "What? He can't have. What's his motive? The sheriff's an idiot! So am I for letting it get this far." She slipped on her jacket. "Have you ever tried a murder case, Delacroix?"

"Not successfully."

"Terrific."

Thirty-eight

Having limited command of Chinese, Mick wasn't sure
what Lu Chan was spouting about, but the thin man was not
a happy camper. The timbre of his voice was so high it
cracked. He gestured with the chopping knife like the demented villain in a slasher film.

"You bring him here."

Technically, Mick had gotten a ride to the restaurant with
the sheriff. They'd about given up on finding Lewes without
a search party or Warren Prouty's pack of hounds, which
Zimmer made sound more ominous than the Hound of the
Baskervilles. They'd tried Lewes's house, Tony's, the community center, cruised the streets of town. Come up empty
until they parked in front of the Great Wall Restaurant.
Through the plate-glass window they saw Frank Lewes
reading the local paper while waiting for Lu Chan to prepare
his take-out.

"He good man. Good worker. Come here every Thursday
for special. You bring evil pig."

"Right, evil pig sheriff. Zimmer's just doing his job. He
has circumstantial evidence against Lewes, that's all. You'll
see, he'll be out of jail after dinner."

"Dinner. What about his dinner? I make for him. I take to
jail. They give to him? Maybe?"

"Sure. Maybe. But not if you take the knife."

Lu Chan muttered under his breath. He slopped gelatinous sweet and sour pork into a foil tin, slapped on a cardboard lid, splattering hot pink sauce on the counter. He crimped the foil edges with a vengeance before sliding it into a thick brown bag and stapling it shut. The restaurant owner yelled something to the tiny girl behind the counter, who was still responding in a high-pitched harangue long after the red door slammed.

Mick's cell phone sounded. He straddled a plastic chair and answered it.

"Hagan. Yeah, Sal, what's up?"

"Maybe nothing, but there's something curious about that judge of yours."

"Reiske?"

"Yeah. But first, tell me how come you're stirring up questions about Semple's death? Captain thought you were going to talk nice to Moore, not reopen the case. Read his lips: It's closed. If you can't drop it, you're on suspension, plus ten more sessions with the shrink. You're tormenting yourself for nothing. You hear me?"

"Guess Sheriff Zimmer called."

"Correcto. Said he got the phone number from you. I says, 'Yeah, well, then you get the file from him as well. But you won't find nothing against Becca Moore. She was just dating the wrong jerk at the wrong time.' You with me, Mick? If she sues the department for harassment, neither the captain nor I will testify in your defense."

Mick leaned across the table and extracted a toothpick from the metal dispenser. "Reiske?"

"I'm giving you good advice, Mick. Listen to your Uncle Sal." He sighed dramatically. "Reiske's hearing *Alonso,* right? Biggest-profile case to come along in the decade. And we all know how the judge loves being front-page news, right?"

"Tom Rush sang it best: 'Like babies love stray dogs.'"

"Well, Shirley over in the court steno pool hears that Reiske is going to recuse himself from it."

"Recuse himself?" Mick swiveled around in the skinny-legged chair, slouched to a comfortable position. "The term originally applied to Catholics in the fifteen, sixteen hundreds who wouldn't attend Church of England services."

Sal cracked a nut. "Well, *recuse* me. Ain't you a fount of knowledge. You know why the judge might not want to hear such a mega-case?"

"Could be he's all choked up over his friend's death?" Though no one, from fellow jurist to social acquaintance, had described Reiske as sentimentalist. Quite the contrary. "Why else? You can't think the judge is being bought off? He's squeaky clean."

"I ain't paid to think. That's your description. Thought you should know the word that's going 'round is all."

"Appreciate it, Sal. You come up with a connection between Stuck and Reiske?"

"Not a glimmer. We even flashed Stuck's picture around the courthouse. If the judge and Stuck were spending Saturdays watching football and chasing dames, they were doing it someplace else." There was a smug lift in Sal's tone. Mick sat up.

"Yeah? Any idea where that might be?"

"So glad you asked. His Honor often spends weekends on his fifty-four-foot sailboat, *Virtue*. Love the name."

Mick smiled. "And you know where said vessel is docked?"

"How's Annapolis sound?"

"Like a coincidence worth checking out."

Sal's admonition to stay away from Moore rankled. Like most good advice, it was tough to choke down. Intellectually, Mick agreed that Moore had not pulled the trigger that ended David's life. She hadn't forced him to do it. She was simply the final straw heaped on the humps of his screwed-up psyche. For months caring friends had mouthed the same refrain. *If Semple hadn't been so weak, or so vain; if he'd had more self-esteem, more faith, whatever. David's death was David's fault.* Mick was sick of the platitudes. They were preaching to the choir. Mick had witnessed David's flaws up close and personal when they were growing up. Seen them. Ignored them. Later tried to correct them. And when he couldn't, dumped David altogether.

Mick wanted to swallow the party line. Let it go. Hearing Moore's public confession had helped, but he was still divided. The cynic in him insisted that Moore had known what she was doing by manipulating David. The romantic in him viewed Moore as an innocent, unaware of David's involvement in the scam or his instability; someone who needed compassion. The cop in him slapped him alongside the head, yelling that if he couldn't blame Moore, he'd have to blame himself. Shut up and live with it.

Maybe he should flip a coin?

Instead, he was spinning his wheels in Head Tide, embroiled in a murder investigation out of his jurisdiction. Fantasizing about an auto mechanic. And talking to the toothpick dispenser in a Chinese restaurant.

Mick snapped a toothpick in half and pitched it into the trash on his way out of the Great Wall. He climbed into the Cherokee. Time was running out. He had only a couple of days to help solve the local crime, stop a murderer and settle things with Moore. Then get out of town. While he still had a job to get back to. He rolled down the side window, pulled into what would have been traffic in any self-respecting city. Rush hour, and his was one of three cars on the street.

Of course, it would be more expeditious to pick up the cell phone now and ask Moore, possibly beg her, to meet with him. Maybe take her someplace for a nice grilled steak or a bowl of crab soup. A bottle of wine. A little chat. Assuming she was at home, not still at the station house trying to bail out her head mechanic. Or cloistered somewhere conferring with her silken-tongued attorney. Or so annoyed with Mick for forcing her to come clean about Semple that she'd never speak to him again.

Mick changed stations on the radio. On second thought, solving the crime in the next few hours seemed much less daunting.

Thirty-nine

Jo was inside the sheriff's station trying to talk sense to Zimmer. Rebecca had abandoned that as a lost cause when the sheriff waved handcuffs in her face, shouting he was going to arrest her as an accessory. She'd stormed outside so she could breathe without screaming. Now she was pacing on the sidewalk like a sixties protester. She didn't care that two youngsters stopped running in the park to gawk at the crazy lady talking to herself.

Make that scolding herself. Naturally, she was upset that Frank had been arrested. She couldn't stand to see him sitting immobile in a jail cell. She should have prevented it, hired an investigator, taken the circumstantial evidence more seriously, tried to defuse the situation before Zimmer arrived at the wrong conclusion. Something.

Frank could not be guilty; she refused to believe it.

Why? Was she worried she couldn't run the shop without him? Or because right now he was the last vestige of stability in her life? Jo feared that Frank would kill for her—she was all the family he had. Wasn't the reverse almost as true?

Frank insisted that the train transformer was an old one—one he'd tried unsuccessfully to fix. It gave off weak shocks when he turned it full on. He'd tinkered with it after work last week. When he couldn't repair it, Frank tossed it in the trash out back along with the extension cord, in case that had a short. Didn't want to set fire to the house. His explanation sounded legit to her. Anyone could buy a transformer. Had they checked nearby hobby shops? Maybe the old True Value stocked them. Or Wal-Mart. Someone should be looking. *Yeah, who?* The sheriff wouldn't bother; he had his suspect behind bars. Hagan was on his team. She hadn't encouraged Jo to hire an investigator—an unnecessary expense when she was sure Frank was innocent. And Jo didn't push it. He wanted Rebecca to investigate the case herself.

Rebecca leaned her shoulder blades against the rough brick front of the sheriff's station. She sucked in the damp air, watched the light fade. Dusk was being hurried along by a heavy mist carried in on the tide. The fog had settled on her brain as well. Freeing the cell phone from a jacket pocket, she punched in her home phone number, hoping Juanita would be there. The girl answered on the second ring, with a giggle and a whispered "*Hola.*" As calmly as she could, Rebecca told Juanita that Frank had been arrested for murder, but that Jo would have him out of jail soon. She hoped. There was nothing Juanita could do at the moment.

"Val's there with you?"

"Yes. He cleans the house, better than my *madre*. And Paulie, he is on his way over. I make enchiladas. And *mole*. We think you need to be cheered up. We wait dinner for you and the lawyer, yes?"

"No. But thanks, Juanita. For the offer, and for picking up the mess. When Paulie arrives, have him call the lawyer at his office, okay?" Mrs. Antrim had offered to help before. It was time to test her sincerity.

Paulie had come to work for the shop because Sylvia Antrim had made Uncle Walt an offer too good to refuse. Walt had had his eye on a second four-post lift which would have set him back ten thousand dollars he'd never have. Sylvia was searching for a place for her son to go and be useful on a regular basis. She assured Walt that Paulie didn't need the paycheck, he needed a place to belong. Over seconds of coconut cream pie at *Flo's*, Walter Moore and Head Tide's only resident aristocrat struck a mutually advantageous deal.

The irony was that Paulie fit in at the shop as smoothly as shifting into top gear. Frank handed him a tiny wrench in welcome, saying, "This here fits 2BA nuts. You gonna need that." Val handed him half of his bologna sandwich and solemnly advised against eating lunch at *Flo's*: too busy around noon and we'd miss you. For his part, Paulie was fascinated by them. He respected their abilities as mechanics. They taught him what they thought he could learn. He lectured them on making drinkable coffee and gave advice on where to buy ties and how to care for white bucks—laughing matters to everyone except Paulie.

Rebecca turned down Jo's suggestion that they grab a bite. She assured him there would be leftovers in the house. She promised to eat, then get some rest. With a light kiss on her cheek, Jo let her slip out of the car and evaporate into the mist.

Rebecca did not go home.

There was a limit to how much abuse she was willing to take from Brad Zimmer in his quest to be king of the molehill. Last year, she'd put up with the DC detectives. The horror of David's suicide and her guilty conscience had thrown her into a state of shock. She'd been polite, patient. She'd answered their questions fully. Graham and Vera Stuck's deaths were different. Rebecca had nothing to do with them. She wasn't going to let them ruin her business, denigrate her employees. Or starve her cat.

Rebecca bypassed the house, cutting through the walnut grove to the back of the darkened shop. In the shadows of the pines she paused and listened. She tried to discern if anything had been disturbed. She wondered if the killer could have fabricated another explosion to be set off unknowingly. Like when she opened the door. Would she recognize a bomb before she triggered it?

Everything looked normal in the gray light.

She reached under the boughs of a towering spruce and

dragged out a chipped cinder block. She lugged it past the charred remains of Graham's Subaru, stood the block on end and braced it against the building. Balancing on the block, she reached for the ledge spanning the back door. She wiggled a loose chunk of stucco near the corner until she could lift it out. Under it, she felt for the key that had been stashed there for years as part of Uncle Walt's open-door policy. Key in hand, she hopped down. She carefully peeled away the yellow police tape and slipped into the car shop. Nothing exploded.

In the empty room the silence was so intense that the soles of her sneakers squeaked on the concrete floor. As she slid open one of the fire doors, Rebecca fancied she could still smell the metallic odor of blood, the tang of rotting flesh, but it was the reek of Paulie's *Stetson* cologne that guided her toward the glass beader and the workbenches beyond it. She banged her hipbone against the corner of a bench and stifled a yelp. Why, there was no one to hear her except Moe. And the ghost of Graham Stuck, if you believed in spirits. She discarded that notion faster than an oil-soaked paper towel. She had enough trouble dealing with the living, thank you.

Rebecca opened the single drawer beneath the work surface and felt around until she found the metal shaft of the Maglite. With its narrow beam pointed at the floor, she walked quickly toward the office. Once she was through the door, Moe's yowl of delight greeted her. Sweeping him up in her free arm, Rebecca extinguished the flashlight. She nibbled on the cat's ear to start him purring.

She closed the office blinds, fed Moe, then risked turning on the computer. As the PC screen flickered to life, Moe sat up like a squirrel beside the monitor to wash his stomach. A necessary prelude to napping. She longed to take him home with her, sink into a warm bed and let him purr her to sleep, but who knew how the Doberman would react to having a cat underfoot? No doubt Moe would voice a few objections of his own. It would be more merciful to leave him in familiar surroundings.

Rebecca signed on to the Internet, entered her password

and was rewarded with the ubiquitous "You've got mail." She quickly located two entries from *phayes* scattered among the junk ads from AOL. Peter's first message was three pages long. Rebecca skimmed it as she hit the print control. It began with Lindeman's bio—born in Scranton, Pennsylvania; degree in electrical engineering from Cornell University—then the e-mail evolved into a rambling description of Hal Lindeman's business dealings. Either his finances were complex or Peter felt they needed lengthy interpretation. She hoped the bottom line was not a zero.

She printed the second message without reading it. She saved both to the file cabinet. Then she replied, thanking Peter and directing him to e-mail her care of her lawyer or call her at home. He didn't need to know that the local law had locked her out of her business.

The LaserJet stopped spewing paper. Rebecca thought she heard a car door slam. She listened. She waited for footsteps on the tarmac, a knock at the door. Nothing. Moe curled happily into a tight fur ball and ignored the sound. Rebecca decided to do the same. She folded the pages into quarters, slid them into her back pocket, then filled the food bowl with Meow Mix for midnight snacking. Putting the cat food back in the cupboard, she saw the tin of brownies from Vera. Good idea. If there were no leftovers in the fridge, she'd make do with dessert.

Flashlight in hand, Rebecca retraced her steps through the machine area, into the car shop and out the back exit. She shivered as she stepped into the damp night. Except for crickets, all was quiet. She was anxious to get home, to be safe among friends. Eat rewarmed enchiladas. And pig out on brownies. She mounted the cinder block and replaced the key above the doorsill. If the sheriff should ask if she had a spare key, she could honestly answer no. The flashlight she'd stash under the tree with the block.

She turned to hop down.

An arm slammed into her stomach. It lifted her off the block and banged her onto the ground. Her teeth snapped shut with the impact. The tin flew from her arm, but she clung on to the flashlight. A body pressed her close from behind. Rebecca swung the flashlight, arcing it upward, back over her head. Not a lot of force, but it connected. Someone screamed.

"Jesus Christ, Moore. What the hell are you doing? You've blinded me." Mick released her to grab for his face.

She whipped around and shoved him away with both hands. "What am I doing? I'm protecting myself." She pushed him again, harder. "What are you doing, sneaking up and grabbing me like that?"

"I was trying to help you down. Like a gentleman. You don't weigh as much as I thought." It hurt to grin. She shoved him again. He held up one hand, stumbling backward.

"What are you doing, lurking around my property in the dark?" She made to push him again. Mick feinted left to avoid it.

"Me? What about you? You're breaking into a police scene."

"To feed my cat. Someone has to."

"Sorry about that. We should have taken care of the cat."

Moore's hands fell to her sides. "Yes, you should have. Tell your pal Zimmer that I'm coming in again tomorrow morning to give Moe breakfast. And dinner tomorrow night if the shop's still cordoned off."

"You won't if I confiscate that key." Mick pointed to the ledge. "How long has it been there?"

Moore sighed and shook her head. Her hair danced. "Years? Check out the mold. Walt stashed keys outside so repairmen could get in if he wasn't here. It was wasted effort, he was always here—all day, every day. When he did go home he usually forgot to lock up anyway."

"I think I would have liked your uncle." Mick massaged the start of a lump above his left eye.

"Most people liked Walt. He was good-hearted, warm and trusting." Even in the dim light of the security lamp he could see the ghost of a smile dance over her lips.

"Unlike you." The words slipped out before Mick could censor them. *Damn it to hell*. He couldn't believe he had said that. Moore's eyes flashed with anger, or hurt.

"The complete opposite of me, Hagan. How perceptive of you."

She spat out the words and spun away before he could pry his foot out of his mouth. He grabbed her wrist on her way by. In approved cop fashion, Mick twirled Moore around, pinned her arm behind her back and pulled her up against him. Her right hand sprang up to claw at his face. He stopped it in midair.

"Shh. Shh." Not original, but it was all he could think of to say before his lips found hers.

Mick wanted to be tender. He wanted to know the feel and taste of her flesh—to prove she was real, someone worth dying for. His greedy mouth was out to devour. She struggled to pull away. She may have said stop, he wasn't listening. He let go of one wrist, slid his fingers up under her hair. He cradled her head, forcing her face to his. Closed his eyes. He caressed her cheek, his thumb trailing along her lower lip. His mouth played on hers. Savoring the warmth and wetness of her as his tongue slid inside and began exploring. He moaned. Or maybe she did. He hoped so.

He sensed her fist rising toward his head.

Oh, hell, let her slug him, he probably deserved it. He wouldn't feel it.

He did, though. Felt the softness of her palm as she touched his cheek. Warmth of her hand as it cupped his face, catching on the stubble. Her fingers lingered behind his ear before circling, clutching his neck. Pulling his face closer as she rose on her toes. He felt the urgency as her tongue began its own exploration.

It was all the invitation Mick needed. He released her other hand, encircled her waist, pulling her body, breasts, hips against his. He planted gentle kisses on her face and eyes and lips. Played his fingers lightly down her neck, feeling the pulse in her throat, the fine bones of her shoulder. His hand moved lower to cup her breast. He could feel the nipple through the layers of cloth. His erection pressed hot against her thigh.

Oh, God. He stopped moving. What was he doing?

Moore sensed his hesitation and pulled back, questioning eyes probing his face. He couldn't answer them. He buried his face in her hair. Moving as one being, he pressed her against the side of the building and held her motionless. Breathing together. They fit so well. Ying and yang.

He ached to finish what they'd started right there in the dark on the damp ground, forgetting that she was the person he held morally responsible for David's death. His more rational self cautioned that David could not be ignored. Better to take it slow. Try to develop a relationship with her that—

Mick never heard him coming. Soggy earth deadened his tread as the Doberman raced across the ground, weaving through the grove of trees. From six feet away the dog launched his taut body into the air toward the man holding his new mistress captive. At the last minute, following Moore's sideward glance, Mick glimpsed the dog flying at him and raised his elbow. He deflected the bared teeth from his neck, but the dog's jaws fastened on his upper arm. Together they hit the ground hard.

Moore pushed away from the building, shouting at the dog. "Down, Wonder. Down." She fell to her knees, grabbed for the dog's collar. "It's okay, boy. Okay."

The dog growled, clamped tighter, eyes darting sideways as she spoke. Mick stopped struggling. Moore's tone softened as she stroked the dog. "Let go, boy. Come on. There's a good boy. Good boy."

The dog released the pressure of his teeth on Mick's arm. He whimpered and looked at Rebecca for approval, quickly turning his head back toward Mick lying motionless on the ground. Front feet prancing, the dog turned toward Moore again. She stroked his neck, murmuring. The dog sat back on his haunches and quivered. Moore continued to mutter endearments until he licked her nose. Good sign. Mick lowered the arm protecting his face. He slithered backward away from the woman and her dog. He sat up, straightened his jacket, fingered his biceps through a tear in the sleeve. No blood, that was a plus—no rabies shot needed.

His voice was strained. "I knew you were protected by ex-cons and a black cat. Where'd he come from?"

"Wonder's staying with me until Billy Lee's out of the hospital."

"I figured that, but where the hell was he?"

"Juanita must have let him out of the house. Are you all right?"

"I'll be black and blue by morning. Nothing broken." He shrugged, getting to his feet. "Except my spirit. I am duly chastised for my behavior." Mick brushed leaves from a pant leg. "Guess I got carried away." He stopped picking debris from his pants to look at her. She had that damn Mona Lisa smile on her face again. The one he couldn't read. It could be an invitation. Or a promise to see him in court for assault. A prudent man would call it time for a dignified exit. If one were possible.

Mick reached down, offering Moore a hand up. As she rose, the dog sidled around to sit beside her leg, eyeing Mick's every movement.

"I'm truly sorry about Frank Lewes. The sheriff will have to let him go. There's no hard evidence against him."

"I hope you're right."

"I'm also sorry about giving your employees a hard time. Despite what it looks like, I am a good investigator. There are a couple of things I need to check out in DC. They might tie in with the murders. I'll let you know." Mick let go of her hand. He crammed both of his into his pockets. "Unless you'd prefer I work through Delacroix?"

Moore hesitated for a second. "Either one of us is fine. Thank you for deciding to help."

Mick nodded. "I owe you. I'm also sorry—"

Moore grinned. "About your behavior just now?"

"No way. I'm sorry the damn dog interrupted."

Forty

After Hagan left, Rebecca stashed the cinder block beneath the fir tree and retrieved the tin. Wonder pranced ahead of her as they wove through the trees up the rise. She held the flashlight close to her side, more as a weapon than to see by. She clicked it off as she approached the house. Light flooded through the multipaned windows at the side, making elongated rectangles of yellow on the dark earth. She climbed the steps. The front door was ajar. Wonder bolted inside and landed on the sofa.

Juanita was in the kitchen singing something in Spanish, the melody punctuated by the clang of pots and the rush of water. The air was redolent with the odors of chili and chocolate. In the dining room, one place was set: woven mat, pottery plate, flatware, pilsner glass and a single candle waiting to be lit. The sight of such consideration almost reduced Rebecca to tears. She dropped the now-dented tin onto the table in passing.

"Hey, *chica, que pasa*?" Rebecca tried sounding cheerful. "Where is everyone?"

Juanita turned from the sink, shaking soap suds from her arms. "You are home. I am so glad." The small girl beamed. "Val goes with Paulie to his mother's. Paulie say she is always more polite in front of strangers. They arrange the money for Frank."

She smiled at Juanita. "That's great news. Any enchiladas left? I'm starving."

That was an understatement. She must be starving—for affection anyway—judging by her reaction to Hagan. She could still feel his mouth on hers, the heat from his torso. Juanita handed her a chilled *Dos Equis* and shoved her out of the kitchen. Rebecca walked to the dining room, sipping the cool beer, amused at herself over the encounter in the dark, wondering what would have happened if the Doberman hadn't rushed in. Hormones were truly peculiar things.

Juanita came right along, carrying a plate of enchiladas and rice. As if tuning in to Rebecca's thoughts, the girl uttered the dreaded words: "Can we talk?"

Before Rebecca could think *What now?* Juanita began. "You know I graduate in June. From school?"

Rebecca placed the napkin in her lap and picked up a fork, as if she still had an appetite. She could guess what was coming.

"I was thinking that maybe then I . . . Val and I . . . well, Val has asked me to . . ."

It was only a matter of time. The kids were young, in love or at least in lust, and Juanita had strong nesting instincts. Why wouldn't she want to live with Val?

At the risk of sounding old-fashioned, Rebecca set down the fork and said, "Are you planning to get married?"

Juanita beamed. "Not for a year or two, until we get money. I will ask Flo to work full-time. When we have enough, we buy a small ranch. The one on Route 468, past the Texaco station. There is land for a garden. And a goat." Juanita danced around like a monkey, spilling out her plans for the future.

Despite the tightness in her throat, there was no way Rebecca could spoil the girl's happiness. She would miss her bubbly presence in the house, terribly. And yes, Val was an ex-drug-using felon. Both he and Juanita were too young. Most adults would agree that Rebecca's objections were real, but they were also hers. Maybe the relationship would work. Juanita had kept Val straight for a year now; maybe she could forever. The love of a good woman and all that. Rebecca drained half of her beer.

Juanita fell to her knees and hugged Rebecca's lap. "I knew you would understand. We will be so happy. You will see."

"Promise me—"

"Anything." Juanita's earnest brown eyes gazed up at Rebecca.

"Promise me that you'll come over every Sunday and cook dinner here."

"*Con mucho gusto.*"

"And leave the leftovers." With a powerful squeeze, Juanita resumed singing as she returned to the kitchen to finish the dishes.

Rebecca couldn't taste the food; it could have been cumin-laced cardboard. The beer went down just fine. When she wandered into the kitchen for a second, Juanita was still bubbling. She hugged Rebecca again with damp arms, then tripped up the stairs to bed, humming what sounded like "I could have danced all night" from *My Fair Lady*. Rebecca reached into the refrigerator for two bottles to save a trip.

She poured the beer straight into the glass, letting the foam ooze over the edge. She pushed away the plate of food. To keep from brooding on all the pitfalls of Juanita's announcement, Rebecca tugged the e-mails from her pocket and spread out the pages.

By candlelight she learned that Hal Lindeman had more riding on the Paris-to-Peking than his ego. He had made a crippling business decision about five years ago, going into limited partnership to purchase an early 1980s Formula One race car. Spent close to a million for the open-wheeled racer. Somehow the car had been misrepresented. By the time Lindeman confirmed that it had never been driven by Alain Prost, or anyone else of championship status, he also discovered that repairing the drive train was going to cost an additional thirty thousand. With no provenance, there was no way he could sell the car for the money he had in it. Peter wasn't sure how much money had actually changed hands, since the lawyers had put a "temporary" halt to the sale.

Peter's missive did not contain the name of the broker who conned Lindeman into buying the car. Rebecca could guess. The deal went sour about the time Lindeman switched restorers, bringing his car to *V&C*. Could Lindeman have been angry enough over the swindle to murder Stuck? Now? They'd been in litigation for years.

Rebecca pushed back from the table, folded her legs into her lap and took a swig. Could Lindeman have run out of money, or patience, and come to Head Tide over the weekend to settle up with Stuck? What if they'd agreed to meet somewhere out of town where they wouldn't be recognized? Stuck says he can't pay what he owes, instead he offers Lindeman a deal. Stuck will scuttle the Bentley so Hal's assured of winning the rally and the side bet. Lindeman agrees but insists on witnessing the sabotage for himself. They return to *Capitol Chassis*, find the Bentley gone and the note directing them to the shop. Once at *V&C*, Graham either refuses, or they quarrel over the terms. Lindeman freaks. One blow and he rids himself of Stuck, squashing him like a bug beneath his foot.

Rebecca nodded. It would play in Peoria. But what about Vera? What would compel Lindeman to kill her? Could she have suspected him of her husband's murder and been foolish enough to confront him when he came to pay his respects? So he tortured her to learn if she'd told anyone else, then tried to erase all evidence with the fire? Was it feasible? Rebecca poured another beer.

Peter ended the message with a pledge to fax more details later. Hopefully, they would contain the assurance that Lindeman was now rolling in dough. Without his money Rebecca wouldn't have enough to pay her lawyer to sue him for her money. Talk about a catch-22. Peter also promised background information on Shelley. So far, Shelley's business dealings were so clean they made Peter's nose twitch.

The second e-mail contained one sentence: *About your pal Hagan, his interest in you may be more personal than professional. Hagan and Semple were stepbrothers. Hagan's mother married Semple's father.*

"Brothers?" The word screamed up from the page. She read it again. Stepbrothers? David had never mentioned a brother of any kind, had he? Rebecca couldn't honestly remember. In the months she'd been with him, she'd focused on David as a financial investor, a contributor to her exposé, not as a person with family connections. Sure, he'd talked about his father and his unreasonable expectations for his son, but not a word about a *brother*.

Rebecca drained her beer. If Hagan was David's brother, he should have been at the funeral. Was he? Admittedly, she'd spent most of that day looking at the floor, unable to tolerate the stares of friends and enemies alike. The President could have been sitting next to her and she wouldn't have noticed.

Peter was too thorough a researcher to be mistaken. Besides, Edna's report on Hagan agreed, at least on the fact that Hagan's mother had remarried. Edna hadn't mention the second husband's name, nor had she reported any siblings. And Rebecca had never asked.

How bloody stale am I?

Friday

→

Petrol Fumes

Forty-one

Bacon is the ultimate weapon against sleeping in.

Eyes closed, Mick inhaled the aroma as it oozed upstairs, insinuating its way through the radiator grilles set in the oak floors. He imagined he could hear it sizzling in the pan. There'd be coffee waiting on the counter. Maybe biscuits. Eggs any style he wanted. Totally unfair. As if he didn't feel enough guilt over David's death. Did his mother have to be so normal?

Mick kicked back the blanket. He crossed the narrow room, stubbing his toe on a shoe box full of buttons. The attic room once had been intended for guests, mainly Mick after his divorce. Thanks to his mother's latest hobby—making costumes for the community theater—it was turning into a prop shop. He felt behind the door for a striped terry robe that always hung on the hook, so worn it was ventilated. If it hadn't been there, the costumier would have some explaining to do.

In the bathroom Mick let both the hot and cold water run into the porcelain sink. He glowered at the mirror. What the hell was he doing here? He'd fled from the farcical scene with Rebecca Moore straight to Mom's doorstep. Why? To receive comfort—a confused little boy needing his mother's understanding? Or to give comfort—was he finally ready to face the woman whose adopted son couldn't live with his own shortcomings? He poked at the lump above his eye.

Mick had been working undercover when David committed suicide. Thirteen frustrating months investigating his way up a ladder of extortion, drugs and murder to finger the capo, Anthony Alonso. One day he was pumped, knowing that one of the worst scumbags was about to go down. The next day he learned that his stepbrother was dead.

Mick hadn't attended the funeral. He hadn't been there to take his mother in his arms and let her cry her heart out on his shirtfront. Later, he couldn't do it. And she made no attempt to seek his comfort.

At the time, he was glad to be apart from it. He didn't have to pretend to be a pillar of strength when what he really felt like was a sparking fuse on a powder keg. Anger swamped his every thought. Anger at Moore for driving David to do it. Anger at his mother for letting it happen. Anger at David for being so weak. And at himself for not having worked harder with the kid, for not seeing it coming, for not stopping it. Anger at—

"Michael Patrick Hagan. This is your long-suffering mother bellowing. I've got bacon, yogurt and strawberries. You want to eat with me, you'd better hurry down. I'm due at St. Cecilia's at eleven. Or did you forget it's Friday?"

When Mick left Head Tide the evening before, he'd taken Route 2 north to Annapolis, home port of Reiske's *Virtue*. Sal said the Judge escaped DC on weekends and entertained on the boat. Mick was curious about his guest list. Starting in the center of town, he flashed photos of the judge, Graham and Vera Stuck, Lewes, Lindeman and Shelley—and, just to cover his bases, Moore—in every quaint tourist bar and bistro. Two frustrating hours with little success. The manager at the *Treaty of Paris Restaurant* said Lindeman looked familiar—his type did anyway—and maybe he remembered the judge, but he saw so many distinguished guests he couldn't swear to it.

Mick had better luck at *Knoll's*, the wine and spirits store on the square. He slipped in just as they were ringing out the cash registers for the night. The owner brushed him off, but his sartorially confused assistant—nose rings and Topsiders—was more helpful.

"Yeah. Oh, yeah. The white-haired guy comes in a lot. Like Saturday once a month, you know? Buys a shitload. Like, a case or two of, like, fine wines. Last time a really primo cognac. A hundred dollars a bottle. Like, to die for. You know?"

"Take your word. Was the last time you saw the guy maybe a couple of weeks ago? Friday or Saturday before Memorial Day?"

"Could be. Definitely. I asked the old dude if he was expecting company. You know, the cognac and all." He scratched at the corner of his lips as he thought about it.

"Was he?"

"He didn't say, dude. Just gave me a look. You know?" He grinned a wide smile, bobbing his shaved head to a tune Mick didn't recognize.

Yeah. Mick knew.

The night security guard at Jason's Boat Yard was even less useful. Sporting a crisp uniform and a ponytail, he leaned against the shack smoking a cigarette. The guardhouse was strategically placed at the head of a long runway connecting the shorter arms sticking into the Back River. About twenty sailboats bobbed gently in their slips. A couple had lights burning. Someone was strumming "Me and Bobby McGee" on a guitar with strings older than the song. There were "Private. No Admittance" signs every ten feet. Anyone wanting to board *Virtue* would have to go past the guard's station unless he swam underwater.

"Nah, don't know 'em. But man, I've only been here a week. Guy who does weekends has been around longer, a couple of years. Len. He's in the box from noon on Friday through Sunday. Ten-hour shifts suck, but it's work. He might talk with you. Then again, he might not."

Mick knew Len could be convinced to talk, if Mick bothered to come back. Probably a waste of time. He wasn't sure what he expected to find out. Or how it could help. He was just scratching an itch.

Mick escorted his mother to her station wagon and kissed her cheek. When she asked if he'd be home for dinner, he hedged. "Depends on what I uncover today, okay? I may have to head back to Maryland."

"Michael, you haven't spoken to that young woman yet, have you? Tell me you're not hanging around harassing her."

"Ma, don't start. It's more complicated than you think." Complicated by the way Moore looked and felt and tasted. "And I'm not harassing her. There's laws against that kind of behavior. And I—"

"Always obey the law. I know that, Michael, just like your father. One time he does something shady, and look what happened." She started to roll up the car window.

Mick stopped the window with his palm. "What are you talking about?"

"Your father should never have kept that gun. If he'd thrown it away, your stepbrother wouldn't have found it when Bill and I moved here. He wouldn't have had such an easy way out."

"The revolver was Dad's?"

"You could say that." His mother sighed as she buckled up. "From some bust or other. I didn't remember the details when David asked. I surely don't want to remember them now. Let it go, Michael."

Mick reached out toward her. "Ma—"

"Don't, Michael. You always were too hard on yourself. You couldn't have saved David. His father and I couldn't. Why don't you put this behind you? Forget the girl. Forgive yourself." His mother twisted the key in the ignition. The V-8 revved to life, spewing exhaust from a hole in the pipe.

Because of the roar she couldn't hear Michael mutter, "I'm trying to do both. It's just not working."

Forty-two

Through her bedroom window, Rebecca watched a hawk circle the meadow out back hoping a field mouse would break from cover. Half an hour before, she'd heard Juanita open and close the refrigerator door in search of orange juice, her idea of a balanced breakfast. The girl insisted that she ate a good lunch and dinner, so what's to worry? But Rebecca did worry. She worried about Juanita's eating habits, and her schoolwork. Now she worried that in three weeks Juanita would graduate from high school, then move in with Val.

She'd like to offer Juanita full-time employment at the shop. If the shop was still in operation, and if she could afford another body on the payroll. It would keep Juanita close where she could watch out for her. It would also put Juanita next to Val all day, every day. That might be good. Maybe they'd get sick of each other. Most likely they wouldn't. What if Juanita got pregnant again? How would they—

"Oh, shut up." Rebecca said aloud. She slid from between the sheets.

Covered in one of Walt's thick long underwear tops and flannel pajama bottoms, she began doing stretches, reaching up, then down to touch her toes, feeling each vertebra as her spine flexed. She delivered her rationalization to the dog. "Juanita and Val are legally adults. In their short lives they've been through enough to know what they want. They can take care of themselves. Their relationship is none of my business."

Down again. Palms touching the floor in front of her toes, Rebecca smiled. If she wanted to agonize over adolescent behavior, she could simply recall last evening and Hagan's amorous attack behind the shop. *Honestly.* Honestly what? She dropped to the braided rug on the pine floor and folded her legs into the lotus position. Wonder wriggled closer and watched, one eyebrow raised, as she breathed in through her nose, exhaled through her mouth. *Honestly?* She'd enjoyed the encounter. How's that for truthfulness? She grinned at the dog, breathed in, exhaled.

Snuggling in the solitude of her great-aunt's sleigh bed, waiting for sleep to come, she'd tried to pretend she wasn't attracted to Hagan. It was months of not talking to a man who wasn't carrying a wrench. Or simply the passion of the moment after abstaining for too long. The primordial urge to couple. But, as the rose-colored dawn filtered through the dark branches of the sycamore, she was willing to admit that the attraction was the person, Michael Hagan. Something about him made her nerve ends tingle, her pulse kick into high gear. He was as cocky as his stepbrother, but less self-preoccupied. As good-looking as David in a more unconventional way. And curiously, he seemed more vulnerable than David, who had hidden his insecurity until pushed too far.

Rebecca breathed out, lowering her forehead to rest on the floor in front of her folded feet, arms extended. She should be furious with Hagan. He'd hounded her and her employees, provided the evidence that got Frank arrested, and exposed her involvement in David's death. All the while neglecting to mention that David had been a relative. She breathed out, returning to an upright position, still grinning. Now Hagan had added sexual assault to the list. Not a poster child for DC's finest.

Rebecca showered and dressed in decent trousers and a blouse, then phoned the sheriff's office for permission to enter the shop and feed Moe. After last night's fiasco, she decided not to violate a crime scene again.

Sandra Olson answered. When she heard Rebecca's concern, she muffled her voice. "Don't worry, doll. I took care of him on my way in. He's fine. Vocal, if you know what I mean."

"Cranky."

"You could say that. But he ate good. I'll call as soon as you can go in, okay? Boeski's there today."

Great. Rebecca thanked the sergeant for looking after the cat. It was very considerate, but Moe wasn't the only reason she wanted back into the shop. Murder or no murder, she had work to do, money to make and creditors to fend off. And a building to defend. If the murderer was still searching for evidence, the shop remained a prime place to look. On the bright side, if she couldn't get in, neither could the killer.

The forced inactivity was driving her nuts. Rebecca paced in the kitchen. After her third cup, she was wired. She had to move. From the hall closet, she fished out a remnant from her former career: her favorite sea-foam-green cashmere blazer that accentuated the color of her eyes. Amid the clutter hastily stuffed back into the upended drawer she found reusable tapes for her recorder. Both the recorder and tapes went in the jacket pocket. For good measure, she grabbed a steno pad and slipped it into her shoulder bag. While waiting for Zimmer to go away, she might as well poke around on her own. Jo would be so pleased. What could it hurt? She used to be good at it.

Halfway out the door, she returned to the kitchen and grabbed shears. She clipped slender stalks of Siberian iris on her way to the car to take to Billy Lee. He'd looked bad the night of the fire. Word at Flo's was that he was doing okay on oxygen and could talk a little despite the hoarseness. Well enough to have been questioned by the police, it seemed. Town opinion was divided on whether the questioning was cruel treatment of Billy Lee or civic-minded zeal on the part of their sheriff.

Rebecca rationalized her visit to the hospital as an act of

charity—easing Billy Lee's mind about his faithful companion, who at the moment was bobbing at her side, eager for a ride anywhere. Selfishly, she was counting on Billy Lee to have an insider's perspective on the lives of Graham and Vera Stuck, and to be willing to share it.

Removing the oxygen mask, the nurse warned her against tiring her patient. As the nurse left the room, Rebecca dumped the deep-blue stems into a leftover vase on the windowsill. She bent over the frail man and lightly squeezed his arm.

"Hey, there, Billy Lee. You up for some two-stepping at the Blue Goose?"

"What time?" Billy's voice was barely audible, but he opened one bloodshot eye.

"You name the day. Until then, I'm keeping that dog of yours. He truly is a wonder."

Billy shut the eye, nodded. "Yup. He's a good one. Does he miss me?"

"Heck, no. He's too busy eating Juanita's burritos. Any day he'll start barking in Spanish. You better claim him soon."

"Plan to." His chuckle turned into a cough.

"Billy, I hate to make you, but could I ask some questions about Graham and Vera?" His hand fluttered in what Rebecca took for agreement. "You just nod yes or no, okay?"

Rebecca leaned against the side of the bed and started the tape recorder. She'd have to vocalize the answers as well as the questions, but it was more reliable than taking notes. She slipped her hand into one of Billy's and rested the other one lightly on his shoulder.

She began the interview with the same futile questions Zimmer must have asked: *Who was Graham going to see over the weekend? Where he was going?* Two no's. She changed tacks, asking if Lindeman or Shelley had visited Vera. Yes to both. Shelley left first to walk back. *Did you give him directions?* No. *How did Shelley know the route using the old bridal path?* Billy shrugged. *Had you seen Vera, talked to her, that last day?* That got her a yes, as tears welled in his eyes. *When?* Six o'clock. Zimmer figured the fire started two hours later, around eight. *Was Vera expecting anyone else later that day?* Billy didn't think so.

When Rebecca asked if Vera had been nervous or upset, she mentally kicked herself. It was a stupid question. Her husband had just been killed, naturally Vera would be upset. In response, though, Billy nodded vigorously and squeezed Rebecca's hand.

"Crying. A lot." Who wouldn't, married to a lech like Graham? Then Billy croaked, "Lindeman." Hal Lindeman made Vera cry? No one believed Lindeman had come to town days early just to save on airfare. Could he have come to call on Vera? Was there an emotional tie between them? Perhaps he knew Graham was out of town and took advantage of it. Was it so hard to believe? Lindeman was between wives. Vera was lonely, fed up with Graham's affairs. Why not have a tryst with one of his ex-customers? Poetic revenge.

Billy Lee moved his hand to reclaim her attention. "Crying music." He coughed and sank back into the pillow as if the last memory exhausted him.

It psyched Rebecca. "Music made her cry? What music, Billy Lee?" His head lolled to the side, facing away from her. "Operettas? Gilbert & Sullivan?"

His head rolled back, eyes flew open.

What were the titles of the CDs they had found in the Bentley? *Come on.* Which ones? Right: *Mikado* and *Pirates of Penzance*. She fed the titles to Billy. At the second one, he nodded firmly. Okay. She had a recent widow crying over *Pirates of Penzance*. Did it mean anything? Maybe it was a sad musical. Or maybe *Pirates* had been one of Graham's favorites which they'd enjoyed together? She asked Billy. "Hated it."

Curious. She kept digging. "Did you see the CDs in the car? In the Bentley?"

He rocked his head from side to side, too worn out to answer.

Rebecca leaned against the side of the bed. What was it

about G&S? The CDs kept showing up where they shouldn't be. First they were found in Shelley's Bentley, a car with no CD player. Now being listened to by the widow who detests operettas. For a second, Rebecca regretted not holding on to them. She made a note to ask Boeski about fingerprints. Were they smudged, unmatchable to any on file, or had the cases been wiped clean?

Billy tried to raise his hand. "Quiet. Too quiet. Made me go. Leave her. Leave her alone." Tears were streaming down his face. His last contact with Vera had been a rejection, and it was breaking the old man's heart.

"Billy Lee, Vera wasn't angry with you. She was upset by Graham's death."

"Should have saved her. Where was Brad?" Billy Lee gulped for breath between sobs.

Rebecca was frankly relieved when the nurse returned to shoo her from the room. She wasn't sure the stress of the interrogation on Billy Lee had been worth the answers. Still, as Rebecca walked through the hushed hallway, her instinct told her she'd been handed another piece for the puzzle. If only she could make it fit.

Forty-three

"Jo, I need access to the shop. Now." Rebecca removed undercooked bacon from a toasted BLT. "With Frank in jail, the rest of us will have to work around the clock to finish. Which is fine by me. At least we'll be there to protect the place."

Delacroix had a breathing space between clients and agreed to meet her at the diner for a late lunch. They had the place to themselves, if you discounted Flo and Priscilla—"Flo and Over-Flo," as the local dubbed mother and daughter. Flo was a big lady, Priscilla an even bigger girl. They were pretending not to eavesdrop as they wiped down the tables.

Jo blew on the bowl of tomato soup, separating the steam into wisps. "True. If the murderer continues his search, the shop is one place he'll hunt again. He might also go to your house again. Have you thought of that?"

"Of course."

"Which leads me to suggest that you leave town."

"Pack up and move out? Me, the cat, dog, Juanita? Did you come up with that brilliant idea before or after you learned Vera had been tortured? Hands and feet bound. Hair and nipples burned off while the rest of her body was untouched by the blaze." She dropped the sandwich on the plate and shoved it away. "Were you planning to tell me?"

"No, I wasn't. Who did?" Jo set down his spoon and glared at Flo. She abruptly scooped up a handful of saltshakers to refill behind the counter. His attention swung back to Rebecca. "I want you to be safe. Leaving town makes good sense."

"Close the shop, put the guys out of work until our wizard of a sheriff solves the case? How long do you think that will take? Reiske and Hagan have already skipped town. Shelley and Lindeman fly to Paris the end of next week to allow them playtime before the cars arrive at the docks. By the time Zimmer pieces it together, the murderer will be long gone. Or will have confessed, published his story and negotiated an appearance on *Oprah*."

Jo, unfazed by her outburst, reached for a package of saltines. Fine, he said, stay. But if she did, then it was up to her to foil the murderer. Uncover his motivation for blackmail, reveal her findings publicly, and put an end to the murderer's search. Help put him behind bars. Jo crumpled crackers into the soup. "In short, return to the profession at which you excel."

"You don't give up, do you? I've got Hayes working on it, isn't that enough?"

"Why do you refuse to help? It's your life."

Rebecca smoothed out her napkin on the table, then began folding it. "Because it is my life, I guess. I don't have a clue as to how it's supposed to play out. I loved reporting until the debacle with David. If I'd been more professional, I could have had the story without driving David to suicide. Doesn't that tell you I'm not fit to be a reporter?"

"It tells me you made a mistake with serious consequences. But so have others. Giving up is not the solution. Learn from it. You'll never make a mistake like that again, will you?"

"I hope not. But how can I be sure?" Rebecca started picking tiny holes from the paper napkin.

"Nothing is certain, Rebecca. We cannot know that the sun will rise tomorrow, only assume that it will because it has every other day."

"Hume."

Jo grinned. "How delightful—an educated skeptic. I'll start citing my sources."

"You do that." Rebecca dropped paper shreds in the ashtray. "Have you ever made a mistake that ended in someone's death?"

Jo removed his glasses. "Yes. But I did not stop being a lawyer. The point is, you go on."

"I'm trying. Right now I'm trying to run a repair shop and not to fail at that."

Jo signaled for Priscilla. "If you sit with me over dessert, I'll call the sheriff and convince him to let you resume work. You may not respect Brad's abilities, but in this case, he will be tenacious."

"Says who?"

"You recall Stella's tale of the young man who fell in love above his station?"

"Zimmer is the man who loved Vera Stuck?"

Jo nodded. Rebecca leaned back in her chair. In a small-town kind of way it made sense. Zimmer had grown up low-class poor. He'd excelled at football in high school but not much else. Vera had been the pretty, quiet child of one of the county's richest families. Didn't the quarterback always get his girl—or think he was entitled to her? Yet Zimmer hadn't gotten Vera. He'd never married. Had he waited all these years for her? According to Jo, Zimmer had respected her marriage to a man disliked by the locals. Then the man was murdered. Would Zimmer have dared to hope that his turn had come? That as adults they might be able to forge the relationship that never materialized in their youth? Then Vera was snatched away from him. Rebecca could well imagine the emotional strain the sheriff must be under.

"How cruel for Zimmer that she died so soon after Graham." What had she heard Lindeman crooning? She tried her hand at imitating the catchy tune, singing, "A policeman's life is not a happy lot."

Jo surprised her by singing in response, " 'When a felon's not engaged in his employment'—or something to that effect."

"What?"

"Gilbert & Sullivan. I assumed you were paying tribute to Stuck."

Rebecca shook her head. She didn't know that the ditty was from G&S. Felons and cops—*Pirates,* naturally. And Lindeman, whom Shelley said called it caterwauling, was singing it just yesterday. Too bizarre. She dragged herself back to Zimmer and resumed picking at the napkin. "Of course, if Vera hadn't been murdered, too, the sheriff would make a convincing suspect."

"Agreed. And it's conceivable that Brad killed Vera as well. Perhaps he went to her, confessed his affection and she rejected him. Or he confessed to killing Stuck for her and she was horrified. After decades, his thwarted passion finally explodes." Jo pushed back from the table. "But it's unlikely. Saturday through Monday, Brad was in Arlington at his sister's. A silver anniversary gathering for them, I understand. Boeski reached him there when you reported finding the body."

"But Arlington's so close—"

"Rebecca, you're clutching at straws. Maybe he could have killed Graham, but can you envision Brad Zimmer torturing, then killing, the woman he's pined for most of his life?"

"More easily than I can see Frank Lewes doing it. Yet you claim they have the same twisted motive."

Jo snatched away her napkin. He held it by one corner and shook it. It fell open, revealing a lacy pattern. He grinned. "Perhaps I'm the one clutching at straws. You seem to prefer snowflakes."

Forty-four

Rebecca left Jo at his office waiting for his four o'clock appointment. The tide was in. She leaned against the stone wall of the one-car bridge and inhaled the salt tang. A tern was running forward and backward, pecking at the water's edge. She empathized with the energetic bird—darting at elusive sea creatures only to have them snatched away by the receding water. Something was teasing her subconscious the same way. Something to do with Vera. Something she'd said. Or someone had said about her.

The air was cooling quickly as the sun faded. Rebecca jogged across Ryder's Mill Road where it intersected Main Street at the bend. She started up the lawn to the house. Once in the walnut grove, she pulled her jacket close, glanced toward the shop. Olson's patrol car was parked alongside the building. Zimmer must have assigned her first shift, keeping an eye on the shop. Rebecca hoped Moe was asleep in the in basket. She'd get him out of there soon. And replace the burned-out security light. Just as soon as she dealt with the glimmer flickering beneath the surface of her brain. A teasing suggestion, floating just out of reach.

Rebecca unlocked the front door and was knocked off balance by a wiggling mass of sleek black fur. She stroked Wonder's ears. "Did you miss me, boy? I'm going to miss you once Billy Lee is back on his feet. Do you have a brother? Or a sister?" Wonder sat, cocked his head and appeared to consider the question in earnest.

Billy Lee. Was it something he'd said about Vera?

Rebecca shrugged off the jacket, hung it in the closet. What did she know about Billy Lee? Good mechanic, solid worker, according to Walt. A man who'd risked his life trying to pull his employer's wife from the fire. Presumably, his impressions of Vera were accurate. He claimed she hated light operettas, yet she was listening to one just days after her husband's death. And crying. Crying so hard she banished Billy Lee from the house. Was she crying over Graham? Or was it just emotional strain? After David died, Rebecca had wept over the verses in Hallmark cards.

The muted sounds of reggae floated down from Juanita's room. Rebecca wandered into the kitchen. *Coffee or beer?* She crossed to the sink. Next to it, on the counter, sat Uncle Walt's wooden train. Someone had resurrected it. The wheels had been pinned onto new axles, the cars recoupled, a coat of paint dabbed on the caboose. Who had repaired it? Jo? More likely Juanita had taken it to Frank. He'd found time to mend it before he was arrested. Would a murderer and arsonist be that sensitive, that giving? She had to get him out of jail.

As she reached out to touch it, Rebecca blinked back tears. She molded her hand over the engine and began rocking the train back and forth on the tiles. Click-clack. Click-clack. The pudgy maple wheels tripped over the grout lines. Back and forth. Back and forth. Linked cars going nowhere. Just like her thoughts, stuck at the station. But perhaps, like the train, she could get rolling again, if she could decipher what was bothering her. She opted for coffee and reached for a clean mug.

The music upstairs shifted to a Spanish lullaby which Juanita loved, though the melody made Rebecca morose. As the soprano turned a high note into a wail, the light bulb clicked on for Rebecca. Vera's crying music—the damn CDs.

What if they weren't CDs at all? Perhaps the CDs were a cover for something else in the cases. A hiding place. Rebecca had read the label on one, then dismissed them both. She hadn't opened the second one. Could something small have been secreted in the case, something worth killing for? Rebecca held the coffeepot in one hand, cord in the other, linking the events like cars on a train:

1. The CDs came to the shop in the Bentley.
2. They were boxed by Boeski.
3. She tried to return them to Todd, who disclaimed them.
4. Juanita picked them up and gave them to Vera when she delivered the casserole.

Then what? Billy Lee witnessed Vera listening to music the afternoon she was murdered, *Pirates of Penzance,* the one Rebecca didn't open. Listening to it after Hal left or while he was there? Was that where he'd heard it, why he was singing that song? Rebecca loaded coffee grounds into the filter. Then the case must have contained music. Assuming the CD she was listening to came from that case. What exactly had Billy Lee said?

Adrenaline started pulsing in her temples. This was it.

She left the pot on the counter and sat at the table to replay her tape of the conversation with Billy Lee. He'd quoted Vera, who called it "crying music." But he also said it was "too quiet." Rebecca assumed he meant Vera was being unnaturally quiet. Had he meant the house was too quiet, that there wasn't any music playing?

Billy thought Vera was going to give him the CD, then changed her mind. Sent him away. Why? Because she didn't want Billy Lee involved, or because she didn't trust him with what she'd found? If not him, whom? Whom would Vera have trusted with damning evidence? Did she know Hal well enough? He'd just left. Could she have given it to Lindeman, then regretted it? Maybe he'd refused to help, which upset her. So Vera was standing in the den, clutching the jewel case, tears streaming down her face. She evicted Billy Lee. What would have been her next option? Try to contact Zimmer—local lawman and old friend—the man who had loved her for years? Vera might well have turned to him. But what was it that Billy Lee had mumbled?

Rebecca fast-forwarded through the tape until she heard his plaintive cry near the end: "Where was Brad?" Good question. Was Billy implying that Vera had called Zimmer, but he hadn't come? Damn it all, why hadn't Rebecca grilled Billy Lee harder? She'd been way too gentle on a dispirited, sick man. Or she'd simply forgotten how to investigate a source.

Rebecca raked her fingers through her hair. If not Zimmer, who? Reiske—judge and family friend?

"*Hola*, Reb." Juanita pounded into the kitchen, sandals flapping on the tile floor. She crossed to the refrigerator and pulled out a carton of milk, then rummaged in the cupboard for a snack. Rebecca watched the girl push aside cans of vegetable soup in her quest for cookies, a package of dough-nuts or anything else for a sweet tooth. She dismissed the granola bar, kept rooting for something stickier. Sweets were Juanita's downfall, as the dentist pointed out twice a year.

Sweets. Of course. Oh, Christ. Not the judge. Vera didn't give it to the judge.

Rebecca bolted from the kitchen. In the dining room she snatched up the red metal tin from the sideboard. The tin Vera had sent home with Juanita—*I am to give it to Miss Rebecca, no one else.* The tin Rebecca had barely opened. It had sat in the cupboard at the shop the night Vera died. Rebecca had carried it to the house after Hagan's seduction. She'd planned to eat the brownies until Juanita announced she was moving in with Val, and she lost her appetite.

With a sinking feeling, Rebecca pried off the lid.

Brownies. Rich, dark, homemade, crumbly squares. She poked at them. Then stopped. Could the tin contain explosives of some kind? Had Vera decided that Rebecca was to be blamed for Graham's death after all—the brownies were her revenge?

Not possible. Hagan had snatched one from the tin, it hadn't exploded. He broke it in half, ate at most of it and was still pestering her, so they weren't poisoned.

Rebecca carried the tin out to the front porch, shutting the Doberman inside. She sat on the top step and carefully lifted out the first layer. She placed it beside her. The dog whined through the screen. Second layer looked as innocent as the first. No wires or nonedible bits amid the squares. No secret messages. She removed the second layer and set it on top of the first. An ant scurried across the porch, lured by a fallen crumb. A protective sheet of aluminum foil lined the bottom of the tin. Rebecca slid it up and out, touching only the edges. She placed it on top of the pile of brownies.

Under the aluminum foil was a black disk.

Not a CD. Not a recording of *Pirates of Penzance*.

A plain, unlabeled three-and-a-half-inch-square floppy computer disk.

Forty-five

Leonard Grikowski, the day guard at Jason's Boat Yard, had been around the block a few times. Hotly pursued by cops on at least one of those occasions, unless Mick was off the mark. Animosity toward the police rippled in the bunched muscles of his jaws. He seemed to think a sentence with more than one word was a waste of consonants. Still, Grikowski put down the sports page and agreed to the interview.

Mick received three "Yeahs" in a row. *Yeah,* he knew the boat, *Virtue. Yeah,* he recognized Reiske by sight. *Yeah,* the judge sometimes entertained guests on board the boat.

After that it started to get sticky. Grikowski wasn't going to exert himself by opening the door to the guard's shed to talk to Mick without a barrier. He leaned on the plywood shelf, glowering through the Plexiglas. Mick plastered photograph after photograph up against the window and got no reaction. He saved the snapshot of Vera and Graham for last.

"These two ever guests of the judge?"

The guard squinted at the photograph. He crossed his arms and settled his haunches on the stool. "That a crime?"

Mick shook his head. "We know they were friends. Both of them visit?"

Grikowski picked at a lower tooth with his fingernail. "Never saw the broad."

"But you know the guy? He come often? Stay the week-end?"

"Sometimes."

"Was he here Memorial Day weekend?"

Grikowski scratched under his chin while nodding. "Saw him around eight Saturday."

"Doing what?"

"Leaving."

Okay, we progress, inch by inch. "Alone? Judge stay on board?"

Grikowski shrugged. "I guess."

"You're not sure?"

Grikowski sighed. This was going to take more words than he liked to use. He tapped the window. "The guy leaves happy. Singing to himself. I nods to him. A bomb goes off. Pier C." He pointed to the farthest arm out. "I snatch a fire extinguisher. Rush over. Guy beats it."

Jesus. Here we go again. "What kind of a bomb?"

"Kid kind. Bottle bomb hits a dinghy. I put it out. No damage. Takes ten minutes."

"During which time the judge could have left his boat?"

"Doubt it. I didn't see him."

"What does he drive?"

"Volvo wagon."

"Volvo still in the lot after the bomb goes off?"

Grikowski shrugged beefy shoulders. "Why would I look? This ain't going to get me in Dutch with the judge? He's a solid tipper."

Mick peeled the photograph off the Plexiglas. "For now, it's between us."

Grikowski slouched back, returned to the sports page.

Mick contemplated the photograph of husband and wife as he walked the length of the wharf toward the parking lot. Attractive couple, prosperous-looking. But man, their rela-tionship made you think twice. Both had been murdered. She was a closet drinker. He was a womanizer or worse, and most likely a blackmailer. Odd that they were friends of a straight-arrow like Reiske. Maybe the good judge liked slumming on occasion. More probably Stuck liked sucking up to those higher up. Memorial Day weekend he's in Annapolis. Drops in on the judge unannounced, checks out the sailboat, drinks a little vintage cognac, makes some connections. Returns to Head Tide, mellow, all puffed up. Finds death waiting. He should have stayed in Annapolis.

Forty-six

Half a day wasted, and he'd accomplished exactly what? Mick had confirmed the obvious—that Stuck and Reiske were friends; that Stuck had been in Annapolis as Vera had guessed; and that he was alive when he and the judge parted company. Heading out at eight P.M. sounded like Stuck should have been on his way to see his latest honey, take her for a late dinner or spend the evening amorously occupied. So, what happened to change his plans? Mick punched in Zimmer's number on the cell phone and started the Jeep. Olson put the call through. No, Zimmer sighed, he had not located Stuck's girlfriend. He didn't have the endless resources of a slick city detective. Heck, he didn't even have the promised services of said slick city detective, who had skipped town without telling him.

Mick guided the Cherokee onto Route 50 heading west. He promised to return as soon as he paid a visit to the courthouse.

Mick arrived at the U.S. district court with minutes to spare. He took a seat in the next-to-last row. The place was packed with reporters and a handful of interested parties willing to risk being photographed in the vicinity of Anthony Alonso. The din from dozens of whispered conversations wafted toward the murals on the high ceiling. The air was electric with supposition and suspicion.

Nothing much was anticipated other than opening arguments, but the fourth estate didn't want to miss a beat of what promised to be the most flamboyant trial of the spring session. If Sal's sources were correct, they'd have a salacious sidebar to include about Reiske stepping down. No explanation would be innocent enough for the media, the suspicious SOBs. *Suspicion,* from the Latin and French: the act or an instance of believing something wrong without proof or on slight evidence. Standard operating procedure for reporters. Believe the worst about someone, then set out to convince the reading public. How could Moore have been one of—

A skinny, bespeckled man in a hand-knit vest and plaid jacket slipped in the bench beside Mick, jostling his arm with his briefcase. The man extracted a steno pad and tiny tape recorder. He smiled at Mick. "Sorry, didn't want to miss this. You press?"

Mick snorted. "No way. Guess you are?"

"Shows, huh? Peter Hayes, *Washington Post*." He tried to wriggle around to shake hands. When Mick just stared at him, the reporter dropped his arm.

Mick cocked his head. "*Post?* I know someone who used to work there. You ever hear of Rebecca Moore?"

Without moving his shoulders, the thin man swiveled his neck to see if anyone was listening. Then he turned close to Mick. "She send you? She needn't have. She should have known I'd be here. Doesn't she trust me? I'd never let her down."

"Relax, I'm here on my own. I heard that Judge Reiske is excusing himself from the case. I wanted to see him do that in the flesh."

"You're the second person today who's mentioned it. Why, do you think?" Without giving Mick a chance to answer, Hayes sped on. "Blackmail." His head bobbed like a dog's in the rear window of a sedan. "That's what I think.

Blackmail. The Mafia's got dirt on the judge and are forcing him to give up the case in favor of someone they can control: Thomas, maybe Crandall. It's said Reiske can't be bought. Maybe he can be squashed if you're powerful enough, like Alonso." Hayes draped his arm along the bench behind Mick and leaned in. "Or clever enough. Or patient enough. You should see what I've uncovered about the illustrious judge's past." Hayes's eyes were glistening.

Forty-seven

Jo chuckled to himself, but the sound lacked mirth. The energy he'd expended trying to convince Rebecca to investigate the murders had boomeranged. Looped around and whizzed back at him. He wanted to duck. He caught it instinctively. With the primitive weapon in one hand, clutching loose straws in the other, Jo felt compelled to join the hunt. Now that Rebecca was on track, he had every confidence she would solve the mystery. But could she do it alone, before the loose straw—all those loose ends—burst into flames?

Jo locked up his office and drove to the Sunset Marina. It was the cocktail hour. He expected to find Lindeman and Shelley hoisting a few in the bar. He would prefer to question them separately—use their competitiveness, pit one against the other. He needed every advantage. Jo knew he was too believing to be an effective investigator.

He buttoned his jacket and entered the lounge. It was nearly empty—one cozy couple at the bar and Fred Dexter, cousin to the funeral director, embalming his liver pre-need. No sign of Rebecca's customers.

Jo tried the front desk. He knew the receptionist; he'd handled her recent divorce. She smiled warmly, wagging a new diamond on her left hand. Sure thing, Mr. Lindeman was registered in Room 110. She hadn't seen him since lunch. Mr. Shelley was in Room 204. He'd requested tea about fifteen minutes ago, so he should be there. Jo thanked her and took the exterior stairs to the second floor.

Todd Shelley answered his knock promptly, a cell phone clamped to his left ear. He continued speaking while motioning Jo into the suite. A four-color, glossy view of the bay dominated the room: undisturbed blue water rippling to the opposite tree-lined shore; a lone sailboat, mast erect, motoring toward windier seas.

The interior was less scenic. Shelley's bed was rumpled, unmade. Dirty coffee cups and plastic cups on every surface. A laptop computer sat open on a narrow table designed for lone dining or paperwork. A spreadsheet flickered on the screen. Official-looking letters were strewn near it. Jo idly picked up one embossed with the address of the U.S. International Development Cooperation Agency. He'd skimmed through the second paragraph before Shelley snatched the sheet from his hand. He cut his phone conversation short.

"Lou, just see that the damn Bolsheviks pay up. We'll make good on the couplings later. If you have to, but get the cash." Shelley clicked off, tossed the phone onto the bed. "You do corporate law, Delacroix? International? Didn't think so. Then my business dealings are none of your business—correct? He turned the letter face down and added it to a pile on the far side of the computer. He closed down the screen. "Why are you here?"

Shelley was miffed, but he agreed to answer questions until his tea arrived. Getting him to talk about Lindeman was easy. Shelley confirmed Rebecca's suspicion that Lindeman and Stuck had parted ways over the Formula One race car. "Served Lindeman right. Thinks he's such a hotshot investor, then he gets fleeced by a minor-league louse like Stuck."

Jo gestured toward the closed computer. "You, on the other hand, are major league? Playing international games of which the government disapproves?"

"Not games, lawyer. Real life. Too real for the bureaucrats to comprehend. If they can't cover it with a restriction, they don't think it can be legitimate. It will blow over." Shelley slid open the glass door and stepped onto the balcony. The sailboat was no longer in sight. Jo leaned against the doorframe and addressed Shelley's back. He asked how Shelley knew Stuck was "minor league," or was he just guessing. Shelley shrugged, continued to watch the sky and sea turn crimson as the sun faded. "Stuck was a petty thorn. I admit he threatened to scuttle my negotiations, go to the trade board, but nothing came of it. If he'd played his card, he'd have lost his power. He was just bright enough to figure that out. All I had to do was ride it out until the rules changed and his trump was rendered useless."

Jo left Room 204 as the waiter arrived with Shelley's tea. Shelley had reiterated his alibi for Saturday—he was with Ms. Spotelli. For Wednesday, he offered none. He'd gone with Lindeman to visit the widow. He was anxious to cut it short since he was expecting an overseas call and needed to refer to data from his computer. Lindeman was dragging his feet with the widow. He didn't mind if Shelley left. Seemed almost relieved when Shelley suggested it. Lindeman described how to find the footpath through the trees down to the shore near the marina. The expected call had never come through. Shelley said he fell asleep waiting. Lindeman pounded on his door around seven, suggesting that they check out the other dive, the Blue Goose.

Jo walked the length of the outside hallway connecting the upper rooms. There was a lazy breeze off the water. From his vantage, he could look over the lilac hedges separating the hotel lot from the marina. Lindeman—ruddy hair glowing in the lowering sun—was standing on the pier, one foot resting on the gunwale of a powerboat. He was guffawing at some quip Ned Tender had tossed him. As manager and chief salesman, Ned was playing Lindeman as a hot prospect for a powerboat. Jo suspected Ned would be disappointed.

By the time Jo reached the wharf, Ned had gone inside. Lindeman was sitting in the captain's seat of a white and maroon boat with twin engines. Dark glasses in place, he was flipping through a glossy brochure. Jo smiled down at him.

"New purchase?"

"Just trying her out for size. Have to, if you're my size." Lindeman patted the paunch stretching a marigold-colored polo shirt to its limit. Jo hunkered down to admire the craft. He nodded his approval to Lindeman.

"Nice. I would have thought your money was tied up in cars. What with the Hisso, the rally and, what was it I heard you had bought—a Formula One racer?"

Lindeman lowered his colored glasses and regarded Jo with one brow raised. He tossed the brochure on the mate's seat. "So, someone's been digging in my sandbox, have they? I'd suspect Rebecca, but she has too much to lose if she pisses me off." He gripped the steering wheel with both hands, played the wheel from side to side. "What you really want to know, Delacroix, is did I kill Graham Stuck for fun or for profit. Right?"

Jo grinned. Hard not to admire such directness in an opponent. "Something like that, Mr. Lindeman. May I buy you a drink?"

The bartender saw them come in. Before they reached Lindeman's habitual stool, he had set two scotches on coasters and slid them into place. Jo moved ice cubes around with a plastic stirrer. Lindeman's first swallow drained half the glass. He sighed with contentment.

"The Formula One deal went sour years ago, Delacroix. Your fraternity brothers have been bleeding me ever since. Between my attorney and Stuck's there won't be a cent left for whomever wins. I admit, I came to town last weekend to cut my losses. For a percentage, I was willing to settle and never have to look at his smarmy face again."

"Stuck wouldn't agree?"

"Never saw him. Phoned on Saturday. Vera said he was

out of town. Wouldn't say where or when he'd return. Too vague." Lindeman drained his drink, lifted the empty glass to catch the bartender's eye. "So I walked over to his place. He wasn't there, just Vera." The bartender set a fresh glass in front of Lindeman, noted Jo's full one and turned away to wait on the young couple still snuggled near the other end of the bar.

Lindeman jiggled the cubes in his glass. "Vera claimed to know nothing about her husband's business deals other than he was expecting a windfall. That made me see red. The swine would get the rest of the money over my dead body." Lindeman raised his glass and grinned wickedly. "Or his."

Lindeman seemed to talk freely in answer to Jo's questions. He admitted that he tried to negotiate with Vera on Wednesday after Shelley left. Yes, it was tasteless to pressure the new widow. Still, he hoped to convince her that a small advance right now would prompt him to drop the lawsuit. Save her the bother. He dismissed his deal with Stuck as dueling penises—not expressed quite like that to the lady—more bluster than it was worth. Vera agreed to discuss it with her lawyer. Lindeman left encouraged if not any richer. He did not confess to torturing or murdering Vera.

Jo took his first sip of the smooth scotch. The burn in his gullet made him shiver. "Now that both of them are dead, the matter seems to be resolved."

"Possibly. As is Shelley's wee problem with the international trade boys. Has anyone really questioned Shelley's silicone bunny, Denise? I overheard her bragging to Glory about last weekend's bachelorette party at some male strip joint. The boys were impossibly well hung, to hear her description. She didn't get back to her apartment until two-thirty Sunday morning. That's right." He winked at Jo. "So, what do we think? Shelley could have gone to bed alone, pining between the sheets for her return. Or he might have been killing time—and Graham Stuck—in Head Tide." Lindeman clinked his glass against Jo's. "Stuck's death has been a blessing to us all. Your friend included."

"Rebecca?"

"Miss Rebecca's floundering business, at least. And possibly that fellow Hagan. What is his game?"

"Assisting the sheriff, as far as I know. What are you implying?"

"Nothing much. Only I wasn't the last person to see the widow alive. Hagan's Jeep passed me as I left Vera's house. I checked the rearview mirror. Watched him turn into her drive. It was just before six."

Forty-eight

After hanging up with Jo, Rebecca dialed the *Post* trying to reach Peter. Naturally he was out of the office. She asked Juanita to turn Bob Marley down low enough to hear the phone. If Peter Hayes called, he was to contact Delacroix at his office. She handed the girl a business card with the number circled.

Rebecca debated taking Wonder along. The dog was bounding waist-high, clearly in favor of going. Juanita would be safer with him in the house. Rebecca snatched a thick flannel shirt from the back of the sofa, buttoned it over her T-shirt and headed out. She locked the door behind her.

Walking under the dense branches of the walnut trees, she rehearsed her story for Sandra Olson. She counted on the sergeant being sympathetic enough to let her go into the shop to bring Moe out. Whether the officer could be cajoled into letting her use the computer was something else. Zimmer's instructions would have forbade anyone meddling with anything that could be evidence. Computer as well as cars.

As Rebecca crossed the bridle path, the town fire siren erupted. She paused, a shiver running down her spine. *Not another fire. Please let it be something minor, like burned toast—the result of carelessness, not malice.* She jogged toward the shop. Olson would be tuned in to the police radio. She'd know what was going on.

Rebecca was too late. She was still twenty yards away when the cruiser pulled out around the far side of the building, spitting gravel, siren blaring, light spinning, heading east toward Blue Marsh. Not good. Zimmer was rallying the troops, calling Olson away from guard duty. On the plus side, Rebecca could let herself into the building and out again without the officers suspecting a thing. She walked quickly to the fir tree for the flashlight. Using the cinder block, she reached for the key stashed over the back door. It wasn't there. She hopped down and twisted the knob, and pulled the door open into the empty shop.

Only it wasn't empty. While the car shop was dark and hushed, light leaked from between the fire doors leading to the machine shop, along with the heavy bass pulse of rock and roll turned down low. Someone swore as a tool clanged onto the concrete floor.

Rebecca tiptoed to the doors and looked through the crack. In the light from his work lamp she could see Val yanking wrenches from a tool chest drawer in search of the proper size, throwing the discards on his bench. Rebecca scraped open the door and marched in. "What are you doing in here? Trying to give Zimmer a real reason to revoke your parole?"

"Hey, Reb, way cool. Come help me finish." Val returned his attention to the car. He tightened the chrome nut holding a headlamp on its stanchion. "Once we test the lights, she's good to go." He grinned proudly at the Bentley.

Rebecca stared at Val like he was speaking Kurdish. "What do you mean? It's done? You've finished the Bentley?"

"Me and Frank. He worked on it yesterday after the fuzz left. Before they arrested him. Made me promise to come back and button her up. So I snuck in last night, again today." Val leaned into the car and twisted a polished switch on the dash marked "S&T." "Side and tail?"

"You moved the cinder block and broke in using the key over the door?"

"Sure. That's why it's there, isn't it? Side and tail, boss."

Dumfounded, Rebecca picked up the routine, walking around the car as she had a hundred times before, checking the lights in order: side and tail, head/side/tail, brake, reverse, center, all on—the final test before sending a car out the door. The lamps glowed on cue—from the turn signals on the front wings to the center light above the bumper. The 3-Litre was ready to go.

She couldn't believe it. She ran her hand over the bonnet, smudging a trace of fingerprint powder. While she had been spinning her wheels fretting about murder, arson and overdue taxes, Frank and Val had defied the sheriff's orders and snuck in to reinstall the magnetos and get the Bentley running. Swallowing a lump in her throat, Rebecca moved toward the boy.

"Val—"

He squashed her in a bear hug before she could utter her thanks. Rebecca folded her arms around him to complete the embrace and muttered into his hair, "Get the hell out of here before Olson comes back. And here." She fished in her jeans pocket for a twenty. "Do me two favors. First carry Moe up to the house. See if he can hide out in Juanita's room until he and the Doberman declare a truce. Then get take-out for dinner tonight—pizza, Chinese, whatever. Stay with Juanita until I get back. Once this is over, we'll all celebrate. Okay?"

For a few seconds they stood side by side, grinning like asylum inmates, as they admired the dark green car. Then Rebecca hurried to the office to snatch up a purring Maurice. She explained the situation to him while nibbling on his ear before thrusting him in Val's arms. "Now go." Rebecca pushed the boy and cat toward the exit. Val saluted her and trotted the length of the car shop. He slipped outside, leaving Rebecca alone in the stillness of the building.

Forty-nine

Rebecca booted up the computer. She slipped the floppy disk, still smelling like brownies, into the drive. It contained only one file, labeled simply with the year. She opened the file and scanned the length of it. Each page was headed with a day and date followed by a paragraph or two. A computer diary: How prosaic. She wasn't sure what she'd expected to find—maybe encrypted messages about arms dealing if it involved Shelley; insider trading if it concerned Lindeman; bribes and kickbacks if it dealt with either cop. Not a common, garden-variety diary. If the daily entries were in code, they were good, because they sure read like an ordinary person's recounting of ordinary events, bad grammar and all.

She returned to the beginning of the file and settled in to read. Page after page was devoted to the details of an affair that had begun months earlier. Dinners, bottles of wine shared, gifts, nights of X-rated sex, talk of plans for the future. Rebecca was eighty-eight percent sure she was reading Graham Stuck's record of his recent love life. The man had been egocentric enough to find himself fascinating. A Balzac he wasn't. Most of his entries were perfunctory; boring, despite the lurid subject matter.

As early as the end of February the glitter was rubbing off, at least for the writer. There were frequent caustic remarks about the lover. Paragraphs dwindled to a sentence. The writing didn't perk up until a third party emerged in April, a mysterious person referred to as "god," small *g*, in quotes. The resulting ménage à trois was a tad lopsided: As far as Rebecca could deduce, the deity apparently wanted Graham (if he was the author) to force his lover to step aside. Since Graham's passion was fading, he was in favor of the move. The snag seemed to be convincing the lover to agree. By the first of May, Graham was still requesting more time to set it up.

Rebecca cracked her neck and checked her watch. She didn't know when, or if, someone from the sheriff's department would return. Most emergencies should keep them busy for at least an hour. If they came back and caught her leaving the building, so what? Still, she was getting prickly. Time to finish and stash the disk somewhere safe.

She scrolled ahead, skimming lines, until she reached the last week of May. Plans had progressed—the first hint of blackmail surfaced three days before Stuck was killed:

> *Mailed locker key to "god." Tomorrow he gets the photographs and tape. Then it's his ball game. Guess who will have to play along?*

On that point, Graham Stuck had fatally misjudged his opponent. The lover-*cum*-murderer was a real sore sport, first killing Stuck, then going on a rampage to find the missing photographs, tape and/or this disk.

In the last entry, Graham finally waxed eloquent, denouncing his former lover:

> *May 27—What a laugh that someone so successful is gullible enough to believe me. If anyone could know me, he should. For a while, I thought we were alike. But he's a fool. When I told him it was the money he was shocked. He thought I cared! That I stayed in this*

twisted relationship for more than I can get out of it.
Should be quite a lot thanks to "god."

Rebecca had seen it coming. What had Paulie said during
the pizza party? *How about a male honey? Some men just
like sex and aren't fussy about the gender.* Stuck would
screw anyone, why would he limit himself to just women?
For one reason, they're more easily intimidated than most
men. More inclined to cave in to betrayal and blackmail
without retaliating. Unlike a powerful, albeit gullible, man.
Successful and gullible. Rebecca could name a few. Like
a rural sheriff who might have wasted years in love with one
of the victims, and was dragging his feet about calling in the
state police on double homicide/arson. Or a city detective
who happened to mosey into town the day all hell broke
loose, harboring mixed emotions over one of the players. Or
Stuck's former business partner, who lost a fortune, rebounded and was attempting to sue him out of existence. Or
a judge, who arrived to console the widow, believing she
was grieving for the two-timing husband that she was poisoning. At a stretch she could make a case against a backwater lawyer who talked a good game, patted you on the back,
but made little progress on your defense. The field was littered with suspects—even after discarding all the women in
the county.

Rebecca bit at a hangnail. The diary didn't prove murder.
It didn't name the murderer. But it sure helped in the motive
department. She needed to keep the disk safe. This morning
she would have taken it to Jo, then gone with him to Zimmer. Until she could eliminate them as suspects, she wasn't
about to risk blowing this case by being naive. If Vera Stuck
had died because of this disk, the least Rebecca could do
was put it in the proper hands. State police tomorrow.

Tonight she'd hand it to the press. She laughed out loud.
Peter Hayes would be delirious. He'd have to wait for the actual disk, but an e-mailed copy would make intriguing bed-

time reading. He'd do the proper thing with the information, of that she was sure. Hayes had no direct involvement in the murders, had no contact with Blue Marsh County or with either victim. To him, the killings were his ticket to a front page byline.

Rebecca sent the file to the printer. She logged on to the Internet and opened up the mail page. She called up the address for Hayes and copied the entire diary entry into the message section. No attachment to get screwed up in the nether regions of the Net. At the top of the file she jotted specifics on where she found the disk and when. She added a brief explanation of what she thought it meant.

Rebecca logged off, slipped the disk into her hip pocket. She left the contents of the diary visible on the screen, the lights on, the hard copy of the file in the top desk drawer—scattering evidence like bread crumbs for Zimmer and crew. She wanted them to know that she'd been in the building and what she'd found.

Time to go.

Rebecca took one last look around, feeling more optimistic than she had in days. It was coming together. With this evidence, the sheriff would have to release Frank. Stuck would never have considered him successful. No one who knew him would call Frank gullible.

The dormant reporter in her hoped she'd get to interview the murderer about how he committed the crimes, and why. This was one story she was willing to come out of retirement to write. She snapped off the light. Had she really promised the byline to Peter? She pushed through the door to the darkened shop. Too bad. He'd just have to share the glor—

A wrench erupted out of the darkness. It missed her upper body, smashing hard against her thighbone. Pain shot upward. Rebecca stumbled. She twirled around the door, tried to fling it shut. She heard a grunt before the door rebounded, the knob smacking her elbow. She grabbed for her wounded arm. Her attacker swung again. Rebecca ducked. The wrench clanged into the metal door, reverberating throughout the shop.

Rebecca pushed off and ran. He was close behind.

With a ragged gait, Rebecca wove her way between benches, dodging car parts. In the dark she had the home-court advantage. She passed the wire wheel, flicked the machine on. The motor grated, a demented toy come to life. She shoved it backward. The wheel and its pedestal toppled into her assailant's path. "Bitch" escaped with a hiss as the man tripped. One for the good guys.

She repeated the procedure with the grinder: snapped it on, pushed it over. She didn't hear her pursuer stumble. Over the noise, she couldn't hear his footfalls but sensed he was there, just feet away. She lunged for the opened fifty-pound bag of glass beads leaning against a center pillar. She tipped it over behind her, spilling beads onto the floor. On the painted concrete, the glass oxide was as slippery as black ice. She thought she heard a thud and a groan, as if a body had collided with something hard. She hoped that meant he was down, and hurt. If she could reach Val's bench, there would be a tool she could use as a weapon. A hammer, spanner, anything to fend off the attacker long enough to escape. If she could slip into the car shop, reach the door opener, someone walking by might—

A hand grabbed Rebecca's hair and yanked, snapping her neck back, wrenching her off balance. Reversing the momentum, he slammed her into the bed of the massive Bridgeport milling machine. She grunted with pain as a rib snapped. Gasping for breath, she twisted to face him, elbows flailing, hands slapping. Strong fingers covered her mouth and nose, cut off her air. She clawed where his face should be. He arched back out of reach, chuckling. His grip tightened on the bones of her face. His body pinned her hard against the metal table, the edge threatening to sever her spine.

Lashing out, she tried to pry his hand from her face. Her elbow hit the work lamp. It snapped on as it toppled, aiming a diffuse beam of light at the ceiling. With her right hand, Rebecca stretched upward, fingers scrabbling to reach the on/off toggle for the machine. Her middle finger connected with the switch and pulled. The mill burst to life, its one-inch-thick cutter spinning at two thousand revolutions per minute. Sharp enough to blast a clean hole through a slab of steel.

The assailant's fingers remained locked into her flesh. Her nails clawed at his hand and arm. He squeezed harder. The cartilage in her nose crunched. She could taste blood. It bubbled in her nostrils, blocking each breath. Her lungs ached. There was no air.

Rebecca stopped fighting. She closed her eyes. Reaching around behind the spinning cutter, she felt for the slick neck of the mill. Bracing her forearm, she shoved. The thrust propelled her body off the far edge of the machine, pulling the murderer with her. Dragging him across the face of the drilling bed and into the spinning cutter.

The fly cutter snagged her assailant's sleeve. Relentlessly it wound the cloth around the shank, reeling in his trapped arm. With mindless efficiency the cutter tore into the bared flesh. Above the cacophony of the motor, like the blast of a noonday whistle, came a scream to wake the dead.

Rebecca was released. She smacked the concrete floor on her back. Lay stunned, gasping. With unexpected fury, her attacker kicked at her ribs. Rebecca screeched in pain. She rolled onto her side.

Screaming like a banshee, he kicked her again, more intent on hurting her than on escaping the cutter. Rebecca felt for the Bridgeport with her foot, made contact and pushed, sliding a few feet on the cold floor. When the next kick came, it missed her. Unbalanced, her assailant fell. Fabric tore. Blood splattered in an arc on the white wall as the cutter whipped around.

The screaming stopped.

Crab-fashion, Rebecca sidled away. Whimpering, a wounded animal, seeking a place to hide or a way out. Pain burned in her ribs; her eyes smarted from blood and sweat. She reached Val's bench, gripped the edge of the worktable and pulled herself up. She bent over the smooth surface, her hand flying, groping for Val's three-bladed upholstery cutter. She knocked the wooden shaft with her fingers. She teased it closer, wrapped her fingers around the handle and spun around, ready for her opponent.

He stood behind her, inches away, mouth pulled back in a death-mask grimace, raised arm dripping blood.

Gripping the cutter, Rebecca lunged for his throat. He swung at the same instant. The wrench connected with her temple. She fell into blackness.

Fifty

Jo returned to the office and wrote up his conversations with Lindeman and Shelley. Then he took his notes and sought refuge at his farm. There he'd removed his jacket and walked to the far edge of the meadow, ripping up a clump of new straw on the way. He sat on a ledge facing his mother's stone marker. He spoke to her, sometimes aloud, as he created four piles of the straw—each strand representing one shred of evidence against the men he considered suspects. He remembered why he hated investigating. He preferred his stories tightly constructed: beginning, middle, end with a moral. All the individual straws held together, no loose ones slipping through his fingers.

When the last vestiges of daylight were replaced by a damp chill, Jo returned to the low stone house, ready to assume the profession for which he'd been educated. Enlisting the help of Edna and a few professional contacts, Jo chipped away like an ice sculptor at the facades of the lead players to reveal the true faces underneath. Character is always key: If you know a man, you know the kind of crimes he can commit.

Jo had narrowed down the list. Despite the arguments he had cited to Rebecca, Jo did not believe Frank Lewes was guilty. Lindeman and or Shelley were more convincing villains. Neither man had an alibi for either death that could not be challenged. Both were ruthless, fueled by egos that were defined by money. Each had a long-standing disagreement with Stuck that could have come to a head recently. Moreover, they knew the back way to Stuck's house from the marina, so could have set the fire and murdered Vera unseen. Their business dealings would have generated any number of damaging bits of evidence worth hiding.

Lindeman, his jovial exterior peeled aside, was a ruthless manipulator. A man who had pulled himself up and wasn't going to be dragged back down. Jo had traced Lindeman's lawyer in Chicago. In cautious phrases, the attorney had verified Lindeman's legal wrangling with Stuck over the expensive race car. In addition to the purchase price and the repair bill, Lindeman had forked over a ten percent finder's fee up front. Even after the car was proven to be a fake, Stuck refused to return the money. Not a vast sum for Lindeman, but the sting of being outwitted by Stuck rankled. The battle was more about saving face than recouping money.

For Shelley, it was all about money, his currency being international contracts. An acquaintance at the State Department uncovered Shelley's name in an investigation into substandard fittings for the pipelines his company was selling to the Russians. There was finger-pointing going on and name-calling in two languages, but nothing that smacked of governmental reprisal, yet. Shelley excelled at playing to win. He was not above cheating. But killing? Jo believed Shelley when he called Stuck a "minor thorn."

Shelley's temperament was more sullen than Lindeman's, less explosive. His game was wait and see. With very little effort Jo could picture Lindeman being pressured by Stuck and pushing back—seek and destroy. Stripping Stuck, leaving his body in the beading machine at Rebecca's, could have been an impromptu attempt to throw the police off the track, the proverbial red herring. But torturing Vera?

Jo poured himself his nightly glass of wine, an Australian Shiraz, appropriately the color of blood. In his mind's eye,

Vera's final moments pulsed with personal intensity. Or with its dramatic opposite—a calculating coldness hard for Jo to fathom. Passion gone rancid brought to mind Brad Zimmer. Jo could make a case for motive; distasteful, but conceivable. What about opportunity? Arlington was only an hour's drive. Zimmer could have left the anniversary celebration Saturday night, driven to Head Tide, killed Stuck, then returned to the Motel 6 where the partygoers were staying. Unnoticed. While investigating the murder scene, Zimmer could have set the bomb to blow up the car. He was in and out of Vera's home questioning her about Graham's death. No one would have found his presence suspicious, or even worth mentioning.

Nor Hagan's. Admittedly, Jo had a selfish reason for wanting Hagan to be guilty. That aside, though, there was a good deal of circumstantial evidence. Hagan had shown up in town at the time of murder. He'd agreed to help Sheriff Zimmer, which gave him access to privileged facts and the ability to slant the evidence. As a cop, he would know how to rig every scene—the fires, ransacking, murder. Though Hagan had no known connection to Graham or Vera, he was tied to Judge Reiske, who was linked to the Stucks.

As was Zimmer. If Lindeman was telling the truth, Hagan was the last person to visit Vera. If he had no motive himself, could he have been working with Zimmer? Hired to do the dirty work for him? Hagan is sent to question the distraught widow, gets too rough, kills her—either accidently or to cover his involvement. Or to obliterate Zimmer's culpability in Graham's. Or both.

Jo closed his eyes and sighed. Mentally he added another straw to the policemen's pile. Then poured a second glass of wine to wash away the taste in his mouth.

Fifty-one

Mosquitoes? Smack. *Where did the mosquitoes come from?*
Smack. *Why are they attacking my face?* Smack. *Go away.*
Rebecca's head rolled with each blow.

"Wake up, Moore. Now."

Smack. She could hear bells ringing in the distance. *Telephone?* She should answer it. Smack. She tried to ward off
the next slap, but her hands wouldn't respond. They were
bound at the wrists with duct tape. She was pinned and wriggling on the floor, held down at the mercy of a man who had
already killed twice. Rebecca blinked her eyes open. He
glowered back. During the chase Rebecca had recognized
his mirthless chortle, the mercilessness of his pursuit. She
was not surprised to face him, just a little sick and a lot
scared.

The Honorable Stewart Thornton Reiske straddled her
bruised body, bony knees squeezing against her sore ribs.
One hand clutched the front of her T-shirt; the other was
poised to strike her again. Her only consolation was noting
that Reiske's left arm sported a tourniquet made from her
flannel shirt. Blood had saturated the fabric. Good, let him
bleed to death. Quickly.

He stood. "Get up."

When she didn't move, he grabbed her bound wrists and

yanked her to her feet. Her leg buckled. She collapsed against him. He clutched a fistful of hair and pulled her face close to his. "I'm in no mood to be crossed. Move." With a shove, Reiske headed her toward the front rooms.

The office looked the way Rebecca felt. Reiske had tossed it and everything he could get his hands on. The desk had been swept clean. Pencils, Rolodex, phone, handbooks, Moe's in basket littered the floor. All drawers were open, some empty. The hard copy of the diary was gone. Remnants of receipts she'd been separating into piles for the IRS littered the floor. *Swine.* Rebecca swung around and kicked at Reiske's shins, missed. He pushed her toward the computer. She landed half on the chair.

"Where's the disk?"

Rebecca studied the Judge, trying to determine how crazy he was. Crazy enough to kill her whether she gave him the disk or not. After the first two deaths, where was the incentive to stop? If he found out she'd sent the file to Peter Hayes, would he go after him, too?

"As I said, Moore, I once admired your journalism. You penned intelligent arguments. Be intelligent now."

"What do you consider intelligent, Judge?"

"Not dying for my secrets. Give me the disk, and I might let you live." The corner of his eye twitched.

She didn't believe him. "You know I've read Stuck's diary. It wasn't hard to figure out that Alonso—'god,' short for *godfather,* presumably—was using Graham to blackmail you into stepping down from his trial. What did he have on you?"

"*What* doesn't matter. Only that he *had* something. Graham actually thought I would acquiesce, that I'd crawl away with my tail between my legs. He deemed it inevitable and sensible because he wanted it. I step down from Alonso's case, my reputation remains pristine. I step down and Graham gets enough money to leave Vera and squander on a lifestyle to which he has grown accustomed, the philistine." The judge coughed up phlegm. He wiped at his mouth with the bloodied shirt, smearing red on his cheek like misplaced war paint. "He underestimated her. Did you know she was poisoning him? She confessed to me. A pinch of arsenic in his nightly Old-Fashioned. She was as fed up with his abuse and his philandering, as he was with her simpering. With a competent attorney they could have worked it out."

Reiske sagged against the edge of the desk, propping the wounded arm against his hip. He needed a rest, or wanted to talk, or both. Fine by Rebecca. The longer she could drag this out, the greater chance that Olson or Boeski would return.

"You and Graham couldn't work things out, though, could you?"

"Entirely different. Once he betrayed me, Graham closed all doors. What he wanted was ascendancy over me, as I once had over him." Reiske winced, drew in a breath. "He was my first client as a trial lawyer. I was a public defender. He was a juvenile caught stealing from a wealthy widow. I got him off, thanks largely to police incompetence. In appreciation, he offered . . . services."

Reiske paused to scrutinize Rebecca. "No raised eyebrow? Too jaded from years of airing dirty laundry to be shocked? I confess, I was. At twenty-six I had no idea I could fancy a man. I'd been too busy studying to date, so I never thought about it. Graham was my first. I was his last. He laughed at me, said he could tell. Graham was always making fatuous statements. He wasn't intuitive. If he had been, he might be alive." Reiske hugged his arm to his body, watching the blood seep. "I tire, Miss Moore. Give me the disk."

"What good is it? Alonso has the evidence, the photographs, right?"

"He won't do anything with them. He's a businessman. He got what he wanted. I stepped down from the case today. Once I formally retire from the bench next week, I'll be of no use to him. Graham was the only one who thought he had long-term leverage."

"What are they? Lewd shots of you two in the throes of sex?"

"The photographs?" The judge shrugged. "I barely glanced at them."

"If they aren't leverage, why step down?"

"Ever the probing journalist, aren't you?" He leaned against the wall. "Because Alonso made certain that I had no choice."

As Reiske told it, Alonso had understood his real vulnerability. In addition to the damning evidence, Alonso had Graham find out the jurist's bank account number. Then Alonso had wired two million dollars into it. The money would be Reiske's free and clear—if he kept quiet. If he caused a problem, the money would be made public and the wire transfer traced to the mob. Everyone who cared would assume it was a bribe.

"What reporter would believe that I had no knowledge of the money, that I did nothing to earn it? Would you have ignored that lead, Moore?"

Rebecca shook her head.

"No. The liaison with Graham impacted my personal life. It would have been unpleasant, but I could have survived. I would not, however, allow his interference to destroy my professional legacy. If people believed I was corrupt enough to accept money from the mob, then the press, and my colleagues, would question every decision I've ever handed down. I would not tolerate it. That is my Achilles' heel."

Rebecca blinked. She was surprised to find that after what she'd gone through last year because of the aborted sting and David's death, she could empathize with the deranged jurist. One's profession and one's ego have an insidious way of entwining and distorting one's perspective.

The phone rang.

Fifty-two

Mick longed for a siren. He'd left Route 4 for 258. The winding two-lane road was pushing the Cherokee's ability to stay upright. The tire tread wasn't the greatest and the sucker was truly top-heavy. Good thing there was little oncoming traffic.

Last night he'd cruised the beltway returning to the District. Halfway back he said to hell with it. He'd get over David's death. Let Rebecca Moore live with what she'd done. Let the sheriff solve his own cases. The sleepy burg could go back to sleep. If he hadn't totally pissed off the captain, Mick still had an important job in the District, friends who understood him and a crime-infested city that felt familiar.

That was last night. Today he knew differently. The deaths of Graham and Vera Stuck hadn't closed the case. Until the murderer found whatever he was looking for, no one connected with it was safe. Now that Mick could name the killer, he was sure he'd never stop. Justice Stewart Thornton Reiske was the personification of thoroughness.

Again Mick punched Moore's home number on the cell phone, fractionally disconcerted to realize that he'd memorized it. After ten rings he gave up. He yanked the SUV across the double lines to pass an overloaded semi he'd been stuck behind for five miles. He'd tried the shop earlier, no luck. And the sheriff—he was at a fire near the county line. Mick left a message with Olson: "Tell Zimmer there wasn't another woman. Ask him what kind of a car Judge Reiske was driving."

Olson jotted down the first part. She responded to the second. "Late-model BMW. Rental. Black, I think." She confirmed that the shop was still off-limits, so Moore should be at home.

Sure thing. When did Moore ever do what was expected of her? Mick dug in the ashtray for a sanitary toothpick. Was he totally sure Reiske was responsible? No way. There were as many gaps in his theory as holes in Swiss cheese. But what he knew, combined with what Peter Hayes had uncovered, was too suspicious to ignore.

At first blush, there had been nothing incriminating in the information Peter Hayes had doled out a sentence at a time between half-chewed mouthfuls of fried squid dripping with cocktail sauce. Calamari might be O'Toole's specialty, but Mick had stayed with liquid refreshment. He sipped a Coors and ogled an underaged cutie in short-shorts as she punched buttons on the music machine. He'd listened to Hayes.

Many would consider Stewart Thornton Reiske's rise from an illegitimate child to superior court justice admirable. He'd been born in 1943 to a would-be dancer, Leslie Thornton, who fled NYC to have her baby upstate. When he was eight, Mom was killed in a car crash. No relatives came forward to claim young Stu. No frustrated, would-be parents itching to adopt the sullen, overly bright boy, so he wound up in foster care near Albany. Presumably, he triumphed over adversity because there was nothing in any official record about him until his senior year of college at SUNY at Albany. He only made it into a footnote then because his foster parents, Gladys and Harold Schiller, died in a house fire.

Mick had stopped playing with his toothpick. He'd had to ask.

"No." Hayes wiped cocktail sauce from his finger. "According to my sources, Reiske was never under suspicion. He was hitchhiking back from school for the Christmas break. Police located the guy who picked him up for the last leg of the trip. The kid arrived home for the holidays to find the house in ashes."

Reiske was left with nothing: no foster family, no house, no souvenirs of his early life. He had been accepted at law school, so the college used part of a slush fund to finance his remaining semester. After graduation, he headed for Columbia University to begin his rise to the top.

"They ever figure out how the fire started?"

Hayes had folded a squid ring into his mouth, chewed, swallowed. "Not really. Best guess, an oil lamp in the kitchen. Neighbors were divided. Half were convinced that the couple had a fight, knocked the lamp over without realizing. Other side of the street claimed the old man finally flipped out and torched the place and them with it. No one wanted to besmirch the dead, *but* they had nothing good to say about Harold Schiller, or the way he treated his family."

"Abuser?"

"Of the wife, definitely. Maybe of Stewart as well. One retired cop swore then—and is still swearing now to anyone who'll listen—that it was murder/suicide. Position of the bodies suggested that the mother was locked inside a closet, pounding to get out. The old man was praying, hands together." Hayes had pushed away the red-smeared plate. "Whatever. They went down as accidental deaths."

Mick had drained his beer. *Accidental death*—another term that didn't set well. Second cousin to a *coincidence*.

Mick gave the phone a rest, tossed it on the passenger's seat. Both hands on the steering wheel, he built the case against the judge out loud, talking to his reflection in the windshield. So, first we have Reiske's foster parents dying in an unexplained house fire, just like Vera Stuck. His stepmother in a closet, dad found in an attitude of prayer—or with his hands tied together like Stuck's. The old man was an abuser. Kid probably flipped. Knocked him unconscious, bound him, locked her in. Set the fire to go off when he was away from the scene. Takes a bus out of town, hitchhikes back. Happens home in time to find the charred ruins, stands around all brokenhearted. Just like at Vera's.

"Next, we have Reiske stepping down from one of the biggest cases of his career. Reiske, uptight prig who's never done anything impulsive in his legal life. Now Alonso will be tried by a less rigid judge, possibly one who's already holding hands with the mob."

Mick shut up as he turned late into the next curve, almost losing the rear end. He corrected the skid, then braked hard to avoid colliding with a rusted camper doddering along at well below the speed limit. Ignoring the double yellow lines, Mick swerved the jeep past the RV. He did not give the driver the finger. Mick should have been concentrating more on his driving, worrying less about the judge.

He returned to his musings. Why would Reiske give up the case? Only if he was being forced, big time. He wasn't the type to fear for his life. Besides, if he was afraid, he could ask for personal protection and get it. He had no family members to be threatened, no one but himself. It had to be blackmail. Which meant there had to be something shady in the judge's life worth killing to keep quiet. Snuffing out his foster parents would do for a start. No statute of limitation on murder.

Mick smiled in the dark and resumed talking to his reflection. "*Okay.* And whom do we suspect is capable of blackmail? Graham Stuck, that's who. The slimy adulterer who took compromising photographs of his lovers and kept them in files labeled 'Insurance.' Not a giant step from there to blackmailing a U.S. justice for fun and profit."

Mick bet the judge's past indiscretions had been filed under 'Life Insurance'."

During his most recent phone call to Sal, Mick had been handed one more piece for the puzzle. Sal had a coincidence he knew Mick would love. He'd wanted to save it until Mick showed up in person. Mick could hear him smiling through the wire. Carole's friend in Albany had refused to unseal the juvie file on Clarence Small, a.k.a. Graham Stuck. Didn't think they had a "legitimate" need. Soft on kids or something. But she was willing to answer one question.

"You owe Carole for this one. Girl knew the question to ask." Sal chuckled.

The hair on Mick's neck tingled. "What?"

"She asked if the name Stewart T. Reiske showed up in the file."

"And?"

"The noble judge's name was there, all right. Outside, on the line. He defended Small/Stuck when he was a minor. Court-appointed lawyer. Those two go way back."

Mick's smile grew broader as he moved on to the matter of opportunity—all those lovely coincidences. Like the bottle bomb going off at the boatyard and distracting the security guard, making it possible for Reiske to slip out unnoticed and tail Stuck home, then on to Head Tide. And the black BMW that was parked in front of the drugstore Tuesday afternoon and again Wednesday evening. Mick had assumed it belonged to the guy who owned the Rite Aid, given the cost of prescription drugs these days. Olson said the owner drove a minivan with a metal stick-on sign advertising condoms for safe sex. So, it looked like the Bimmer was Reiske's rental. Which meant he was hanging around the shop before the Stuck's station wagon was rigged to explode. And again the next evening when Moore's house was ransacked. The BMW was never seen at Vera's, which could be explained. According to the valet, Reiske drove Vera home in her Jag the first night he was in town. He must have returned the car to her later, then walked back to the Marina. Easy stroll, like Moore said.

Mick reached for the cell phone and tried Moore's number again. He jammed the phone against his shoulder so he could drive with both hands. Muttering to himself, he willed the phone to be answered. His neck was cramping just as he heard a soft voice say, "Hello." Mick spit out the toothpick.

"Moore? That you?"

"No, is Juanita. Who is this, please?"

"Where's Moore? I have to speak with her."

There was static on the line, but Mick was sure he heard the girl correctly: Moore had left the house several hours ago. She'd gone to the shop.

Then why wasn't she answering? He punched in the number for Vintage & Classics. Nothing but dead air. What did he expect? After a third try with no response, Mick dialed the number listed on the reverse of Moore's business card. Mick did not want to speak with Jo Delacroix, Esquire. However, it was just possible that Moore was with him, safe, drinking white wine, listening to Mozart and brainstorming about the case. Or whatever.

He got the office recording. *Shit*. Didn't anyone work twelve-hour days? The secretary's taped voice gave him a number to call in case of an emergency. Mick spotted a wide patch at the side of the road and slowed the Cherokee. He pulled off, rolled down the window as the semi lumbered past. Breathing in gulps of night air laced with diesel fumes, he redialed Delacroix's office to retrieve the emergency number.

When it rang, Delacroix answered like he was waiting by the phone. Mick expelled a breath. First person he'd reached all day. Last person he wanted to ask for help.

"Delacroix, is Moore with you?"

"Who is this? Hagan? Is that you?"

"Yes. Answer my question."

"Why should I? Why are you pestering me? Brad said you'd returned to DC."

"Save the questions for the courtroom, lawyer. Moore is in deep and serious trouble. Or she's going to be. She's not at the house. Girl said she'd gone to the shop. No one's answering there. Is she with you?" The last four words were spaced, as if he were talking to the village idiot.

Delacroix's denial was too quick to be a lie.

"You got any ideas where she could be? I'm still forty minutes away."

"You know who the murderer is?" The attorney was leapfrogging to conclusions. Reluctantly, it occurred to Mick that Delacroix was probably a damn bright lawyer.

"Got a real good guess. He isn't going to quit until all the loose ends are tied tight." Mick could hear the jangle of keys as Delacroix rummaged for them.

"I'll meet you at the shop. I'm at my farm, I can be there in twenty minutes." Delacroix hung up.

Curious. The lawyer didn't ask who Mick suspected.

Fifty-three

The phone rang again.

In unison, Rebecca and Reiske turned toward it. Neither moved. Twelve rings. Not a casual customer or a telemarketer. Rebecca prayed the caller was anxious enough to come to the shop on the run.

Reiske must have had the same thought. He rose and crossed to a duffel bag lying near the wall. He dropped the wrench inside. From a side pocket he pulled out a gun. It looked real. He looked comfortable with it. He pointed it at Rebecca.

"The disk."

From hammer, to wrench, to gun—the judge was versatile with weapons. Too many years on the bench hearing about proven methods for dispensing with one's enemies. The gun was an ominous sign. Reiske's demeanor changed as he clutched it. Patience was gone. He wanted to conclude his business quickly.

She had to keep him talking.

"You've given up the bench, you're not concerned about your private life, why worry about the disk?"

"Loose ends annoy me, Moore."

"You tortured, then killed Vera to tie up a loose end?"

"You find that extreme? Vera was surprisingly stubborn."

He wound the soaked shirt tighter around his arm. "I'm a tad disappointed that she made me kill her, though. I fantasized about defending Vera for her husband's murder. It would have been amusing to get back in front of a jury, one last time. Leak just enough 'facts' so they would see her guilt in stark black and white, like a forties film."

Reiske chuckled. He stared off into the distance, watching the projector roll. "It's midnight. Delicate Vera Stuck wakes suddenly. She thinks she's alone in the house, until she hears someone moving about. She's nervous. Tying her robe, she creeps downstairs. She spies her husband, which is curious, since he's not supposed to be home. Vera starts to call out, then watches as he turns and leaves again almost immediately. On impulse, she decides to follow him, most likely out of jealousy. She's fed up with his womanizing. She hastily buttons a trench coat over her night clothes, grabs her keys and runs to the car.

"Graham drives to Vintage & Classics, a rival business run by a sultry ex-reporter. Parks around in back of the darkened shop. Vera follows. Leaves the Jaguar just off the verge of the road. She watches him take out a key, unlock the door and go in. She hesitates a fraction of a moment, then steels herself. She's come this far, she must know the truth. Music swells. Vera bursts into the shop expecting to catch her husband in *flagrante delicto*. Instead, he's alone, searching through an old car. Graham is furious, incensed that she followed him. They argue. He grabs her. No, he slaps her. She lashes out at him in response. He strikes her again. She totters backwards, falls against a workbench. Fumbles, feeling behind her for some kind of weapon. Her hand connects with the hammer. Without hesitation she strikes Graham a fatal blow. Fade to black."

Reiske grimaced. "It could have happened that way. Hypothetically. I'd plead self-defense, diminished capacity. Of course, I would have to lose the case in the end, which was not appealing. So, Vera and I had a little chat. Once death seemed preferable, she told me that you had the disk, the missing piece." With a stride he closed the distance between them. "You should be flattered, she actually thought you could help her. That you would make me pay for murdering Graham. Even I fretted that you'd spoil my plans too soon. Seems neither Vera nor I realized that you've lost your edge."

Reiske brought the gun alongside Rebecca's face. Lightly, he rubbed the barrel up her cheek, resting the tip in her hair. She shivered from the touch on her scalp. He whispered in her ear.

"I'm about to realize my earliest fantasy. I can't bear the thought of a nosy reporter hounding me into paradise like one of the furies. If you don't give me the disk, I'll assume that someone close to you has it. I will keep searching. How many people are you willing to sacrifice to your bravado?"

Unbidden, the list flitted through Rebecca's mind: Juanita, Frank, Val, Paulie, Jo, Hagan, Peter. There was no reason to think that Reiske wouldn't keep hunting and killing. His quest wasn't logical; it was an obsession.

Bracing her bound hands on the desk, Rebecca stood. The gun moved with her. Every part of her body and spirit ached. She moistened her lips.

"I'll give you the disk. Promise not to torch the building." She hated to beg, but it seemed imperative she leave something behind for the guys. Walt's legacy was all she had.

"Agreed. I don't have time to set it up."

Rebecca nodded. "In my right hip pocket."

Reiske pressed the gun to her temple as he insinuated fingers into the pocket and extracted the disk. He showed no emotion as he tossed the floppy into the opened duffel bag. He clutched the back of her neck. In a dancers' embrace they moved together, first to pick up the bag, then into the machine shop. Blood from his arm oozed through her shirt— warm and cloying.

"You know, Becca, in a perverse way, Graham did me a favor. I've tired of adjudicating. His meddling caused me to give it up. But more than that, for the first time in my adult life I had to act impulsively—kill him, then destroy everything he touched. I'd forgotten the thrill of lashing out blindly without premeditation, without thought of consequences, Zeus-like. With Alonso's two-million-dollar contribution I shall sail to Greece. Take up residence in the islands. Read the classics. Write some poetry. Sounds idyllic, doesn't it?"

He had maneuvered her across the machine shop to the driver's side of the Bentley. "Get in."

"It doesn't run."

Reiske regarded the car: buttoned up, waxed, smelling of leather polish. "I don't believe you. Get in." He yanked at the driver's-side door and shoved her in. He snatched a roll of duct tape from the bench, used it to lash her left hand loosely to the steering wheel. With a utility knife he cut the bonds between her hands. Released, her right hand fell into her lap, numb.

"Put it on the wheel."

"You expect me to drive or just sit here?" She didn't care if she angered Reiske. She'd be dead soon anyway. She nodded at the long shift lever snug against the right-hand door. "I have to shift, don't I?"

Without comment, Reiske used more duct tape to lash her right wrist to the shift. He cut another length of tape, holding it in his teeth while he unwrapped her blood-soaked shirt from his arm and dropped it to the floor. From the duffel bag he produced an opened bottle of cognac. Muttering, "Waste," he braced the bottle under his arm and extricated the cork stopper one-handed. He sloshed the alcohol onto the wound and hissed in anguish as the liquid burned the shredded, raw skin. Using duct tape he sealed up the wound, then took a healthy slug of the brandy for himself.

"Medicinal, wouldn't you say? Though it was intended to be celebratory. Until Graham told me about the money. I'm afraid I was rude. I cut our weekend short and threw him out."

He tossed his duffel into the back seat and added the bottle to it, wedging it upright. From the far wall he retrieved two new red plastic gas cans, hoisting them to gauge their contents. Heavy. Paulie must have filled them in case they needed to put more test miles on the cars. Reiske stored the cans behind the front seats.

He pulled apart the double fire doors between the shops. He walked to the back window, then checked a front one. Satisfied, he hit the door opener mounted on the wall. The motor whirred, raising the garage door to admit crisp air. Dusk had deepened to dark. The photoelectric security lights glowed yellow in the parking area. Rebecca could hear a pickup's subwoofers throbbing with country-western as it turned down Ryder's Mill—best parking spot in town. Nothing else. No pedestrians out for a stroll. Not a patrol car in sight.

Reiske snatched the garage door remote from its holder. He returned to the Bentley and got in. He dredged a windbreaker from the duffel and eased it on over his wound. Shifting sideways, he laid his arm along the back of the seat behind her shoulders, like a lover. Lower down he planted the gun in her gut.

"Start the car, Becca. Drive out slowly. At the street, turn right."

Rebecca depressed the clutch. One-handed she moved the shift lever into neutral. With her thumb, she adjusted the throttle control and ignition levers on the center steering hub.

"Did you set the fire to lure the police away?"

Reiske frowned, then lightened. He almost smiled. "Fire's a hobby of mine. A passion, really. So many uses. To alchemists, it was one of the four basic elements. Throughout history it's been lauded: as a weapon—think Greek fire; as a rite of purification—funeral pyres, for example. My favorite use is to cleanse, the way spontaneous forest fires make room for new growth. It's also handy as a diversion." He squeezed her neck. "Stop stalling. There'll be no eleventh-hour rescue."

Rebecca adjusted the carburetor control. "You'll have to

press the starter button. The large one in the center of the dash."

As he did so, the 3-Litre roared to life. First push. Rebecca was inappropriately pleased. The car was indeed good to go, as Val had proclaimed. She was proud of the guys' dedication. They had finished the car on time, though Todd Shelley would probably never enjoy the fruits of their labor. She doubted Reiske would spare the Bentley. Rebecca could feel a traffic accident coming. A blazing one.

Reiske prodded her with the gun. "Becca, think of your friends. Do this my way, you will be my final act of cleansing. My retribution will be complete." He looked calm, a hint of a grin twitching at one corner of his mouth. Only his cold blue eyes revealed how demented he was.

Rebecca slipped the shift into first, gave it gas. The Bentley roared through the open door.

Fifty-four

Jo eased the Saab onto the bridle path midway between V&C and Rebecca's home on the knoll. There were lights in the kitchen. He fancied he could hear music. If it were a week earlier, Rebecca and Juanita would be fixing dinner, talking about their days at school, the diner, the shop. How could such innocence have been destroyed so inexplicably by happenstance? Vengeance Jo understood. But this seemed so arbitrary. If the Bentley had not been brought to the shop, all of this horror might have bypassed Rebecca and her friends.

Jo exited the car. He walked silently into the grove of trees, waited to let his eyes adjust to the night. The leaves danced on an unfelt breeze. One tickled his neck. Jo started, then batted it away.

A faint glow came from inside the machine shop. Lights were on in the front office. Was it possible that everything was fine? Could Rebecca be in there working on the car, or on her taxes, or feeding the cat? Hagan might have misdialed the number. Or perhaps she didn't hear the phone over the drone of machinery. It was possible. Jo could walk in and find Rebecca frazzled but alive, wryly amused at his concern. He turned up the collar of his coat and headed toward the building. He didn't believe in his fantasy for a minute. He wished he believed in guns and had one with him.

No one answered the bell. The front door was locked. Jo circled around back. The rear door was not locked, though it should have been. He entered, crossed to the machine shop and paused at the open fire doors. The Bentley was gone. Surely that was a good sign? Rebecca had finished the car and snuck out for a test drive. After dark? Unlikely, but Brad's interference might have compelled her to do it. *What a Pollyanna I am.* But he prayed he'd have a happy ending to assign to Stella. She harbored too many sad stories. He hoped that one day the storytelling doll would amuse others with the saga of the mad judge and his murderous rampage. For Jo had no doubt that Stewart Thornton Reiske had murdered Graham and Vera Stuck, as he had his foster parents when he was just twenty. The pattern was established in his youth, held in check until he was pushed too far.

Minutes before Hagan's phone call, Jo had hung up from speaking with a college roommate who worked in the hall of records in Albany. Donald had been the first person Jo called, the last to respond with pertinent information.

To divert himself away from dwelling on Brad Zimmer's possible guilt, Jo had begun another imaginery pile of straw, this one for Judge Reiske. The judge had not been seen in town the night Graham died, though that didn't prove he hadn't been there. According to Edna, the jurist owned a Volvo station wagon, yet he rented a car for the trip down to console Vera. Why? Was he afraid his car had been noticed in town on Saturday? Could the station wagon Rebecca saw parked on the street with its hood raised have been a Volvo? She hadn't said.

Reiske had been at Vera's most of the day she died. Helping with papers; looking over things in the garage. He admitted discussing work schedules with Billy Lee, assuring the worker that he would be paid until Vera disposed of the business. Since he'd walked over from the marina, not driven, who could say when Reiske left? He could have been in the garage while Lindeman and Hagan called.

And motive? Reiske had known Graham for a number of years. It was plausible that Graham had stolen something from the judge, or was threatening him. How in character it would be for the judge to simply destroy that which offended him?

Jo had slipped off his glasses and rubbed his eyes. He could only imagine what it must be like to have absolute power when it came to meting out punishment. Such a damning indulgence. What would that kind of power do to a person's sense of self-worth after thirty years? Would it make him capable of committing murder? Of torture and destruction? As Jo knew from Stella and the other dolls, stories begin internally. Each of us carries within us the seeds for our own fate. Life determines which seeds we sow. And nurture.

Then Donald had called. And the straws mounted.

Mick's Jeep clipped the curb and screeched to a stop in front of V&C. He was out of the door before the vehicle settled. Mick lunged for the front door. The knob hit him on the hand. Joachim Delacroix was moving out. The lawyer carried a plaid shirt drenched with blood.

"No one's here. Most of the machinery is running. The computer is on. The office has been tossed. The Bentley is gone. As is the cat. And her shirt is dripping blood." He strode to the Cherokee, hopped in, dropped the shirt at his feet.

Mick climbed back into the driver's seat. "Cat's at the house."

"That's something."

As Mick turned the key, Delacroix spewed out directions. "Go right. Then take Route 2 south till it intersects 422, then go east on, I think he said Dead Eagle Road. Never heard of it."

"You know where she is?" Mick slammed the SUV into reverse.

"I hope so." Jo grabbed hold of the door grip as Mick peeled out.

Jo had come out of his reverie when the noise of the running machines finally penetrated. He took in the knocked-over tools, the bloodied shirt on the floor, the arc of sprayed blood sweeping the wall behind the mill. His heart sank. He'd quickly searched the rest of the building, then picked up the phone. He had called the sheriff's office. Sandra Olson answered. Jo described what he'd found at V&C. Told Olson to contact Zimmer. "Then I demanded to speak with Frank Lewes. My tone apparently convinced Olson to hand the receiver to the prisoner."

Mick glimpsed the signpost for Dead Eagle Road a fraction late. Tires squealed. The Jeep lurched to the left but stayed upright through the turn.

"What does Lewes have to do with Moore's disappearance?"

"Will you agree that the good judge enjoys constructing the scenes of his crimes? He favors motifs involving fire, preferably accidental. He made a barbecue out of Graham's car. Vera's death would have looked like an accidental house fire, but for the rain. And there was an earlier recorded incident as well."

"Death of his foster parents? You heard about that?"

"One of my college roommates lives in Slingerlands, west of Albany. He remembered the case because there was so much local gossip about the parents and their bizarre end. Watch it." Waddling quickly, a possum disappeared into the underbrush at the road's edge.

Delacroix continued. "Given Reiske's propensity for flaming theatrics, what's more logical than crashing while road-testing a high-performance car? The car conveniently bursts into flames, obliterating the driver and all evidence."

"Pretty flimsy reasoning, Delacroix."

"Do you have a more substantial suggestion?"

Mick snorted.

What the lawyer had asked for and gotten from Frank Lewes were local driving routes with winding roads and preferably a precipice. Lewes's best guess was Dead Eagle—it had both. It was also flanked by the Salmons Wild Life Preserve, so the road was nearly deserted. And for a short stretch, the coastline had eroded away. Tricky to drive in the dark. "In short, the judge couldn't have designed a better road for a fatal crash."

Mick braked hard, flying around a curve. "I hope your theory's right. We won't get a second chance to find them in time."

"With your driving, we may not have a first."

Fifty-five

Reiske jabbed Rebecca in the ribs. He pointed to a sandy pull-off on the bend ahead. She slowed, double-clutched to downshift. She eased the car off to the side and let it idle at the edge of the cliff, its headlamps shooting yellow beams into the low mist rising off the water.

The exhilaration of speed combined with the night wind had cleared Rebecca's head. Though each breath was painful and she was stiff and chilled, she felt calm. The Bentley had run like a Thoroughbred, drifting through uphill S-curves—tires squealing, engine roaring, power to spare. The car's vitality was so strong Rebecca rejected the easy way out at the forty-five-degree bend. Driving head on into a sturdy trunk was too iffy a route to suicide, too much like giving up. Besides, she couldn't do that to the car. Destroying the Bentley would be an inexcusable waste.

A fat moon balanced at the edge of the water. A screech owl complained from the top of a wind-crippled pine. On the far point she could see lights from the fishing community of Denton's Cove. Closer, running down the bank to a rocky beach, tenacious daylilies poked up through the loose dirt. Their fronds rustled, toyed with by a breeze from the water. In a few weeks they would cover the hillside with orange blooms. Rebecca adjusted the controls to smooth out the engine. Small consolation, but this was a truly scenic place to die. She'd thought about death often following David's suicide. Some days it seemed a welcomed alternative to going on. But in her fantasies, ending her life had been her decision, not the whim of a demented jurist with an urge to tidy up.

Reiske rummaged in his bag. He retrieved a heavy industrial flashlight. Standing, he played the light out in front of the long bonnet and over the surface of the water below—searching or signaling. He replaced the light in the duffel, hoisting it out onto the dirt. Then he climbed stiffly from the car and walked to Rebecca's side.

Blood from the wounded arm had seeped around the duct tape, a dark stain soaking the thin fabric of his jacket. Reiske didn't seem to notice. He shifted the gun to his weak hand and pulled out the utility knife. He slashed at the tape holding Rebecca's right hand to the shift, nicking the inside of her wrist. Any deeper and the suspense would have been over.

Reiske stepped back. With every movement he splatted blood. "Unwrap your other hand. Quickly. Then out."

Rebecca was glad to comply. With her hands free she'd have some sort of chance. For what, she didn't know. He had the gun. Her cracked ribs and bruised thigh made running futile. Diving over the bank and rolling over toward the water might be her only chance. A slim one, which assumed that the judge was a lousy shot. Reiske waved the gun in her face to get her moving. "Leave the car running, lights on."

Rebecca climbed down from the 3-Litre. She tested her leg for strength. It buckled. Standing by the running board, Rebecca hugged the side of the car and sifted through the loose ends to come up with a question that might distract Reiske, buy her some time. She kept coming back to one thing that had bothered her from the beginning. "Why did you stuff Graham into the glass beader?"

Reiske jerked upright, startled, as if he had forgotten all about that. "Can't quit, can you?" He laughed with genuine mirth. "I'd planned to burn him in his car until I heard noises from the front office. That was you? I imagined it was."

He inclined his head in a courtly bow. "The glass beader was a gesture of love." Having uttered that, Reiske laughed again and ended up choking. He wiped at the spittle with the back of his gun hand, then retrained it on Rebecca.

"Not convinced, I see? Neither was I. But that's what my foster father swore each time he locked me in the basement cupboard. 'I only do this because I love you, boy. You got to learn respect. Learn not to lie.' Words to that effect. I don't think I ever believed Harold. Perhaps if he'd been my real father?"

Reiske let the gun sag downward. "From the first, he forced me to strip. Ostensibly to better feel the punishment he would inflict. And the cold. I got used to the confinement, used to the whippings—people do adapt—but I never got used to the cold. Nor, I expect, to the degradation of being bound naked. Harold began binding my hands the first time he suspected I was capable of an erection. Didn't want me playing with my privates." Reiske's breath was rasping as he lingered in the past, stewing in a goulash of unpleasant memories.

Slowly Rebecca turned to face him, braced her back against the Bentley, gauging the distance between them, considering making a break. As if sensing her decision, the judge lurched closer, pinned her shoulder against the car. She could smell his sour breath. He hissed. "Picked at scabs as a child, didn't you?" Reiske snapped the gun upward into the flesh under her chin. Rebecca flinched.

Instead of squeezing the trigger, Reiske focused on the gun as if it were a pesky fly. He sighed, lowered the weapon along his leg. "I shouldn't blame you; it was Graham's betrayal that reignited those odious memories. For forty years I've kept them buried in the backyard of my soul. That's really why I bound his hands with his necktie. The same way I did Harold's. I wish Graham had been alive to appreciate that touch. He knew all about Harold." Reiske winked at her like a fellow conspirator. "Enough reminiscing. I have a yacht to meet."

The judge backed away from Rebecca and the car. "Lift out the gas cans. Place them on the ground. Good girl. Beginning at the front, douse the car with the gasoline. Use both cans; saturate the seats. I want the bonfire to light up the coast when the car strikes the rocks. It will signal Swen. Think of this as your funeral pyre, Becca, your suttee. Make it worthy."

Rebecca blinked away the moisture pooling in her eyes. She was out of questions, out of ideas, nearly out of strength. Reiske waved the gun at her to get moving.

She bent forward and unscrewed the cap on the first can. She hoisted it to rest on her knee. The heavy can was awkward in her grip, her right hand numb from the tape. The can slipped back to the ground, sloshing fuel on her foot.

"Stop fumbling. Hurry."

Rebecca lifted the gas can again. The Bentley looked posed, its sleek lines silhouetted against the rising moon. Less than a week ago she'd thought this car's arrival was the sign of good fortune. Instead it had been a Trojan horse containing furies that would end lives, bring down her company and cause its own destruction. She wondered if the analogy had occurred to Reiske, lover of Greek history. It was almost funny, if it weren't so tragic. *Damn it.* It would be a tragedy to destroy the 3-Litre. For nearly seventy years it had raced around tracks and over highways, quickening the pulses of driver and spectators alike. Now that it was restored and primed for new adventures, some dysfunctional pyromaniac wanted to torch it for his own amusement. Her own death seemed more comprehensible.

Screw him. She would not be a party to it. Reiske would have to destroy the Bentley without her help.

Giving rein to her anger, Rebecca lifted the gas can with both hands and whipped it away from the car, toward the judge. Gasoline erupted from the opened container and flew at Reiske.

The first stream fell short.

The second burst splashed on his arm.

The third soaked his chest. Reiske raised the gun.

The fourth sprayed into his eyes. He yipped in pain, wiped at his face.

Rebecca hobbled closer to splash him again. Reiske pointed the gun and fired.

The bullet slammed into her left shoulder. She stumbled from the impact, toppled backward, losing her grip on the canister at the height of its arc. Momentum completed the trajectory for her, carrying the can straight toward the half-blind judge. Reiske sensed the object flying at him. Squinting, he fired at the shape. Then fired again. The bullets missed the airborne gas can. It didn't matter.

As the gun detonated, the sparks ignited the gas vaporized on Reiske's clothes. With a whoosh, the fumes burst into flames. Fire raced up his gun arm, melting the nylon jacket in its wake. It licked at his neck, chin, lips, ears, eyebrows. A high-pitched wail escaped as his hair caught. Reiske dropped the gun. He batted at the fire with both his hands, smothering the flames on his head with his arms. He tore at the smoldering jacket, ripping it from his body. He flung the shreds to the ground, where they landed in a puddle. Added a hot wick to the fuel. Flames erupted once more. Leaping streaks of fire attacked his feet and ignited the legs of his trousers.

Rebecca scrambled backward. She stumbled to her feet and ran toward the car. She hoisted the second gas can from it and heaved it over the cliff, away from the heat. Running back to the Bentley, she reached in and shut the car down. From the rear seat she unsnapped the leather tonneau, fumbling as she ripped the closures apart.

Circling around the spilled gasoline, Rebecca approached Reiske from behind. She slapped at his body with the tonneau covering, trying to smother the flames while urging him farther from the oozing fuel and the five-gallon can, farther away from the car. She beat at Reiske, first from one side, then the other. As fast as one flame died down, another erupted. She could feel the heat blistering her hands and forehead. Hear his keening over the sizzle. Smell the charred flesh. Tears streamed down her face: tears caused by the smoke, by her fear, by the frustration of it all.

Reiske fought off the tonneau. He staggered, then twirled around, holding his body impossibly straight, hands clenched into fists. His clothing was nearly gone, a few charred strips fused and hanging from his flesh. The bones of his rib cage were blackened where the skin had dissolved. Already half of his face resembled a skull. He stopped keening.

Slowly, Reiske raised his arms high in a victory salute.

Rebecca sank to her knees, hands covering her mouth, eyes locked on his face. Compelled by the horror, she watched the Honorable Stewart Thornton Reiske embrace the fire that was consuming him. At the final moment, Rebecca would have sworn he was smiling.

Fifty-six

Mick smelled the smoke before he navigated around the bend. He spotted the Bentley at the edge of the road. The Cherokee fishtailed on loose gravel as he slammed to a stop just beyond the vintage car. Grabbing Delacroix's shoulder, he pressed his cell phone into the lawyer's hands. He ordered him to call Zimmer, request a fire truck and ambulance. And for God's sake stay in the car.

Mick rummaged in the glove box for a flashlight. He checked his gun. Keeping low, he broke from the cover of the Jeep and ran toward the Bentley. It was poised on a cliff, one tire inching off the crumbling edge. It looked intact. He flashed the light over the interior. No bodies. He fingered a wet spot on the seat, sniffed—blood, but not a lot.

Nearby, a gas can lay on its side. Someone had kicked dirt over it. Someone had also scuffed up the ground around the pull-off, as if building a dike of earth, a fire break, to protect the racer. Blots of gasoline oozed to the surface through the dirt. There was no longer any fire. Just the smell of gas fumes. And burned flesh.

Mick sidled away from the Bentley. Clouds drifted in front of the moon, obscuring the misty light. He used the flashlight's narrow beam to inch his way around the perimeter of the parking area. A group of boulders loomed at the opposite edge. And something else. Formless, dark and out of place. Bigger than the bags of trash left by picnickers.

Mick quickened his pace. Cutting diagonally across the open, he stubbed his toe on a revolver lying on the ground. It spun feebly, then came to a rest, pointing at the mound of trash like the marker on a Ouija board. Mick bent down to smell the gun. It had been fired. He left it in the dirt.

When he reached the dark mound, he squatted in front of it. The stench told him what was under the covering. He stifled a cough, tried to even his breathing. Tried to think positive thoughts, willing the bundle not to be Moore.

Delacroix rustled up behind him. Mick didn't look up. "I told you to stay in the car. You're contaminating the crime scene."

The lawyer stopped a foot away. "I have to know," he said quietly. "Is it Rebecca?"

That was the very question preventing Mick from lifting the leather covering. Mick wanted to believe that if the Bentley was intact, then so was Moore. She was tough and resourceful. Somehow she had—

Mick shook his head. He was cold, tired and suddenly very afraid of what was underneath.

"We have to know, Hagan. Shall I do it?"

Goaded by the lawyer, Mick had no choice. He positioned his back to block Delacroix's view. He set down his flashlight, holstered his gun. Taking a deep breath, Mick lifted one end of the covering.

After a frantic search, Mick spotted Rebecca floating a few yards out to sea. A speck of flotsam in the black. Stumbling down the bank toward the cove, he tried not to think about the gun he'd found; about how much blood she might have lost; how close she might have been to the fire. Moonlight shone on her pale face, on her shoulders clad in a clinging T-shirt. The rest of her body was dark like the water, like the night. Rising and falling with the waves—otherwise motionless.

He dropped the flashlight on the sand, stripped off his

jacket, hopped out of his shoes and sprinted to the water's edge. Cold waves slapped at his thighs as he scrambled through the phosphorescent surf to reach her. He had one hand on her shoulder when she gasped and sank.

Moore resurfaced, spewing water. She shook her head repeatedly, but no words came out. Eyes wide and unblinking, she shivered without end.

Mick gathered her to him and pressed his lips to her damp, blistered forehead. When he touched her ribs, she moaned. He slid an arm behind her back, under her knees, and lifted her gently to his chest. Together they emerged from the sea streaming water, as Delacroix scrambled down the embankment and stumbled toward them through the sand.

From the distance came the wail of sirens.

Saturday

Bound for Paris

Fifty-seven

Against the advice of her doctor, lawyer, co-workers and the curious who came to visit, Rebecca talked her way out of the hospital after a stay of fewer than fourteen hours. Hagan didn't waste his breath arguing, which showed he might be smarter than she gave him credit for. She had a concussion, a deviated septum, a bullet hole in her left shoulder, two broken ribs, a bruised femur, second-degree burns on her hands, foot and ankle and a slashed right wrist. And the left side of her hair had been seared off, so she'd have to get a haircut. She would heal, physically.

After that, she would do something about the nightmares—clammy dreams of drowning, triggered by floating in the cove after the judge incinerated. She'd raced blindly for the water, hoping that its coolness would soothe her scorched skin. Not suspecting that the ripples would inflame the irrational panic that had plagued her since childhood.

It was Saturday. Intercity Lines' transporter was arriving at three P.M. to pick up both the Hisso and the Bentley. No way she was missing that. Frank and Val were swiping at imaginary dust motes on the cars glistening in the afternoon sun. Only things brighter than the Hisso's chrome bumper were the faces of the owners. Todd Shelley and Hal Linde-man were grinning like the fools she suspected they were.

Todd was particularly pleased. Twice he made Rebecca recount the story of the Bentley's near miss: Reiske's con-fession, the wild ride, the cliff, the sloshed gasoline, the gunshots, the death by burning of a superior court judge. He nudged Hal and pointed with glee at the bloodstains on the seat. He refused to let Val clean the leather. Todd wasn't planning to buy a drink the entire trek. Rebecca wondered how many times he would tell the tale, how distorted it would become by the time they reached Beijing.

Todd wiggled closer. "You don't have any pressing plans for the next few months, do you?"

"Don't even think it, Shelley. If the cars break down in Ankara, you two are on your own."

Hal hugged her gently around the shoulders. "But Re-becca, darling, you know you love to travel. It would be an adventure. Think of the tales you could write. Velvet nights around the campfire in the desert. Haggling in the open mar-ketplace for exotic treasures."

Frank snorted. "Mending linkages with safety pins. Hoof-ing sixty miles for a gallon of watered-down tractor gas. Some adventure. No, sir, Mr. Lindeman, Reb's got a busi-ness needs running right here."

Yes, she did. And the means to run it, for a while.

Folded into her back pocket was a handsome check from Todd Shelley. As promised, he'd added a hefty bonus in ap-preciation for the "speedy work under difficult circum-stances." Nice understatement. She planned to split the tip between Frank and Val. She was still touched that they'd snuck into the shop to finish the car.

She'd made Hal have his payment transferred electroni-cally, even if it was a Saturday. He grumbled, but placed the necessary calls on his cell phone. Frank and Paulie had walked to the bank and leaned against the wall next to the drive-through window waiting for confirmation of the de-posit. It wasn't that Rebecca didn't trust Hal. But after she read Peter's final e-mail on Hal's finances, she wasn't convinced he was good for it, even if he won the Paris-to-Peking rally.

She had hoped the money would buy her some breathing space, time to regroup and get back on her feet, literally. Didn't look like it. Two owners with cars in Graham's shop had called about having them moved over to V&C once the police and the insurance company finished poking through the fire scene. Frank was working out the schedule. Jo was spending more time at the shop than his law office, handling the contracts—something new for the shop—and pacifying her accountant. Rebecca experienced only minor twinges fretting over what he might be committing her to do. She had her own commitments to worry about. For starters, she hadn't told the guys, or Moe, that a new employee would begin work soon.

During her stay in the hospital, Billy Lee had wheeled his oxygen down the hall and into her room. He was weak and weepy and feeling real bad about everything. When she asked him about his plans with both Graham and Vera gone, he hung his head and sniffed. "I should have gone to work with Walt."

"Why didn't you? I know he offered."

"I was a bigot. I told Walt he was a dithering old fool to hire criminals to work on expensive cars. Kill his business. Probably get himself killed as well. Took me years to see what Walt knew back then. You got to judge the whole man, not his mistakes."

"So you went to work for Stuck. Was it better?"

Billy straightened. "He was a worse bigot than me. Worse criminal than the cons. Once Graham set up shop, Walt started missing tools. Nothing common—no Craftsman wrenches. Some of them single-purpose, Brit tools. Your uncle asked me about it. Casual. Didn't accuse me, mind you, but I saw red. Never spoke to Walt again." Billy Lee sank down on the edge of her bed.

"Walt never said a bad word about you, Billy. I know he missed your friendship."

"Later I figured out he was really asking me if Stuck took them. Should of gone to Walt when I saw Graham using the hinged "C" spanner on an Alfa, damn near bent it. Smug when he owned up to taking it. Had been helping himself to tools at night. Who knows what else. Sneaky bastard."

Rebecca covered Billy's arthritic knuckles with her bandaged hand. "It's not too late to make amends. Walt's shop is still around. Looks like we'll have enough work to hire another mechanic."

Billy Lee regarded her for a long minute. "You offering me a job?"

"Maybe. You'd have to work with prior offenders. Think you could handle that?"

The mechanic's head bobbed. "I seen the way Frank Lewes twists a wrench. Be proud to work alongside him."

"Good. Bring your tools. I'm keeping that dog of yours until you show up.

"In that case, boss, see you Monday."

As the white transporter with its blue stripe pulled up in front of V&C, Frank strolled over to greet the driver and sign the papers. Juanita passed around a tray with stuffed mushrooms, duck pâté and mini burritos. Paulie handed out champagne. Rebecca sighed. Hagan slipped an arm around her waist and pressed a plastic flute into her hand. Just as quickly, Jo removed it. He mumbled about mixing liquor with pain medications, then pointedly asked Hagan how soon he would be returning to Washington. Rebecca licked the spilled foam from her fingertips. She'd been wondering the same thing.

She hadn't told Jo, but Zimmer had offered Hagan the job as head deputy. The sheriff corralled him at the hospital as she was checking out. Gleeful that the state had approved replacing Dale Hemphill.

"Politicos figured with the unsavory types making headlines in the county we could use the help. Course I played up your part in solving the murders to make you look good. If you come on board right away, I might be able to backdate the hiring papers, get you paid for the time you spent investigating the Stucks' murders."

Hagan had trouble suppressing his laughter. "Sheriff, that's a tempting offer, and—"

"Pay's not what you're used to, I expect. But neither's the work. Blue Marsh County is a real peaceable place."

"I've heard that before."

"Cost of living's a lot less than in DC. Way fewer politicians. Good weather. Great fishing. Nice bunch of people, some of them even worth protecting."

The sheriff turned his gaze on Rebecca leaning against the counter, signing the release forms. Hagan followed suit. She kept her face neutral. She was staying out of that discussion.

Zimmer played with the brim of his hat. "Of course, we don't have all the fancy equipment you're used to. No experts sitting around just waiting to answer difficult questions. We have to do it ourselves. Real detective work. Makes a man proud."

Hagan chewed on a toothpick, staring at Rebecca's profile while he appeared to consider the proposition. She dropped the pen and handed the papers over to the billing clerk. Hagan was all show. He wasn't staying. He had to testify at Alonso's trial. Peter said they were going ahead on schedule; Justice Thomas had been appointed to hear the case. Besides, Hagan was a city slicker who'd be out of his element down here. Like her.

Hagan removed the toothpick and turned to the sheriff. "I don't know, Zimmer. It's awful quiet around here. Makes it hard to sleep."

"Hell, man. There's cures for insomnia: hard work, long hours, clear conscience, good woman." He winked at Rebecca. "We'll fix you up in no time."

Hagan roared. "That's what I'm afraid of, Sheriff."

Rebecca wasn't sure how she felt about the possibility of

having Hagan underfoot. The attraction was definitely there. So was the shadow of David Semple. She and Hagan had talked about it briefly this morning—his guilt and hers. Afterward, Hagan seemed more at peace in her company, but was she in his? If he could forgive her, possibly she could forgive herself. But could she ever look at him and not be reminded?

That was something to mull over tonight in her own bed—Moe purring on the pillow, Wonder guarding the door. That would be her true celebration—a good night's rest. Tomorrow she'd put her notes on the crimes in order and have Juanita enter them into the computer, then e-mail them to Peter Hayes. He called hourly. Let him write the story with his byline and her blessing. The case was closed.

So was that chapter in her life.

It was time to try settling in to the future her uncle had willed her. View tinkering with old cars as a worthy challenge. A beginning, not a dead end. If she could get the business out of hock and keep the crew employed—and out of jail—she would have accomplished something more durable than all the cynical, sensationalistic stories she forced into print. Something lasting for herself, and for Walt.

Besides, Head Tide was a good place to work on an attitude adjustment. She needed to relax. Learn to face life with more laughter, view friends with more compassion and treat customers with more trust—as soon as she activated the security system.

And if another dead body showed up, she'd take Frank's advice and pitch it out with the trash.

Rebecca grinned as she leaned in front of Jo to snatch a flute from Paulie's tray. She clutched the stem unsteadily in a gauzed mitt and raised the glass—to Mick and Jo, to her family of employees and to the fickle customers gathered around.

"To life."

Lindeman hoisted his glass in response. "To Paris."